10/17

Ghost on the Case

Ghost on the Case

Carolyn Hart

BERKLEY PRIME CRIME
New York

BERKLEY PRIME CRIME
Published by Berkley
An imprint of Penguin Random House LLC
375 Hudson Street, New York, New York 10014

Copyright © 2017 by Carolyn Hart

Penguin Random House supports copyright. Copyright fuels creativity, encourages diverse voices, promotes free speech, and creates a vibrant culture. Thank you for buying an authorized edition of this book and for complying with copyright laws by not reproducing, scanning, or distributing any part of it in any form without permission. You are supporting writers and allowing Penguin Random House to continue to publish books for every reader.

BERKLEY is a registered trademark and BERKLEY PRIME CRIME and the B colophon are trademarks of Penguin Random House LLC.

Library of Congress Cataloging-in-Publication Data

Names: Hart, Carolyn G., author.
Title: Ghost on the case / Carolyn Hart.
Description: First edition. | New York : Berkley, 2017. | Series: A Bailey
Ruth ghost novel ; 8 |
Identifiers: LCCN 2017024251 (print) | LCCN 2017027212 (ebook) | ISBN
9780451488572 (eBook) | ISBN 9780451488565 (hardcover)
Subjects: LCSH: Women detectives—Fiction. | Mediums—Fiction. |
Kidnapping—Fiction. | Murder—Investigation—Fiction. | GSAFD: Mystery
fiction. | Ghost stories.
Classification: LCC PS3558.A676 (ebook) | LCC PS3558.A676 G48 2017 (print) |
DDC 813/.54—dc23
LC record available at https://lccn.loc.gov/2017024251

First Edition: October 2017

Printed in the United States of America
1   3   5   7   9   10   8   6   4   2

Cover art: *Clock* by sociologas/Shutterstock Images
Cover design by Diana Klosky
Book design by Laura K. Corless

In memory of my husband, Phil.
We sang our song for 58 wonderful years.

Ghost on the Case

Chapter 1

Imagine a maple leaf tinged with red and gold drifting in air buoyant as a salty sea. That effortless lightness is as near as I can come to sharing my feeling on another lovely day in Paradise.

Do I see a startled stare? Think what you wish, but Heaven is as real as the sound of a melody or the joy of effort or the welling of love when you see your special other. There is the reality of atoms and there is the reality of spirit.

I simply wish to explain this particular moment. A brief introduction is in order.

I, Bailey Ruth Raeburn, late of Adelaide, Oklahoma, am not in hog heaven, as we used to say in Adelaide when enjoying a succulent baby back rib or holding a winning hand at bridge, but in God's Heaven. Not, I am quick to say, because of merit.

Heavens no. But when our cabin cruiser sank in the Gulf during a storm and Bobby Mac and I made our way here, we were welcomed with open arms.

I shaded my eyes as I strolled on a sandy beach with Mimi, our nippy wirehaired terrier, and gentlemanly Sleuth, a gleaming black Lab. Mr. Easy, our golden retriever, bounded into the surf. Ahead an umbrella shaded two beach chairs. Bobby Mac, my tarpon-seeking husband, was out in the bay in *Serendipity*, our cabin cruiser. Curled next to my chair were Spoofer One and Two and Three and Four. We always called our cats Spoofer. Now they have various nicknames, Mama Spoo, Spoof, S. G. (Spoofer Grande), and S. P. (Spoofer Primus). The cats, instinctively attuned to our thoughts, knew my destination and arrived to relax comfortably until I reached them.

I detect skepticism. I am aware that some on earth darkly say, "Don't expect to see your dogs and cats in Heaven." I can state declaratively (I once taught English) that this claim is false and cruel. Dogs, cats, llamas, goats, parakeets, animal friends of whatever persuasion, are here. Saint Francis wouldn't have it any other way. As he prayed, "Praised be You my Lord with all Your creatures." And talk about creatures! I saw Saint Francis recently with a goldfinch on one shoulder, a rabbit hopping nearby, and— Oh, I forgot. According to the Precepts for Earthly Visitation, I'm not supposed to share everything I know about Heaven.

Perhaps my realization that I was being a bit too forthcoming about my surroundings accounts for my summons from Wiggins. It is my honor to work for Heaven's Department of

Good Intentions, and Paul Wiggins is my supervisor. Wiggins, as he prefers to be addressed, dispatches emissaries from Heaven to help those in trouble, and each emissary is charged to reticence about Heavenly ways. After all, each soul's day will come when all will be known.

Or perhaps the paperback book tucked in my beach bag caught Wiggins's attention. I enjoy Dickens and Trollope and Galsworthy, Emily Brontë, Pearl Buck, and Theodore Dreiser, all suitable to peruse in an English class. But beach reading? Give me a good Erle Stanley Gardner, Brett Halliday, or Donald Hamilton while I wiggle my toes in the sand. The '30s, '40s, and '50s were the heyday of the private-eye novel with a fifth of rye (preferred by John J. Malone) in the bottom desk drawer and a come-hither blonde in the shadows (present in ninety-nine point nine percent of tough-guy books).

In any event, one moment I was heading for a lazy day with a fast-paced hard-boiled novel and the next I was reading a telegram from Wiggins. Wiggins is a man of his time. Telegrams heralded important news in the early twentieth century. Black letters streamed on a flimsy yellow sheet: *In a dilemma. Little choice. Please hasten for consultation.*

"Yoo-hoo." Not dignified but I was ecstatic. My shout reached Bobby Mac. He looked toward the shore. His midnight black hair gleamed in the sun. He is stocky and powerful, as handsome now as when he was a senior and I was a sophomore and he told me firmly that he was taking me to the prom. We've been dancing together ever since. His hand lifted in a generous farewell wave that said: *That's my gal. Go do your stuff. Nobody takes care of business like you do.* What a man. Always on my side. And vice versa. That's the secret to a happy marriage.

One of Heaven's charms is the ability to go from here to there as quick as a thought. Picture your destination, you are there. I quickly changed from a one-piece swimsuit, the Esther Williams style is my preference, and fetching Hawaiian cover-up and white sandals, to a suitable costume to visit the Department of Good Intentions. Wiggins admires modesty. I keep up with earth's fashions. Wiggins would be most approving of the new style of longer skirts. I could dress appropriately and yet feel quite swanky. A blue box-top blouse with cute cap sleeves and an almost ankle-length slim knit skirt made me feel like a model. Tall heels with a beaded strap and open toes were a perfect match. Choose your costume. Dress is our choice and is subject to any whim. If I am in an elegant Bergdorf black dress mood, presto. If I prefer a subdued tweed suit and a silk blouse with pearls and sensible heels, presto. Paradise affords joy for fashionistas.

The heels rat-a-tatted as I hurried up the steps. On earth Wiggins ran a country train station. He had re-created his station to serve as the departure point for the gleaming Rescue Express that rumbles on silver rails to carry emissaries to earth.

I burst through the waiting room and into his office, which overlooks the platform. Wiggins strode toward me, big hand outstretched. Wiggins's florid face looked perplexed. His reddish brows were drawn in a worried frown. His walrus mustache seemed to quiver with uncertainty. "Bailey Ruth." He came to a full stop. On his desk the telegraph sounder clattered.

"I'm here," I said brightly. "Ready to go."

He did not appear reassured. His frown deepened. "I need a skilled detective. C. Auguste Dupin. Sherlock Holmes. Allan Pinkerton."

I was familiar with the authors Wiggins enjoyed. Obviously Wiggins sought ratiocination. Well, I can ratiocinate with the best of them. My turn for a full stop. Heaven compels honesty. Perhaps my claim was an exaggeration. Okay. I'm no equal to his heroes. But I didn't spend all my time as an English teacher reading *Ivanhoe* and *A Tale of Two Cities* (though my heart will always belong to Charles Darnay). A copy of Brett Halliday's *Bodies Are Where You Find Them* sprouted in my hand, a red-haired man leaning forward to support the body of a blonde on the cover. The all-cap title in stark black letters ran down the right side of the cover.

I thrust the book at Wiggins. "I've read them all." It pleased me that Mike Shayne, the Miami PI, was a redhead. I considered that a good omen. I fluffed my own shining red curls. For the record, I'm five foot five of energy and enthusiasm with curious green eyes in a skinny freckled face. Since in Heaven we can be what we wish to be, I chose myself at twenty-seven. It was a very good year.

Wiggins held the paperback in his hand, looked down. Clearly he found the cover a trifle shocking.

I hastened to explain. "Mike Shayne outfoxed the bad guys. Simple. Direct. No b——" I started to say *bull* but feared Wiggins might find the term unladylike. "——boring diversions. Give Shayne a problem and he waded right in. He figured out who was pulling the strings, tracked down the bad guys. What he did, I can do."

The telegraph sounder clacked louder. Wiggins shoved his rounded stiff blue cap with its black brim to the back of a thick shock of russet hair and strode to his desk, looked down. When he faced me, his kind face held despair. "Susan loves her little sister. She'll risk everything. I don't see any way out. An impossible situation. But"—his gaze was imploring—"you always do your best."

I stood a little taller, was tempted to salute.

In two long steps he was at the cabinet with tickets in slots. He reached up, grabbed a red ticket.

A rumble of wheels announced the arrival of the Rescue Express. The deep-throated whoo was a clarion call. The telegraph sounder clattered at a frantic pace.

Wiggins hurried to his desk, stamped the ticket, held it out for me.

I grabbed the red piece of cardboard.

A final shout as I headed for the platform, "Try to remain invisible."

"I will." I meant every word of the brave declaration. This time I would make every effort to be unseen, which is the preferred mode of Wiggins's emissaries. Emissaries have the ability to appear in earthly form. We arrive, of course, unseen. However, if we wish to be present, we simply think *Appear.* When it is better to be unseen, we think *Disappear.* There was one time, I remember my sense of panic, when I lost my ability to disappear. That was a challenge. Being able to appear and disappear is terrific. I suppressed a squiggle of eagerness. I sometimes—oh well, let me be frank—I often feel that I can better assist my charge if I am actually on the earth. This time I would try hard to curb that instinct.

I clutched the red piece of cardboard. I didn't need to look at my destination. I was on my way to Adelaide, my old hometown in the rolling hills of east central Oklahoma. On the platform, I rushed to climb aboard, welcomed the conductor's boost. As the Rescue Express began to roll, I didn't try to suppress my excitement. Wiggins was sending me into an *Impossible Situation* that required the skills—and toughness?—of a private eye. Move over Mike Shayne. Bailey Ruth Raeburn is on the case.

⁓

She was perhaps my height, about five foot five. Ebony black hair framed a face with character, deep-set intelligent eyes, high cheekbones, determined chin. She wasn't conventionally pretty. Hers was an interesting face, shapely black brows, a high forehead, rather thin nose, a generous mouth. She looked like a tennis player or golfer with an aura of easy movement, of quickness. I liked her indigo wool sweater with alternating lines of gold and rose in a zigzag pattern above black wool slacks and indigo leather flats. She stood stiffly in the center of a small living room, a very ordinary room not suited for high drama. A leather shoulder bag was tossed on the seat of a worn wooden rocking chair. Two easy chairs, one with plaid upholstery, the other a nondescript tan, were unoccupied. Library books were scattered on a coffee table, a biography of Douglas MacArthur,

Lives of the Poets by Samuel Johnson, a thriller by Hank Phillippi Ryan, a collection of e. e. cummings poetry. An inexpensive grandfather clock near the front door ticked loudly.

A comfortable room except for the stricken young woman, her face the color of putty, the hand holding a cell phone shaking. "Please"—her voice was uneven, scarcely more than a whisper—"you won't hurt her?" The cell phone was pressed against her face. "Where is she? . . . A hundred . . ." Her left hand rose to her throat. "I don't have that kind of money. I don't have a key. I can't—" She began to shiver. "I can't do that."

She moved unsteadily to the sofa, dropped down, braced herself against the armrest, the phone still hard against her face. A voice was speaking to her, a voice was telling her something that drained her youthful body of strength. "I can't—" Her shoulders drew tight as if in defense. "Tonight? He's having a party. How—" She broke off. Perhaps her caller had interrupted, told her to listen, told her she had no choice.

I knew when the call ended. Her hand, still shaking hard, came away from her face. She stared down at the cell phone, touched the screen, touched again, likely calling a Favorite number. Her trembling hand held the phone close. She listened, then her shoulders slumped. Clearly her call had not been answered and she was being invited to leave a message. Her voice frantic, she cried, "Sylvie, call me. Tell me you're all right. Please." A tap. She stared down at the phone, as if willing her message to be heard. She rose, slipped the phone into the pocket of her slacks. She stood indecisively for a moment, then hurried across the room. She stepped into a narrow hall, passed one room. She stopped at a closed door to a second room. She turned the knob, reached for the light switch.

I blinked as the light revealed a strikingly different milieu. Nothing shabby and worn here, though the furnishings were inexpensive: bright white furniture, a dresser, a chest, a bed with a red satin coverlet. A lop-eared teddy bear with a missing eye sat in an angular metal chair on a fluorescent-bright orange cushion. On the dresser every inch of space was crowded with bottles of perfume and lotions. Heaps of clothes dotted the floor. I had a feeling that the room's inhabitant arrived with armloads of clean laundry and carelessly deposited them wherever, a mound of jeans here, a tangle of panties and bras there, cotton tees loosely strewn on a fuzzy throw rug. It might have been just a messy bedroom except for the watercolors tacked to every bit of free wall space. The work was amateurish, but oh, what a feast of color, magenta, cobalt, royal blue. The paintings weren't simply splashes of color but almost childlike evocations of sunrises, parrots, maple leaves, a football jersey, a yellow brick road rising to the sky, and a huge red question mark surrounded by happy faces.

Happy faces, a happy room. I didn't know the occupant, but the casual disorderliness and vibrant watercolors suggested warmth and originality and unquenchable eagerness.

"Sylvie. Oh, Silly, Silly." The words were a cry of heartbreak from the woman who clung to the doorframe. Her gaze swept the careless, chaotic room. Then she drew in a sharp breath. She darted to the dresser, reached out among the bottles of lotions and sprays and jars of cream to pick up a bright red cell phone.

It took only a moment, and the message she'd left on this phone played and she listened to her own voice, shaking with stress, "Sylvie, call me. Tell me you're all right. Please." Woodenly, she replaced the phone on the dresser.

I was at her shoulder when she picked up a note written in bright red crayon: *Will have lots* (underlined three times) *to tell you tomorrow!!!!*

Sylvie's cell phone was here. Today's youth clings to devices. What prompted her to leave the cell phone behind? Yet she'd left a cheery note. Apparently when she left the light-filled room, she'd been eager and happy. Where was she now?

A muffled peal.

Susan yanked out her own cell phone, swiped, lifted it to listen. "I haven't left yet. . . . I'll go now." She looked down at the phone, its screen now dark. She used a thumbnail to turn off the ringer, shoved the phone in her pocket as she rushed across the room, into the hall, turned to another door.

As she flipped the light switch, I took an instant to look at her. Her narrow face was devoid of color, her brown eyes pools of desperation, a woman laboring under intense emotion.

I popped into the living room, gazed about. I hurried to a side table and picked up a shoulder bag. It took only an instant to open the purse and fish out a brown leather billfold. I flipped it open and there was a driver's license, Susan Mary Gilbert. The photo showed a much happier face, but instantly familiar with the striking dark brows and narrow nose and decided chin. She was smiling. I glanced at the birth date. She was twenty-four. When the shutter clicked to record her image, she'd been twenty-four and confident, not crushed by fear. I wouldn't forget her stricken plea, *Please, you won't hurt her?*

I joined Susan in a very different bedroom. I never doubted the room was hers, a simple maple bed and dresser and chest, pale blue walls, white dimity curtains at the windows. A serene room. No clutter. Susan pulled off her pretty wool sweater and yanked a black sweater from the chest. Atop the chest were two studio photographs in silver frames. I found both faces intriguing. One was a woman in her late forties or early fifties, a mass of blonde hair, huge blue eyes, crimson lips, almost a smile, not quite. The heart-shaped face had a haunting quality, as if there could be laughter but tears were not far behind. The second was young, perhaps not more than seventeen. Blonde curls framed the same heart-shaped face, but this one was bright and eager and the wide blue eyes brimmed with delight.

Susan tugged at the neck of the sweater, slid her cell phone into a pocket. She moved jerkily, hurrying, hurrying.

Wiggins had feared I might be too late to help Susan. I was in a quandary. What would a wise emissary do? Clearly, she was distraught, but I knew too little to be of help now, though I yearned to slip a comforting arm around her taut shoulders. But I must be patient. I had to know more. What was the content of the call she'd received? Obviously she feared for someone's safety. She'd hurried to a bedroom, said raggedly, "Sylvie. Oh, Silly, Silly." The love was clear in her stricken voice when she called out, "Silly, Silly." I was sure this was a big sister's nickname for the girl who had the happy bedroom, the girl she begged the caller not to harm.

Susan was dressed now in dark clothing, dark sneakers as well. She wound a black scarf around her head. At the dresser, she opened the top drawer, pulled out supple black leather gloves, shoved them in a pocket. She hurried out of the bedroom, up the hallway, into the small living room. She paused only long enough to take the billfold from her purse and slide it into a pocket. She plucked car keys from a ceramic bowl and ran into an old-fashioned kitchen, think 1950s, skirted a white wooden table. At the back door, she turned the knob, looked out into the night.

A huge moon silvered a separate frame garage. A small sedan was parked in the drive. The air was chilly. I gauged the temperature in the high fifties. I rather felt that it was late October or early November. Even in darkness, the trees looked as if the branches were mostly bare. I changed into a gray cashmere pullover, navy wool slacks, and ankle boots.

Susan took a moment on the back steps to gaze about. Did she perhaps have a nosy neighbor? After that quick check, she slipped quietly down the stairs. Leaves crunched beneath her feet as she crossed the yard to the car.

I was settled in the front passenger seat when she slid behind the wheel. The car was immaculately kept though obviously an older model. I missed the days when I was a gadabout in Adelaide. Cars were simple to recognize. You drove a Ford or a Chevy or a Dodge. If you rubbed shoulders with the upper crust, you glided in a Lincoln or Cadillac. In my recent forays to Adelaide, I'd gained some familiarity with the plethora of modern cars. All I could say with certainty about Susan's car was that it was modest, in keeping with her home, and likely ten or twelve years old. How did I know? She put an actual key in the ignition and there wasn't a little screen set above the radio. I knew I was distracting myself from the panic that emanated from the rigid figure beside me. She gripped the steering wheel tightly with gloved hands.

I didn't like the gloves. It might be early November and chilly, but no one needed gloves. I didn't like her dark garb. I had a feeling of foreboding right up there with ravens wheeling in the sky or the scrape of a dungeon door. I especially didn't like the car backing from the drive without headlights. The car eased into the street. Susan hunched forward. Peering out into the moonlit street, she drove without lights.

I almost put out a hand then steeled myself. No doubt her progress would end in a jamming of brakes if an unseen hand gripped her arm. Perhaps her stealth was caused by fear for the safety of Sylvie, whom she called Silly. Sylvie was in danger, and Susan was setting out to do something that might assure her safety. This was not the time for me to intervene. I hoped her actions saved Sylvie, but I remembered Wiggins's somber *Impossible Situation.*

I leaned forward in the passenger seat, still unseen. Yes, I can appear, but the Precepts for Earthly Visitation are clear on the subject: "Become visible only when absolutely necessary." That instruction was rather a sore point between Wiggins and me. It isn't that I am eager to appear. Oh. Honesty requires full disclosure. I will admit I like being visible. I like being on earth, a twenty-seven-year-old redhead eager to help. I will also admit I often appeared on past missions, but in those instances I'd not felt I had a choice. Oh. Was that always true? Not exactly. Perhaps Wiggins was hovering near. I've never been certain whether Wiggins actually knows my thoughts at any given moment or not. Just in case, I repeated the Precepts silently to myself as the car turned a corner.

Precepts for Earthly Visitation

1. *Avoid public notice.*
2. *Do not consort with other departed spirits.*
3. *Work behind the scenes without making your presence known.*
4. *Become visible only when absolutely necessary.*
5. *Do not succumb to the temptation to confound those who appear to oppose you.*
6. *Make every effort not to alarm earthly creatures.*
7. *Information about Heaven is not yours to impart. Simply smile and say, "Time will tell."*
8. *Remember always that you are on the earth, not of the earth.*

Susan turned on the headlights and pressed the accelerator. As the car picked up speed, we passed modest bungalows and small frame houses. I recognized the one-story frame home where my beautician had lived. A few houses down was the home of the gawky, pimply faced paperboy who faithfully delivered the *Gazette* and the *Oklahoman* promptly at five every morning. He grew up to be a lawyer and went on to a distinguished career as a federal judge. That stucco home with a tiled roof was the home of soft-spoken, kind Maisie Whistler, who worked in my dad's drugstore.

Susan swung onto a wide street and started up a hill. I don't know how it is in most small towns, but the best homes in Adelaide are on high ground. We drove around a clump of willows, and I spotted some familiar homes. The car continued up the hill, curved to the right. Susan slowed, perhaps because cars were parked on both sides of the street. Lights blazed from a Mediterranean mansion set far up on the hillside. The circular drive was filled with cars. Susan drove perhaps a quarter mile past the drive. She flicked off the headlights as she turned the car into a narrow road.

In the pale wash of light from the dashboard, her face was set. There was no mistaking the tight urgency that propelled her or the barely lashed panic rigidly held in abeyance.

I knew where we were. The mansion blazing with light and the drive filled with cars had once been the home of an Adelaide oil baron, Luke Torman, and later of his ebullient widow, Celine, who had a taste for younger men and loved to rhumba. The house was indeed high on the hill and separated from neighbors by a thick wood. The road we now traveled led to a private lake behind the house.

The dark was so intense in the wooded area that Susan turned on the fog lights, which provided enough illumination to follow the blacktop road past a cabin to a deserted parking area near some picnic tables. Susan nudged the car into the shadow of a pavilion. When she turned off the motor, she tucked the keys into a pocket, pulled out the leather gloves, slipped them on. She opened the glove compartment, grabbed a pencil flashlight.

I was right beside her as she slid from the driver's seat. She gently clicked the car door shut and turned on the flashlight long enough to spot a blacktop path. She knew the way, walked swiftly. The path curved along the shore of the lake. The water looked dark and motionless. The sound of music grew louder. We came around a curve, and the mansion rose to the left. Two wings extended from the broad center portion. The third floor was ablaze with lights shining out in wide swaths from ceiling-tall windows. Guests in formal attire, some dancing, some in convivial clumps, were visible. I left Susan long enough to rise in the air for a quick peek into an elegant ballroom that overlooked the terrace. I admired enormous chandeliers that likely had once graced a grand British country home. Drums thrummed, trumpets blared. The music sounded like a mixture of banshee wails and a buzz saw needing grease. I turned to see Susan picking her way from dark shadow to dark shadow, moving toward the wing where only an occasional light shone. I joined her as she reached the far side of the house.

Susan puffed out a sigh of relief and hurried up a paved walk. The music was now muffled, though the heavy boom of the drums was audible as thumps. Occasional windows were lighted in this wing, two on the second floor, one on the ground floor. A soft glow rimmed drawn curtains in a room near the back of the house. A few feet from the rectangle of light, she stopped so abruptly I bumped into her. She gave a startled gasp.

"Sor—" I broke off the instinctive apology as she stiffened into a hunted posture. Her head jerked back and forth as she sought the source of the voice.

I scarcely breathed and cautiously eased away from her.

The thin sharp beam of the flashlight flared. She twisted and turned the beam all around her, but the light revealed nothing more than drifting leaves on the flagstones and dense shadows beneath the evergreens that bordered the walk. The hand holding the flashlight trembled. She remained in that strained, tight posture for a moment longer, then with a sharply drawn breath turned and walked toward a door next to the rectangle of light. She stopped, slowly reached out. She took a deep breath, used her gloved right hand to grip the handle. She turned it and gave a little puff of relief when the door opened.

I was already inside when she stepped over the sill. A Tiffany lamp on a side table glowed, providing some light.

The large room was masculine, oak-paneled walls, heavy leather furniture, a desk as large as a pool table, wooden filing cabinets, thick floor-length red velvet curtains. One wall was covered by a glass case. Rows of bright fishing lures glittered on pale pine. A stuffed marlin mounted on more pinewood hung above the mantel of a fireplace. The opposite wall of bookcases was filled with knickknacks, likely souvenirs from travels. In a quick glance, I saw a bronze gong on a teak base, a porcelain elephant, a diorama of the Great Wall of China, a mud-stained polo stick, a lariat, a Cubs baseball cap, a miniature wooden sailboat with a plastic sail, a worn small teddy bear with a bow tie.

My nose wrinkled. I like the smell of coal smoke, but this

room held the memory of smoldering cigars. An oversize brass ashtray was on one corner of the mahogany desk.

Susan closed the door gently. Her gaze flickered around the room, but there was no movement, no sound beyond the muffled thump from the faraway music. She took a quick breath, hurried across the room to the hall door, punched in the lock. Some of the tension eased from her body. Whirling, she looked across the room at an oil painting that hung behind the desk. An eighteenth-century highwayman looked masterful astride a rearing black stallion. He was attired in a red coat and black breeches, a musket in one hand. He gazed across the years, his lips curved in a cruel smile.

Susan took slow steps across the Oriental rug, skirted the desk, came up between the red leather desk chair and the painting. She gave a quick glance over her shoulder at the hall door, now securely locked.

Fumbling a little, she ran her left hand behind the frame of the painting.

I heard a click.

She gripped the beveled frame and pulled. The painting swung away from the wall to reveal a large safe inset in the wall. Quickly she tapped a keypad in the center of the safe door. There was not the slightest sound as she pulled the safe door open.

To say I was disturbed can scarcely attest to the turmoil in my mind. Clearly, this was not Susan's house. Even more clearly, this was not her safe. She was dressed in black. She'd slipped into this room, and now with gloved hands she was reaching into a safe. If I appeared, asked her what she was doing, I could easily thwart what was obviously a robbery. Was that the course I should take?

If I'd ever wished for Wiggins it was now.

It was almost as if he whispered in my ear. Precept Three: "Work behind the scenes without making your presence known."

Wiggins clearly had been concerned for Susan. Moreover, his expression was dismal when he concluded she was in an Impossible Situation. She received a phone call that made her fear for her little sister's safety, and now, dressed in the modern equivalent of the eighteenth-century highwayman's garb, she was reaching with both gloved hands into a safe hidden behind a painting in a grand mansion. I hardly had to jump to any conclusions to understand that Susan must have access to this safe because she worked for its owner and that she was willing to commit a crime to do what she must to protect her sister.

Her hands came out of the safe holding a shoe box, a bright red, white, and blue Reebok running shoe box. She tucked the box beneath one arm, closed the safe, pushed the painting back against the wall. A soft click.

I was quite sure that it wasn't Heaven's intent to facilitate crime. Perhaps that was the reason for my presence. I could at any time arrange the return of the shoe box. I felt a whoosh of relief. Of course I would protect the interests of the safe's owner. Reassured, I watched as Susan returned to the hall door, turned the knob to pop the lock. In a flash she crossed the room to the exterior door. I was right behind her as she slipped into the night. I didn't intend to let that shoe box out of my sight.

Chapter 2

Susan stood in the middle of her small living room, clutching the shoe box in a tight grip. Her memorable face with
its high cheekbones and bold chin looked intense, obdurate.
She'd removed—perhaps *stolen* was the correct verb—a cardboard container from a safe that clearly was not hers. I expected
her to look for a hiding place, though there are few spots that
can conceal a shoe box if a searcher is diligent. Would she go out
into the night again, find a trowel in her garage, dig in the
ground? She'd left her home in darkness and returned the same
way, dousing the headlights when she turned onto her street. If
she was concerned about a watchful neighbor, digging a hole—
I glanced at a clock on a side table—at a quarter to midnight
was not an option.

Her next move surprised me.

She walked swiftly to a card table in one corner. She moved aside a chess set, placed the box in the open space. Her entire body tensed as she lifted the lid. She held an indrawn breath.

I hovered above her right shoulder. My eyes widened.

She lifted out stacks of bills, each stack held by a rubber band. The top bill on each stack was a fifty. She fluffed the ends of one stack. All fifties.

I counted the stacks. The box held at least a hundred thousand dollars, perhaps closer to a hundred and fifty thousand. I gazed at her, trying to reconcile the reality of a thief with a woman whose face was generous, kind, serious.

The gloved hands moved swiftly, returning the bundled bills to the box, slapping the lid back in place. She glanced at the grandfather clock. Twelve minutes to midnight. She pressed fingers to her temples, then seemed to realize she still wore gloves. She stripped them off, flung them on the table.

An inexpensive chess set with plastic pieces, limp black leather gloves, and a shoe box crammed with bundles of fifty-dollar bills made an incongruous tableau. The chess set, if used, suggested intelligence. The cheapness of the set indicated a lack of money for extravagance, no ivory or brass here. The gloves were not needed for the weather, were chosen to aid in a crime. The shoe box held thousands of dollars that should not be on the table in this small house.

Susan stood by the table, arms tightly crossed. She stared at the clock. Nine minutes to midnight. She began to pace, six steps, turn, six steps back, six steps, turn, six steps back. The minute hand edged nearer and nearer twelve.

Two minutes to go.

Susan yanked the cell phone from her pocket, held it in her hand.

One minute to go.

Midnight.

She lifted the phone, one hand poised to swipe.

One minute after the hour.

Two minutes after the hour.

Her face quivered as she stared at the silent cell phone.

Three minutes after the hour.

With a shaking hand she swiped, touched Recent Calls, tapped. She held the phone to her ear. A minute passed. Another. She began to tremble. She looked wildly toward the table with the shoe box. She hunched her shoulders. With stiff fingers she tried the call again. Finally, the hand with the cell phone dropped to her side. Stumbling a little, she walked to the sofa, blindly sank down. Tears slid down her cheeks. "Oh God, what am I going to do?"

"There's always something to do." I spoke firmly.

Her head jerked up. Her gaze swung all around the room. Panic flared in her eyes.

I didn't hesitate. Susan needed help. It was time to join her. I swirled into being. Appearing and disappearing are as easy as thinking *Here* and *Gone* or *Visible* and *Invisible* or *Appear* or— But you get the point. When I wish to be, I am. That isn't to say the process can't be disconcerting for the uninitiated. Lights swirl, rose and gold and ivory. The soft bands coalesce and here I am.

Susan shrank back against the sofa, her face slack.

I spoke rapidly. "Don't be afraid. I'm here to help you."

"How did you get in?" She barely managed a whisper.

My smile was a bit chiding, but I hope kindly. "You strike me as a woman who knows what she sees. What did you see?"

"Colors swirling. Rose and gold and ivory and you were here."

I nodded approvingly. "I'm from Heaven's Department of Good Intentions. My mission is to assist you."

She sat as if chipped from ice. Her face was starkly white.

I hurried to the sofa, sat down beside her, and put my hand on her arm. "Don't be frightened."

She jerked away. "This is crazy. I'm breaking down. Everything's crazy. That call and now you. I don't know who you are, but please leave. Right now. I have to— I have things I have to do." She rose, a hostess ready to speed a departing guest.

I remained on the sofa. "Tell me about the call." I used my firm voice, which quelled football players in the back of the class as we discussed *Silas Marner.*

She slowly sank down on the cushion. "A voice said fast, very fast: *Don't hang up if you want to see your sister alive.* I felt like I was frozen and it hurt to breathe. The voice was kind of inhuman, high and thin and metallic."

In my past missions, I've learned a bit from Adelaide's police, especially Chief Sam Cobb and his stalwart second-in-command, Hal Price. I know a thing or two that would surprise Mike Shayne, including how voices on a phone can be electronically altered so the caller is unrecognizable.

"The voice said Sylvie was in a safe place but bad things

could happen to her. If I wanted her to come home, I had to get a hundred thousand dollars. I said I didn't have that kind of money. The voice said, *You can get it out of the safe.* I said I didn't have a key, and the voice said the garden door will be open. The deadline to have the money was twelve o'clock. I had to get the money, and then I'd get a call about where to bring it, and if I did, Sylvie would be safe." She looked at the clock and pressed her lips tightly together.

Susan followed instructions, but no call came at midnight. She turned to me with haunted eyes. "They didn't call. Maybe nothing matters now. Maybe she's—" She lifted her hands, pressed them against her cheeks. "She's silly and wild and kind of goofy and sweet, and I never know what she's going to do next, and now someone has her and I don't know what to do."

"Call the police."

Susan grabbed my arm. "The caller said she'll die if I tell anyone, she'll bleed to death. I can't call the police."

"You won't save her by sitting here doing nothing."

"Maybe"—her voice was wobbly—"there's been a delay. Maybe I'll get a call in a minute or two. I'll take the money wherever they say, and they'll let Sylvie go. I have to wait. There's nothing else I can do."

She was too distraught for me to point out that everything has a beginning. Someone knew Susan Gilbert could open a safe and take a box full of money. Someone unlocked the door to that large, masculine room. "How did the kidnapper know you could open that safe?"

"I work for Wilbur Fitch." She spoke as if that simple answer was all I needed to know.

"Wilbur Fitch?"

She looked surprised. "Don't you know Wilbur Fitch?" She blinked when I shook my head. "Everyone in Adelaide—" She broke off, swallowed. "I know you said something about Heaven, but you don't expect me to believe that, do you?"

I looked into her eyes, nodded decisively.

She lifted a hand to her face, fingers touching a cheek. "All right. If that's how you want to play it. You're from Heaven"—clearly she didn't believe me, had no idea how I'd arrived, knew only that I didn't seem bent on notifying the police about the box from the safe—"so here's the truth. Funny, I have a feeling I'm supposed to tell you the truth. And maybe the phone will ring in a minute and I can take that money wherever it has to go and Sylvie will come home. Right now I might as well talk to you. My name is Susan Gilbert. I work for a really, really rich man. Wilbur Fitch owns a lot of Adelaide, what isn't owned by the Chickasaws. He's a self-made man. Never went to college. I don't think he finished high school. But he hung around a computer shop, and that's when computers were just getting started and they cost a lot. He worked in the back, and he must have spent all his time figuring out about whatever's inside the console or whatever they call it." She waved a hand as if the inner workings of computers didn't matter to her. I felt the same way about light bulbs and television sets. They worked and I couldn't care less why. "Anyway, the store owner let Wilbur haul off all the useless pieces, but Wilbur figured out he could salvage this and that, and he started selling the stuff all over the country. From that he made a contact in China, and the first thing you know, he's buying up old shacks and warehouses all over town and filling them with discarded computers from everywhere and hiring kids with horn rims and baseball caps to sort through the stuff and package it up and off it goes. Long story short, he's worth maybe fifty million dollars."

"Why those bundles of fifties in his safe?"

She glanced at the table with the chess set and gloves and shoe box. When she looked back at me, her face was furrowed and her gaze uncertain. "How do you know what kind of bills are in the box?"

"I've been beside you ever since you received the call telling you to get the money. You didn't use your lights when you backed out of the drive. You turned them on after you drove around the corner. You drove to this huge mansion, but you went in a back way, parked by a pav—"

She scarcely breathed. Her eyes were huge. "How did you see all of that?"

For an answer, I disappeared.

She pressed the back of one hand against her lips.

"I'm still here." I made my voice cheery. "Think of me as your unseen companion." Colors swirled and I was back beside her. This time I chose a pink turtleneck, gray slacks, and pink leather ankle boots. I like to lighten up the fall, though I'm fond of russets and oranges as well. I smoothed my hair and beamed at her. Possibly I looked a bit windblown, but that's always the norm in Oklahoma.

She reached out, gripped my arm. "Okay. You're here now. You weren't a minute ago. Maybe you can come and go. Maybe I'm nuts. Maybe I'm making you up because I'm scared to pieces and that damn phone doesn't ring and Sylvie's gone. If I'm making you up, then sure, you know everything I did because I know what I did so my imaginary person knows what I know. But if you aren't some kind of figment of my imagination and you can go anywhere, go find Sylvie."

This wasn't the moment to discuss my limitations. Although I could easily picture Wilbur Fitch's house and be there in a heartbeat, I had to have a physical destination in mind. Although perhaps— "What kind of car does Sylvie drive?"

"A 2007 Camry. Tan."

"I'll be back." I disappeared.

I stood beside a 2007 tan Camry parked in a lot across from one of the girls' dorms at our local college. Streetlamps provided ample visibility in front of the dorms and in the parking lot. Locked car doors are no hindrance. I flowed inside. A backpack rested in the passenger seat. In case anyone was near, I became visible. I flipped on an interior light, pulled the backpack close, lifted the flap. It took only a moment to empty the contents. A laptop. Four textbooks. Colonial American history. Psychology. American lit. French. I would have expected a welter of crumpled sheets in keeping with the disorderliness of Sylvie's room. I glanced at the laptop. Likely she made notes on her device and paper wasn't a part of her world. I turned it on, checked her calendar. Three classes MWF, a single eight o'clock class TTh. In

Notes three assignments were listed. And, at the end of the page, a cryptic: *I Can Do It!*

I replaced the textbooks and laptop in the backpack. Outside the car, I studied the quiet scene. An almost full bike rack at the end of the sidewalk was illuminated beneath a streetlamp. Across the street there were only two lighted windows in the three-story dormitory. No pedestrians were visible. I looked back at the car, but there was nothing to give me any hint as to its owner's actions after she parked, locked the doors, and walked away.

I glanced again at the row of dorms. Was it possible Sylvie lived in one of the dorms? I gave it a try, thought Sylvie's room.

I stood in the center of the room with the lop-eared bear and the casually dispersed clothes. I walked into the hall. The bedroom door made a slight squeak.

Running steps sounded. Susan plunged into the hall. "Sylvie? Are you home?"

"It's me. I'm back." I appeared.

"I heard her door. I hoped it was Sylvie. When you left, you said something about Sylvie's car." She stood with her hands balled into tight fists.

"Her car is parked across from a dorm on the campus. Her backpack is in the passenger seat."

"That's where she parks when she goes to class. That means she was on the campus today. If she didn't take her car after class, she must have left the campus with someone." Susan looked sick. "If she knows who kidnapped her, they can't let her go."

I very much feared that would be true, but as my mama always told us, "Don't borrow trouble."

I was crisp. "A smart kidnapper will be certain she never gets a glimpse of him. Or her. Sylvie won't know anything to reveal their identity. Now tell me why Mr. Fitch keeps a box filled with cash in his safe. Is he engaged in nefarious activities?"

For an instant, her wide mouth quirked in amusement. "He'd love the way you talk. Maybe if everything ever gets sorted out and Sylvie is okay and I can explain to him and promise to pay back the money, maybe he'll think the whole thing's a hoot. He's like that. Nefarious? He'll boom, *Hell, no. I'm not anybody's crook. Every penny I have is a penny I earned. But I remember when a five-dollar bill was big money to me. Now I've got stacks of fifty-dollar bills right where I can get to them anytime I want. If I take it in my mind to buy a new car, I can walk right in and slap the money down on the counter.* He'll roar with laughter. He knows he's over the top, but he's proud of what he's done. It makes me mad when people act like anybody who's rich is somehow bad and the government should take all their money and pass it out. Nobody does more for people in trouble than Wilbur. He doesn't tell everybody about his generosity. You know how they list donors for charities and a bunch of them are Anonymous. He's Anonymous behind the soup kitchen and the Salvation Army and the fund for homeless schoolkids and the dog and cat rescue society and lots of other things. I know because I'm his secretary and I put the checks in the mail."

"Does he work out of his home?"

"He has an office at the main building, but mostly he works from home. He knows everything that's going on. He gets reports and spreadsheets and has me keep up with the markets around the world and how the yuan is doing. He's very big in China."

"Why do you know the combination to his safe?"

"Wilbur likes to sit at his huge desk or in the big leather chair on the other side of the room and have things brought to him. He trusts me." Her lips quivered. "He's always trusted me. Now I'm a thief. But"—her voice was forlorn—"if we get Sylvie back, he'll understand. I'll pay him back no matter how long it takes. I can sell the house for maybe sixty thousand and then— oh, I don't know how I'll get the rest, but I will. But that doesn't matter now." She whirled, hurried back to the living room. She stopped and stared at the clock. Almost twenty after twelve. She yanked her cell from her pocket, tapped numbers again. She listened and listened, finally swiped to end the call. "Why haven't they called me?"

Susan found the failure of the cell to ring terrifying. "Perhaps you misunderstood. Perhaps the call will come at twelve noon tomorrow. Did the caller say midnight or twelve o'clock?"

I felt the prick of tears behind my eyes at the spurt of hope in her face.

She spoke rapidly. "The voice said twelve o'clock. Not midnight. Maybe"—and her tone was feverish—"maybe they wanted to give me plenty of time to get the money. Maybe they're trying to decide where I should leave the box and how they can let Sylvie go."

Whether this was fool's gold or not, she now had hope. I would work fast, learn what I could while she was able to focus on something beyond her fear. I gave her a reassuring smile. "I'm sure you will hear by noon tomorrow, and that gives us time to figure out what happened. Let's go to the kitchen, fix some coffee, have something to eat."

✑

Susan served a crisp waffle to each plate along with three slices of thick-cut well-cooked bacon. I poured steaming coffee into her mug and mine. I was pleased that she tucked into our post-midnight repast with alacrity.

I drizzled strawberry syrup—earth does have its pleasures—on my waffle. "Tell me about you and Sylvie." I was quite certain Sylvie's abduction was not a matter of chance, because the caller knew Susan could obtain a hundred thousand dollars that very night. That revealed several hugely important facts: The caller knew the cash was in Wilbur Fitch's safe. The caller knew Susan had a younger sister she would do anything to protect. Therefore the caller was someone who intersected the lives of both the wealthy businessman and Susan Gilbert. My task was simple. Discover that link.

Comfortable in her belief that a call would come at noon tomorrow and she could pay the ransom and Sylvie would be freed, Susan managed a quirky smile. "They say all families are dysfunctional no matter how they look from outside. For all anyone knew for years, our family was ordinary. Like they say, move along, nothing to see here, just a postman and his lovely wife with two little girls. Kind of a cottage-in-the-trees perfect life. It sounds bland and boring, but there was a lot of longing and dreams and foolishness."

I murmured, *"And Richard Cory, one calm summer night, / Went home and put a bullet through his head."* Edward Arlington Robinson's poem was a cameo of outward appearances and inward despair.

She put down her fork. Her long face held a mixture of melancholy and ruefulness and understanding. "Sylvie and me. We're as different as our mom and dad were. Dad was a postman. Never missed a day of work. Not ever. Ice storm. Tornado. Blizzard. Hot enough to blister your feet on the sidewalk. He did his route. A dogged man. Serious. Read history. Loved ancient Greece. Liked to quote Edith Hamilton. A favorite: *None so good that he has no faults, / None so wicked that he is worth naught.* I guess that's why no matter what Mom did, he was kind. Mom—well, she must have been gorgeous when she was young. Masses of blonde curls. Just like Sylvie. And a heart-shaped face and huge blue eyes. But she lived in an imaginary world. She waited tables at the Rendezvous, a bar on the outskirts of town, and she was sure in her heart that someday someone would come in and see her and take her to Hollywood. She ran off with a guy when I was twelve and Sylvie was six. We didn't know where she was for a couple of years, and then we got a call from Reno. She was broke, sick. Dad went out and brought her home, and she died from cancer. After she was gone, he sat us down and said, *Your mama did the best she could. Remember how pretty she was and how kind. She was always proud of you girls. So you keep on making her proud.* Whenever something happened that was really nice, he'd say, *Mama is smiling for you.* He never said a bad thing about her, but when he was in the hospital and knew he didn't have much time left, he asked Sylvie to go down to the little shop and get him a Baby Ruth. When she left the room, he moved his hand, wanted me to come close, and he whispered, *Take care of Sylvie. She's like her mama, doesn't have the sense God gave a sparrow, but she can fly mighty high if someone takes good care of her.*" A deep breath. "And he died. I was holding his hand and suddenly it went slack. So"— she looked at me with luminous eyes—"I have to take care of Sylvie. And she is like Mom. She's sweet and silly and credulous, but she sees the world in bright colors and she has a gift. Maybe her paintings won't ever sell. I don't know how any artist makes a living, but she's good and the watercolors make her happy. She's majoring in education so she can get a teaching job." A rueful smile. "She did that to please me. She wants to please people. I think she'll make a happy life, because she can paint and she won't be like Mama, who was sure something magical would happen to her one day. Sylvie lives magic with her paintbrush. I've tried so hard to take care of her and now this happens. It will break my heart if Sylvie is frightened, if she comes home scared to go out. She's never been scared. I'd tell her not to be out past midnight because that's when the drunks are driving, that bad people do bad things in the dark, and she laughs and says I'm an old stick-in-the-mud. When we were little and Mama wanted to do something on the spur of the moment, maybe run up to the City and eat at Spaghetti Warehouse, Dad would hem and haw and say, *Takes a lot of gas to drive up to the City. We can go to the park and the girls can ride the merry-go-round. The merry-go-round is free.* And Mama would say, *Albert, don't be a stick-in-the-mud.*" Tears slipped down Susan's cheeks.

She cried for her mom and dad as well as for Sylvie and for long-ago days when two little girls were loved by a rock-solid father and a mercurial well-meaning mother.

She swiped at her face with a handful of tissues. "Anyway, I promised Daddy."

"You've kept your promise and"—I was emphatic—"you will keep your promise. We will find Sylvie. In fact, we may be able to find her right now if you can answer two questions."

Susan leaned forward. "Ask me anything."

"Who could arrange to open the outer door to the study tonight?"

For an instant she looked eager, then she shook her head. "On a regular night it would be a very short list. But tonight? Everybody who's anybody in Adelaide is at the dance in the grand ballroom. Plus there's catering staff. Someone could slip downstairs and go into that wing. The study door to the hall isn't locked. It would be easy."

My hope was dashed. I thought perhaps the kidnapper might easily be singled out. I asked swiftly, "How many people know you can open Wilbur Fitch's safe?"

Her face was suddenly still. Her eyes widened. "Everyone in

town probably knows about the box of money. Wilbur loves to say offhandedly, *You need five thousand for the Thanksgiving dinner for the homeless? I'll go home and get it.*"

"I doubt a casual bystander is aware Wilbur's secretary could open the safe and bring the money. I doubt a casual bystander even knows you work for Wilbur Fitch."

Realization transformed her face. "You mean someone I know took Sylvie?"

"Yes."

There was a feeling of coldness in the small kitchen as Susan realized Sylvie's captor must be someone she knew, not a nameless faceless stranger. The kidnapper was knowledgeable about her little sister and knew as well that Susan had access to the shoe box full of money.

"When did Wilbur reveal that you can open the safe?"

Susan stared as if I'd suddenly perched a crystal ball in my lap. "How did you know?"

"Sylvie is a very unlikely kidnap victim to be held for ransom."

Susan scarcely breathed. "Only Wilbur knew I could open the safe. Until last week."

"Did Sylvie know?"

That almost brought a smile. "Sylvie loves me and she wants to know about my day, but she asks whether I saw a deer in the park on my way to work or if I've heard the new marimba album or would I like for her to make a lemon meringue pie or, and this is really important to her, what is a better color for a unicorn, sea green or sunrise vermilion. I ask her if she's learned the lines for a play she's going to be in or whether the new professor really understands Faulkner. She knows I work for Wilbur, but she only has a dim idea what he does, and she assumes that being a secretary is a lot of keyboarding. She lives in a world of color and emotion. The neat thing is, Wilbur does, too. It's just a different world. He's considering a plan now to start up a new company to manufacture no-frill cars. Alan Douglas—he's the vice president of projects and designs—came up with the idea that loads of people don't want to pay for cars with TV screens and audio systems and so much electronic capacity a customer needs a three-hour tutorial before driving off the lot. Alan's different. You never know what he'll think of next. He's tall and lanky and diffident. And nice. I was surprised Wilbur was interested because he's made his fortune from computer parts. Everything in our office is the latest, but he says Alan's onto something, that marketers get it wrong sometimes. Sure, people with money want to be cool and have the latest gadgets, but there are plenty of people who like to eat in diners and shop at Stein Mart and get their books from the library. Like Sylvie and me. I'll buy one of those cars if it happens, and if Wilbur decides it's going to happen, it will. You'll roll the windows up and down with a handle, click a knob to turn on the radio. Ditto the heater. You'll use a key to unlock the door and start the car. Alan wants to squeeze out every unneeded computer part. Wilbur says computerizing the world is a big damn risk, that computers can be hacked, jammed. They glitch. Alan brought him a proposal entitled 'Keep it SIMPLE.' The name of the new company will be SIMPLE Cars. Alan has a slogan ready: *Save money for your dreams. Drive SIMPLE and keep the extra cash.* Wilbur had a big luncheon last week in Alan's honor. That doesn't mean he'll agree to the project, but he likes for his employees to be innovative. And, of course, Wilbur likes having people for luncheons. He enjoys holding court in the dining room. It's pretty spectacular, very similar to the dining room at Hearst Castle. High ceiling. Banners hang from the walls. A long oak table seats twenty. There are huge paintings and a stone fireplace and tall silver candlesticks on the table. I love the banners. There's a checkerboard flag from NASCAR, the Oklahoma flag, a Dodgers pennant, the racing colors from a stable he owns. The biggest one is white silk with FITCH in big red letters. He often entertains at lunch. Sometimes it's business, sometimes family, sometimes both. That's how it was last Monday."

"You were there?"

She shook her head. "Sometimes I run errands over my lunch hour. Sometimes I have to eat at my desk. When I do that, he insists I leave an hour early in the afternoon. That day I had lunch out on the terrace. It was a beautiful fall day. The kitchen brings lunch to me if I ask. I was just finishing a bowl of soup when he called me on my cell. My ringtone for him is a bugle blast so I knew it was Wilbur. I always hold the phone a bit away from my ear because he has a deep voice and he booms. I heard him clearly. Everyone at the table heard him. He said, *Susan, I need for you to open the safe. Look next to the money box. There's a velvet bag. Red velvet. Perfect for a king's ransom. Guess it would have been an emperor's ransom back then. I want to show off those Roman coins. They came out of an old shipwreck they found off Malta. I got the best coins of the lot. Bring the bag to me*

ASAP. He clicked off. I went straight to the study, opened the safe, got the velvet bag. I took the bag to the dining room. Everybody looked at me as I walked in."

A secretary opened a safe and carried the requested item to her employer and someone watched and remembered.

"Who was there?"

I shooed Susan from the kitchen. "I'll take care of the dishes. You go to bed."

"I can't sleep." Her lips quivered. While we talked, she'd held tight to the thought that tomorrow a call would come and she could deliver the money and Sylvie would be safe. Now fatigue plucked behind her eyes, fatigue and the possible horrors of a night she could not control.

I was firm. "You have to go to work in the morning."

Her hands clenched. "I can't."

"You have to act as if it's an ordinary day and keep your usual routine. Find out everything you can about Wilbur Fitch's recent contacts with those on our list." Because we had a list. The guests at the luncheon knew Susan could open the safe. One of them was almost certainly Sylvie's kidnapper. I dismissed the possibility that Wilbur Fitch gratuitously informed an unknown person that his secretary knew the combination to his safe. Why would he? The tidbit *My secretary can open my safe* was unlikely in casual conversation. That information came about incidentally because he wanted to show off a new acquisition to his coin collections.

With the list of names, I was tempted to immediately pop to the location of each person, but at a quarter after one in the morning it was unlikely they would be engaged in revealing activity. I doubted the kidnapper was anywhere near Sylvie. If Sylvie was to return safely, it was essential that she not know the identity of her kidnapper.

I declined the offer of Sylvie's room. "I'll sleep on the sofa." Susan provided sheets and a quilt and pillow. I finished the dishes and made certain Susan was settled in her bedroom. I spread the sheet and quilt on the sofa, arranged the pillow at one end, turned off the light, and disappeared.

Chapter 3

The luminous glow of the moon through the windows provided enough light to find the desk and turn on a droopy gooseneck lamp with a green metal shade. I immediately felt at home. I was quite familiar with Sam Cobb's office, the battered oak desk stained by coffee rings and long-ago cigarette burn scars, the wall with the detailed city map of Adelaide and assorted Impressionist prints, an old-fashioned green blackboard with white chalk in the tray—Sam once taught high school math and disdained modern grease boards—and a worn leather couch near the windows that looked out over Main Street.

I settled into his desk chair, opened the center drawer. I found a sheet of paper with a list of scratched-out words except for the most recent addition. Sam loathed passwords, often demanded aloud in his deep voice, *If a computer's not secure in the police*

station, where the hell is it secure? But Mayor Neva Lumpkin demanded that city employees change passwords each week. This
week's password was *Curlicue*. I wondered if Sam was hungry
when he came up with that one. I pictured him at Lulu's, dip-
ping a clump of the cafe's signature curly french fries in heavily
peppered ketchup.

I turned the chair, tapped the mouse, entered the password.
I wished he was here and I could tell him about the missing
girl, but that would entail revealing the theft of more than a
hundred thousand dollars. Sam was an understanding police
chief, willing to listen, but a stolen box of money would certainly propel him to action, which very likely would see Susan
jailed, the money returned to Wilbur Fitch. I had every intention of making sure the mass of cash ended up in the safe. Susan
could pay the ransom, Sylvie would come home, and I, unseen,
would have easy access to the money. As soon as Sylvie was free,
I would hijack the ransom and a kidnapper would be outwitted.

I imagined the kidnapper's call to Susan. *Come alone. You
will be watched. If you want to see Sylvie again, do precisely as
instructed. Put the box inside the Prichard mausoleum next to the
greyhound.*

Every Adelaidean is familiar with the mausoleum that houses
the stone tombs of Maurice and his wife, Hannah. His resting
place is graced by a statue of his faithful greyhound, hers by a
statue of her Abyssinian cat. The instructions would allow Susan
only minutes to arrive to preclude a police trap. The cemetery
offered many vantage points where Susan could be observed.

If not the cemetery, there were other possibilities around

town. There was open space near the merry-go-round in the park. Or possibly a country road could be used: Leave the box at mile marker 7.

Whatever the venue, I would be there, Susan's unseen companion. I pictured her hurried placement of the box, Susan getting into her car, driving away, the cell phone in her lap. Perhaps she would be told to drive downtown, park at the library or near the cement plant, anywhere far from the location of the ransom. She would drive away, park, await the call signaling Sylvie's release, but I would remain with the box and I would discover the identity of the kidnapper.

However, I like to hedge my bets. Now that I had a specific list of suspects, I intended to discover every scrap of information possible just in case . . . I pushed away the thought that the call might never come, that it might be too late for Sylvie. I would hold to the hope that such a meticulously planned enterprise would run according to schedule. The objective was a box full of money and that depended upon contacting Susan.

The temperature was chilly in Sam's office. Buildings do love to lower the thermostat at night. I swirled present in a rose-marled crewneck sweater, gray heather wool trousers, rose leather ankle-top boots, and warm argyle socks. As a pepper upper I added a ceramic necklace, five colorful oblongs on a beaded chain. I stifled a yawn. My eyes felt grainy with fatigue. Yes, a ghost—excuse me, Wiggins—emissary needs slumber, too. Wiggins dislikes the use of *ghost* to describe his emissaries. But as Mama always told us, "Calling a spade an excavation implement doesn't change what it is." As for appearing, I needed any boost I could manage, and the sweater—I smoothed one sleeve—was elegant. For a burst of energy, I opened Sam's lower left desk drawer, found his big sack of M&M'S, poured myself a handful.

Buoyed by sugar, I pulled a sheet of paper from my pocket. Susan had given me her insights about the luncheon guests. I wanted to refresh my memory of each of the seven before I utilized Sam's computer to do a more extensive search. I placed the sheet with Susan's information on Sam's desk.

Present at Luncheon

George Kelly—Wilbur's lawyer. Flamboyant. As tall as Wilbur, but lanky. Wears Tony Lama cowboy boots. As loud as Wilbur, too. An all-purpose lawyer. He won a couple of big oil and gas cases for Wilbur. The company doesn't have in-house counsel, so George pretty much oversees everything. He bills Wilbur at least a hundred thousand a year, sometimes more. He thinks he's God's gift to women, looks at me a little too closely, calls me hon. He and his wife divorced a couple years ago, and he asked me out a few times. I told him I had a steady boyfriend. I don't think he believed me.

Todd Garrett—Chief operating officer of Fitch Enterprises. Thinning brown hair, pudgy face, thousand-watt smile. Knows everybody in the company from the guy who fixes the toilets to the shop foreman to the personnel director. Divorced. Spends his weekends at his cabin down at Lake Texoma. Loves to hunt and fish.

Alan Douglas, twenty-seven. Vice president in charge of projects and designs. He has short-cut brown hair and a long face. He stoops when he comes through doorways, so I guess he's a little taller than Wilbur. He joined the company just over two years ago. MBA from OU. He carved a model of the SIMPLE Car out of wood that he carries around with him. Wilbur said it looks like a Studebaker.

Harry Hubbard, twenty-four. Wilbur's stepson by his second wife, Hayley. Wilbur's been married twice. No wife presently. Neither ex lives in town. I guess they both ended up with plenty of money. Hayley's apartment overlooks Central Park. Linda lives on her yacht, and I think it's in the Mediterranean right now. Harry's tall, blond, handsome, smiles a lot, flatters Wilbur, a good golfer, but, funny thing, Wilbur always wins.

Minerva Lloyd. Mid-thirties. Wilbur calls her a good companion. For that you can read mistress. *Blonde by choice. Definitely not skinny. Maybe that's why he has a Rubens nude in his bedroom, and before you ask, I only visited it last year when he had the flu and needed to dictate some letters.*

Juliet Rodriguez. Hired to inventory his library. Teaches psychology at Goddard. Drop-dead gorgeous, tawny hair, olive complexion, dark chocolate eyes, an enigmatic smile.

Ben Fitch—Wilbur's son. He doesn't look anything like Wilbur. Dark hair. Handsome. Regular features. Blue eyes that are really bright and really look at you. He's about six feet tall. Not nearly as big as Wilbur. There's something about him that makes you tense. Like when a storm's coming and you can feel electricity in the air. He came in a week ago from Hawaii. I'd never met him. I don't think they were in close contact. Wilbur never mentioned him.

Feeling well briefed by Susan, I turned to Google. I found *Gazette* stories, checked addresses on Zillow for value, looked at Facebook pages. In my day private was private and you didn't put your undies out to dry on the backyard clothesline. I suppose these days Mike Shayne would do his first search online. I made notes, filling in some blanks.

George Kelly, forty-seven, a partner in Kelly and Wallis law firm, president of the Rotary Club, a golf champion at the country club, a bulldog rodeo champion. Divorced two years ago. No children. Decree awarded six-hundred-thousand-dollar house to ex-wife and substantial monthly alimony. Pictured in society pages with several different women.

Todd Garrett, forty-eight, was active in a half dozen service groups and chief pancake flipper for the annual Kiwanis supper, owned a collection of antique cars, was divorced, no children.

His FB page sported a half dozen photos of him waterskiing. Lived in a condo but owned a cabin at Lake Texoma and a spiffy Bayliner 285 Cruiser.

Alan Douglas. Math major. Won science competitions in school. Received an MBA from OU. Joined Fitch Enterprises two years ago. Single. No civic clubs. Belongs to a chess club. Likes to ski. Lives in an apartment house near downtown. If he had a significant other, there was no mention. An interior shot of a small windowless room—a rented storage space?—featured a SIMPLE Car made from plywood. The model was painted bright orange. I remembered Studebakers and nodded in recognition. I wondered if he chose that similar design as a tribute to the simplicity of the past.

Harry Hubbard. No service organizations, no church, but he sported a photo album on FB: Harry bowling. Harry at Playa del Mar. Harry snorkeling. Harry on Maui. Harry in Munich, beer stein hoisted. Harry playing poker with some cool-eyed dudes who didn't look like frat boys. Harry's tousled hair and boyish face exuded charm except in the poker pic.

Minerva Lloyd modeled in charity fashion shows. One outfit in particular appealed to me, a sweater beaded with sparkling fleur-de-lis, a pencil-thin camel hair skirt, and scalloped oatmeal textured flats. But there was something lacking. . . . Of course. I would set the sweater off with a multi-chain necklace and a teardrop crystal pendant. Interspersed with fashion shots were pictures of the interior of her store, Dare to Dress. Likely she modeled clothes available at her store. Running a small business takes hours of effort, care, and diligence. The income might be nice but not spectacular. Susan made the point that Minerva was Wilbur's mistress. He might be generous, but she wouldn't have access to the money available to a wife.

Juliet Rodriguez. Her FB entries featured a very serious photograph, hair drawn in a bun, horn-rimmed glasses, and a high-neck blouse, and a series of essays on what in my day might be called pep talks. They explored in a very bright manner: How to Deal with Adversity, The Beginning of a New You, Applying Psychology to Everyday Dilemmas, Leaving the Past Behind, Knowing Your Limits, The Magic of Smiles. I read several. Oh my, she meant so well. She not only saw the world through rose-colored glasses, she added spangles of gold and silver. I never doubted Sylvie adored her class.

Ben Fitch, twenty-eight. BBA from OU. His FB page was heavy on sports. Ben playing tennis. Ben rock climbing. Ben skiing. Ben on a boogie board as a breaker curled and foamed. Ben with a bikini-clad blonde on a catamaran. Ben with a gorgeous brunette in a gondola. Ben standing by a stack of deck chairs with Diamond Head in the background.

I added Wilbur Fitch's name to the list. Google showed enough results to warrant a week of reading. I was more interested in a full-length portrait recently hung in the library at the college. Short curly reddish hair flecked with silver, big face, broad forehead, bold nose, blunt chin. Instead of a formal blue suit, white shirt, and red tie, he wore a baggy gray sweater, khaki slacks, and Adidas sans socks. The artist captured the eagle sharpness of dark brown eyes, the steel strong determination of firmly closed lips. He stood near a table littered with old computer parts, balancing a mouse on one big palm. The image radiated energy. I could picture him striding up and down the aisles in a warehouse or negotiating deals. I would be very interested to learn what Wilbur Fitch, intense, engaged, observant, noted about his guests when he called for his secretary to bring the coins from the safe to the dining room.

～

I woke up, grateful for the warmth of a cotton nightgown. Susan kept her house chilly at night, too. I was deliberately up very early. I neatly folded the sheets and blanket, placed them atop a pillow at one end of the couch. To start a day that would likely demand quick wits and a steady hand, I needed a hot shower, fresh clothes, and a first-class breakfast. I made sure Susan's alarm was on and disappeared.

I arrived at Rose Bower, a forty-room limestone mansion with extensive formal gardens on fifty acres of woodlands. The grand estate is used for honored visitors and special events. I'd spent time there—mostly unseen—when in Adelaide to tidy up concerns about vandalism at the library. I appeared in a stately upstairs bedroom that was flamboyantly red, a Victorian sofa in red damask, a four-poster bed with red bolsters, velvet hangings in red. The fire engine brightness was surely a supercharged way to start the day. After a luxurious hot shower, I appreciated the oversize fluffy towel. I appeared and chose a costume for a good day. I'm afraid Wiggins considers my interest in fashion frivolous, but appropriate dress supports successful action. This was a day to settle down to business: Bring Sylvie safely home.

49

Arrange the arrest of a kidnapper. Return the box of cash to Wilbur's safe.

I pirouetted in front a charming full-length Victorian mirror in an oak frame and nodded approvingly at a bright red cowl-neck sweater, a plaid bouclé skirt, blue and red squares against a fawn background, and red suede wedgies. My red curls were shiny, my green eyes eager. Confident I was well-dressed, I disappeared.

Lulu's Cafe on Main Street was the best place in town for breakfast, lunch, and dinner in my day. Happily for me, Lulu's continues to thrive. Outside Lulu's, I ducked into a dark doorway and became visible. I pushed through the front door. It's nice that some things don't change. The plate glass mirror reflected the counter with a row of red leather stools, a few tables in the center, and four booths against the opposite wall. The smell of bacon and sausage and coffee tantalized. There was only one space at the counter, the tables were filled with Adelaide's movers and shakers. I looked at the booths.

Wiggins lifted a hand in a summoning gesture.

Uh-oh. How did he know I was coming here? But I knew the answer. Wiggins keeps close track of his emissaries. Usually, he isn't in touch unless he is displeased or uneasy. I sped to the back of the room and slid onto the smooth leather opposite him. Instead of his stiff blue cap and heavy white shirt and flannel trousers, he was appropriately attired in a plaid flannel shirt open at the neck and brown trousers. His big face was a bit chiding. But only a bit.

I believe in setting the tone. "Fancy meeting you here."

"Precept Four."

"Become visible only when absolutely necessary." I spoke rapidly and put heartfelt emphasis on the final word.

He raised a thick reddish eyebrow. "Necessary?"

"Susan's only twenty-four." My tone evoked the image of a pitiful waif in a dungeon. "She's terrified for her little sister. She needed reassurance. I was compelled to comfort her."

"Umph."

His response was noncommittal but not a resounding negative. I pressed my case. "Alone. Late at night. No call from the kidnappers. She felt hopeless."

As he slowly nodded, a tall, thin waitress arrived with a pot of coffee. She filled our cups. Her long face was a road map of lost illusions softened by the willingness to smile and be kind. "You folks good today?" Her voice was raspy.

"We're fine." Wiggins smiled.

"Heavenly," I added.

She gave me a quick look. "Now that's a new one. I like that. *Heavenly.* Next time my smart-mouth boyfriend texts me he ain't coming, I'll text back: *Having a Heavenly day.* That'll bring him running. He'll think I got a slab of ribs or a hot blackjack hand. Now, what can I get you folks?"

I ordered sausage, grits, fried eggs, and Texas toast. Wiggins chose bacon, scrambled eggs, corned beef hash, and biscuits with cream gravy. She saw my envious look. "You want some gravy, hon?" I nodded.

As she moved away, I avoided his gaze and hurried to speak. "Of course I was desolate to contravene Precept Four"—if my language was somewhat stilted, it was deliberately chosen for my listener—"because—"

A rumble of laugher interrupted me.

I looked up at him.

Wiggins's spaniel brown eyes were kind. "I remind myself that you mean well. And"—he brightened—"Susan clings to the thought that she is imagining you. Certainly that perception is better than for her to truly recognize your status. And"—now his tone warmed—"that's the only time you have appeared. One transgression does not destroy a mission. We all"—magnanimity here—"must be granted some understanding."

The implication is that we both knew I was a wobbly emissary but one strike didn't send me to the bench.

Our plates arrived and we tucked into our magnificent Lulu breakfast. I was delighting in the excellence of cream gravy on Texas toast when Wiggins gave an avuncular nod. "Your appearance to reassure Susan is understandable. In the main, you have done excellent work."

I felt like Donald Lam when Bertha Cool admired his efforts.

"However."

The Texas toast remained poised in the air.

"I have a grave concern." His face creased in a troubled frown.

I replaced the toast on my plate, waited apprehensively.

"The box." His glance was conspiratorial, and his voice dropped. "You know the box to which I refer?"

I nodded and pictured the red, white, and blue box on the card table in Susan's living room.

"We cannot"—his voice was firm—"be complicit in the execution of grand theft. I have a solution."

I began to breathe again. "Solution?"

"Find a store that sells that kind of shoe. Surely some boxes are discarded. Taking such a box isn't theft. If the disappearance is noticed, it will simply be one of those puzzles that occur in everyday life." His look was hopeful. "A box is missing. They will find a solution." He gave a casual wave of the hand holding a strip of bacon.

Shoe stores display their wares. There would be discarded boxes. I would procure one. I said quickly, "That's easy to arrange."

He beamed approval. "Fill the box with folded sheets of newspaper or anything that makes the weight similar to the box filled with bills. If you hurry you can take care of this before Susan arises. She will leave the box with paper wherever the kidnapper directs, and you can return the original box to its owner."

And in my spare time I could solve the problems of globalism and climate change. However, as my mama always told us kids: "To change a man's plan, start with praise."

"Wiggins"—I gazed with wide-eyed admiration—"that is simply a splendid solution." I paused as if struck by a thought. "But Susan is quite a good secretary, and good secretaries double-check. I can't make the substitution until she looks to be sure the money is in the box. Then I'm sure there will be a moment when I can make the switch." Another pause. Did I appear to have a thought balloon above my head? "Oh. I just realized what will happen. The kidnapper will tell Susan to leave the box in a particular place and then depart. The kidnapper will come and get the box and open it. If the money isn't in there, Sylvie won't be released, and—it's frightening to imagine—the kidnapper might follow through on the threat to harm her." I pressed fingertips against my cheeks. "I know!" Triumph lifted my voice. "I will remain with the box, follow the kidnapper to be sure Sylvie is released, and then I will take the box."

Wiggins nodded judiciously. "A good plan, Bailey Ruth, a very good plan."

I didn't tell him it was my original plan. I simply looked modestly pleased.

○

Susan was attractive in a turquoise cashmere sweater and gray slacks. But the fingers holding a pin to fasten a matching cashmere scarf shook, and her face was drawn and forlorn. She managed to fasten the scarf then whirled and walked to the card table. She started to pick up the box, her hand inches away from the cardboard side, froze. Instead she grabbed the black leather gloves lying there, pulled them on. True to my warning to Wiggins, she lifted the lid, slapped it back in place. She stood beside the card table, her shoulders hunched, and held the box tightly in her gloved hands. Her dark eyes scanned the room.

It would be daunting to have in your possession more than a

hundred thousand dollars in a modest house with ordinary door locks and windows that likely could easily be pushed up. Was she thinking what might happen if a thief chose this morning to break in? She tucked the box under her arm and walked across the room to a hall closet. She opened the closet door, pulled out a canvas book bag, slid the box in. She glanced at the clock, put an arm through the bag's cotton straps, grabbed her purse, and hurried outside. When she reached the car, she struggled again with indecision, finally opened the trunk, put the book bag inside. She removed the gloves and dropped them beside the carryall.

In the car she gripped the wheel tightly, backed out, drove fast, the same route we'd taken the night before. She stared straight ahead, her shoulders rigid.

"Think of Waikiki and ukuleles."

Her head jerked toward the apparently empty passenger seat. "The sheets and blanket were folded on top of the pillow this morning on the couch. I thought maybe I'd dreamed you and put the bed things out."

"I'm here." I made my voice deliberately cheery. "It's a beautiful day." The air was November thin, but sunlight spilled through the trees and onto the street. "Soon Sylvie will be home and we'll put the money back in the safe and—"

One gloved hand swept from the wheel, fumbled, found my arm, gripped. "Are you sure?" Her voice was heartbreakingly husky.

"Of course." I prayed my hope was true, that a bright young life was safe, would be safe. "You'll get a call—"

Her grip on my arm tightened. "That's what I thought." The words came in jerks. "That's why I put the money in the trunk. Sometimes I go home for lunch, but I thought if the call came at noon and I already had the money in the car, I could take it wherever. It's almost eight now. Four more hours and Sylvie will come home." Her hand let go of my arm, returned to the wheel. "Then I'll tell Wilbur what happened and promise to pay him back. If he calls the police, I don't care, not if Sylvie is safe."

"Everything will go according to plan." I felt relaxed as Susan turned onto Hillside, the wide street that curved through trees to the ridge where Wilbur Fitch's mansion stood. The car came around the willows.

Susan drew in a sharp breath and braked. The mansion spread in three-story grandeur atop the hill, golden walls gilded by the early morning sun. Cars filled the circular drive: a half dozen police cars, a silver Lexus, a brown sedan that looked familiar to me. A police cruiser was parked sideways at either end of the drive, blocking access or departure. Red beacons flashed.

"Continue toward the house." I was firm. "You can't drive away. The policeman saw you."

"Do you think"—she scarcely managed the words—"Wilbur knows the money's gone?"

"You are coming to work. You have to act as though you don't know anything about a robbery. Go on up to the foot of the drive."

I knew it took every ounce of Susan's will to drive forward, to pull up beside the police car. She rolled down her window.

The officer, young with short-cut brown hair, a thin face, and brown eyes alive with excitement, stepped up to the window. "Access to this residence is closed, ma'am."

"What's happened?" She looked at the cars in the drive, the many official cars.

"No visitors are allowed. An investigation is in progress."

That could mean anything from a hunt for a rabid dog to a domestic incident to a homicide. But I found it hard to believe the police presence had nothing to do with a missing shoe box crammed with fifties. I poked Susan.

She managed to speak. "I'm Susan Gilbert, Mr. Fitch's secretary. I'm due at work at eight thirty."

I hoped he didn't notice that her voice was wobbly.

"Wait here." He walked away, pulled a cell phone from his belt.

Susan stared up the drive. "What am I going to do?"

"You are a secretary. You are here to work. Get that terrified look off your face."

"What if—"

I placed a cautionary finger on her lips as the young policeman strode back to the car. "You can go up. I'll move the cruiser."

Susan turned the car into the drive. She glanced in the rearview mirror, saw the cruiser once again move into position to block the drive. "I'm trapped." Her voice was toneless.

"Don't worry. Somehow everything will work out. If you have to stay here"—she shot me a panicked glance—"I'll take your cell and keys and see that the money gets where it needs to go." I wasn't sure how I could manage that legerdemain, but my objective at the moment was to keep Susan from crumbling.

She had to deal with whatever awaited us in the mansion basking in sunlight.

A stone-faced officer with midnight black hair in a ponytail waved her to a parking spot behind the gleaming silver Lexus. She was crisp. "Go straight ahead, up the steps. Inside turn right."

As we walked, Susan murmured, "That's the main living room. Maybe there's a gas leak or something." Her voice was hopeful. "They send out lots of cars for something like that."

But I was looking at the brown sedan, and its presence didn't reassure me. However, Wilbur Fitch was an important citizen, and a crime at his home—theft from his safe?—might well bring out the Adelaide chief of police.

Waiting near the broad front steps was Joan Crandall, the *Gazette*'s star reporter, obviously alerted by the police scanner in the newsroom. The breeze stirred her silver-streaked brown hair, tugged at a shapeless cardigan. As we started up the steps, she called out to Susan, "Name?"

Susan ducked her head, ignored the question, hurried to the front door, which stood open. She stepped inside, and an officer with blond hair and a pleasant face gestured at an archway.

The archway opened into a magnificent room with Louis XVI furniture and paintings that would look at home at the Louvre. Six chairs were filled. A balding man with alert brown eyes sat with his powerful arms folded, his broad face impassive. He was unshaven in a gray sweatshirt and sweatpants and sneakers. A woman in a red jumper and an apron flicked uneasy glances toward the hallway. A statuesque blonde, her coronet

braids precise, fingered a pearl necklace at the throat of an attractive gray cashmere turtleneck. Her slender face was distressed. Occupying straight chairs were three women in neat
gray uniforms with *Acme Cleaning* stitched on the left shirt
pocket. Three very different faces but in common each stared
with rounded eyes at the policewoman in the doorway. Standing
near a fireplace was Wilbur's son Ben, his dark hair scarcely
combed, barefoot in a T-shirt and jeans. He was clearly in a
state of shock, his hands placed on the back of a straight chair
in a viselike grip.

There was not a vestige of sound.

Susan stopped in the archway. One hand rose to her throat.
"Ben, what's happened?"

He looked at her. His eyes held anguish and disbelief. "Susan, Dad's—"

A hefty officer in his late twenties was brusque. "No talking.
Each person will be interviewed. Until then, no conversation."

Susan walked to a straight-backed chair beneath a tropical
Gauguin. She sat down, clutching her purse, her face tight with
anxiety.

I knew terror tugged at her heart. Had Wilbur Fitch discovered the theft? She must feel like a desperate animal trapped in
quicksand. Could she leave this room? Would she be stopped? If
she was held here, how could she deliver the ransom and save
Sylvie?

Chapter 4

I bent near, whispered, "Don't be afraid. I'll be back."

Her response was a quick intake of breath. The rigidity of her body didn't lessen. Perhaps my unseen presence was some comfort. Or perhaps she was concerned about what I might do. She was overwhelmed by her fear for Sylvie and a desperate need to be free when the ransom call came. Likely she was terrified that the theft of the box filled with cash accounted for the police presence and the sequestering of those present in a room heavy with forced silence.

I needed to find out what I could as quickly as I could, perhaps devise some means of escape for Susan.

Several police officers and forensic techs clustered in the hallway. Near the open door to Wilbur Fitch's study I saw two detectives I recognized, tall lanky Don Smith and sturdy Judy

Weitz. Don was a computer-savvy detective with a sardonic worldview. Judy, placid faced and cheerful, was always pleasant and even-tempered, but it would be a mistake to equate her stolidity with stupidity. Don's strong-boned face squinted in thought. Judy gazed into the study, watched with bright observant eyes.

Inside the study, Adelaide police chief Sam Cobb stood next to the massive mahogany desk. On the wall behind the desk, the painting was pulled to one side to reveal the open door to the safe. I felt a squeezing in my chest. Susan had definitely closed the safe last night. Now the safe was open. Also open was the door to the garden. A slight breeze stirred the long velvet drape nearest the door.

Sam's grizzled black hair looked unruly, as if he'd received an early call and scarcely paused to use a comb. Sam is a big, solid, muscular man. His face is blunt with bold features. His brown suit was wrinkled, perhaps from several days' wear. I thought the white shirt was fresh. His red tie was already loosened and yanked to one side. Sam wasn't looking at the pulled-back painting or the interior of the safe or the open door. He stared at the floor next to the desk.

Susan would not have the chance to tell Wilbur Fitch about the ransom call or promise somehow to return the stolen money. Wilbur Fitch lay stretched on the floor, the back of his head a mass of dried blood and lacerated tissue. He appeared smaller in death, the body slumped heavily face forward. He wore a white tuxedo shirt, the collar and back now stained with blood, tuxedo trousers, black socks, and navy blue house shoes.

Brisk steps sounded. Tall, blond Detective Sergeant Hal Price strode into the study. I am very fond of Hal and take no small credit for his recent marriage. He stopped next to the chief, gazed at the still body. "Damn."

Sam gave him an inquiring look.

Hal jammed his hands into his slacks pockets. "Deirdre and I were here last night. Wilbur loved to throw big parties. This was to celebrate the thirtieth anniversary of the founding of Fitch Enterprises. He started in a ten-by-twelve-foot decrepit old shed down by the railroad tracks. That was his first warehouse. He described the rats that fought him for possession, and I mean real rats with six-inch tails. He had a hell of a good time. Like he said, *From rat house to this house.* He was a complicated guy. Down-home, liked his grits, no pretense, but he filled a room. You knew he was there, and you knew he could buy and sell anybody anytime he chose. He worked like a demon. He liked to brag about never getting more than three or four hours' sleep, yet he had more energy than anyone around him." A pause. "Last night he didn't look like a man who was going to be murdered. Danced every dance, mostly with Minerva Lloyd. They've been an item for five, six years. Ever since his last divorce. He also danced with a really good-looking gal. Deirdre knows her out at the college. Juliet Rodriguez, a psychology prof." Hal's gaze flickered to the safe, then the body. "I'd say he opened the safe and somebody took him out with a blackjack."

The slap of sneakers. A wiry bundle of energy in a ratty sweatshirt, faded jeans, and sneakers hurtled through the door. Jacob Brandt was the local medical examiner. He stopped just inside the door, gave a low whistle. "I got the call. Didn't know it was the master of the manse. Somehow you don't expect Croesus to get offed." He was across the room, dropping to one knee and pushing up the sleeve of the baggy gray sweatshirt. He pulled a pair of plastic gloves from a back pocket, picked up a flaccid arm, held the wrist. "Yeah. Dead. Probably"—he moved the limp arm—"about five to seven hours ago. At the earliest around one a.m. Back of his skull crushed. Likely never knew what hit him."

"A blackjack?" Hal asked.

"Could be. Or wet sand knotted in a sock. Great weapon. Whack, empty out the sand, throw the sock in the wash. Good to go. Nobody will ever prove a connection to murder." He came to his feet. "I'll get you a report. But pretty obvious. Blunt trauma. Now I got to get out to the high school. A body found in the football stands. No sign of foul play. But opiates are about as foul as it comes." His young face was bleak as he headed into the hall.

As Brandt left, death officially established, the uniformed phalanx from the hall entered, free now to begin slow careful measurements, take pictures, lift fingerprints, collect evidence.

Sam gave the open safe another look, then lumbered toward the hall door, skirting Wilbur Fitch's outflung hand. Hal walked beside him. When they stepped into the hall, Weitz and Smith both stood a little taller and straighter.

I was at Sam's elbow when he said to Hal, "I want to know what was in that safe."

Hal nodded, checked his phone. "Wilbur's secretary arrived about ten minutes ago. She may be able to help. She's in with the people who were on the premises when we arrived."

"Who was in the house when the body was discovered?"

Hal used a thumb to slide the screen. "Carl Ross, Fitch's butler. Marta Jones, cook. She arrived at the house shortly after six, never left the kitchen. The housekeeper, Rosalind Millbrook. Three employees of a local maid service, Emma Edwards, JoAnn Harmon, and Ellen Garcia. The housekeeper oversees their work. They come daily. One houseguest, Ben Fitch, his son."

Weitz spoke up. "Dispatcher was notified at a quarter to eight." She pulled a slim notebook from a pocket. "Fitch's butler reported a homicide, identified victim as Wilbur Fitch. Ross told dispatch he was looking for Mr. Fitch, that his bed had not been slept in. He came downstairs, saw a light shining out into the hall from the study. When he walked into the study, he found Mr. Fitch lying on the floor with the back of his head caved in. Ross said he was unable to find any sign of life. First officers on the scene were Holliday and Cain. Three cruisers followed and an ambulance. Officer Holliday directed the occupants of the house to gather in the living room and remain silent until called for an interview. Officer Holliday remains on duty there. Officer Cain directed a search of the house and found no one in any of the rooms. The officers in Cars Three and Four searched the grounds. No one found."

Sam looked up and down the hall. "Where can we talk to these people?"

Detective Smith gestured down the long hallway. "The dining room."

Sam nodded. "Get the secretary."

⌇

The banners hung still and straight. Sunlight slanted through huge east windows, making the crimson letters FITCH vivid against white silk, the blue Dodgers pennant bright as the day it was made, the Oklahoma flag glorious with seven red-tipped eagle feathers dangling from an Osage buffalo hide shield on a blue field.

Sam wasn't diminished by the length of the long table. He sat at the head of the table, solid, stalwart, and commanding. The chair to his right was empty. Hal Price sat next to the unoccupied seat. Judy Weitz lifted out a recorder, checked to be sure it was in working order, placed it on the table, took her place across from Hal.

Officer Holliday held the massive dining room door open as Susan stepped inside. She paused, eyes wide, glanced around as if seeking someone. She stood in a shaft of sunlight, young and appealing in her blue sweater and gray slacks.

Sam rose. "We appreciate speaking to you, Miss Gilbert. I'm Sam Cobb, chief of police." He nodded at Hal, who also rose. "Detective Sergeant Hal Price. Detective Judy Weitz." He gestured at the empty chair to his right. "Please sit here."

Judy Weitz turned on the recorder, spoke in a low clear voice: "Interview with Susan Gilbert, 9:28 a.m., Wednesday, November 16."

It seemed to take a long time for Susan to walk the length of the table. The clip of her shoes on the flagstone floor sounded loud in the utter quiet. She knew every eye watched her. She managed to appear composed though concerned. Obviously anyone would be concerned to come to work and be greeted by a police presence. Her gaze moved from face to unrevealing face.

Hal pulled out the chair for her. She nodded her thanks as she sat down. The oblong pin holding her scarf glittered in the sunlight. I hoped the flash of red and blue and green stones didn't emphasize the paleness of her face.

The massive grandfather clock at the far end of the room tolled the half hour. Nine thirty.

Susan gripped her hands together. She spoke in a rush. "I have an appointment at noon. I need to leave here at a quarter to twelve."

"That shouldn't be a problem, Miss Gilbert. Now for a few particulars." Sam quickly obtained name, age, address, education, marital status, work history.

Susan replied as quickly, then leaned forward, her face anxious. "Where is Wilbur? Did he call you here?" Her voice was shaky.

Sam watched her with interest. He was always quick to sense unease, the telltale tension that betrays knowledge or fear or, sometimes, guilt.

"Why would Mr. Fitch call us?" His tone was guileless, as if he were merely inquiring, but his brown eyes were intent.

Susan burst out, "Something's wrong. Why are you here? What's going on? Why were we kept in the living room and told not to talk? Where's Wilbur? He's always in charge. What's happened?"

Sam's deep voice was pleasant. "We are conducting an investigation. We received a nine-one-one call at seven forty-five this morning. Carl Ross entered the study—"

Susan's face was suddenly sunken.

Sam watched her reaction, as focused as a hawk circling above a rabbit.

"—and he found Mr. Fitch's body near his desk."

Susan stared at him in horror. She leaned forward, held to the edge of the table. "In the study?" The words were scarcely audible. "That can't be true." She repeated, "That can't be true." But Sam Cobb's face told her she had not been the only visitor to the study last night, that she had come and gone, and that Wilbur entered the study later and never left.

Sam was now on full alert. Susan's response wasn't quite right. Instead of shock at murder, she was shocked at the site of the discovery. "Are you surprised Mr. Fitch was in the study late at night?"

Susan shifted in the chair. "Sometimes when I come—came—to work I'd find notes on my desk. I have a desk in a little alcove on one side of the room. He didn't sleep much. Everyone knew that. It would be like him to come to the study to work without thinking about the time. And you said he was found there?"

"Or perhaps"—Sam's gaze was riveted on her pale face—"he found someone in his study." When she made no reply, he pressed her. "What do you think?"

"I don't know. I can't believe this has happened." Her face crumpled. "I can't believe he's gone. I never knew anyone more alive. When he walked into the room, it was as if the lights were suddenly brighter and the music louder. Everything was better. He shouted a lot"—tears slipped down her cheeks—"but he was kind and generous."

"Apparently he was struck down after he opened the safe."

"The safe?" She scarcely managed to speak. "The safe was open?"

"Yes." Sam's stare was hard. "You know about the painting that conceals the safe?"

"The painting moves." Her voice was thin and shaky.

Sam's eyes narrowed as he tried to figure out what caused the look of devastation that followed his mention of the safe. "Do you know why he would open the safe?"

She shook her head.

"Please answer yes or no."

"No."

"Are you familiar with the contents of the safe?"

"Yes." The reply was barely audible.

Sam leaned forward. "How do you know the contents of the safe?"

"Sometimes Wilbur asked me to bring things from the safe."

"Such as?"

"He has two valuable coin collections. American Gold Eagles and Roman coins from the time of Julius Caesar. When he worked"—she edged her tongue over dry lips—"he'd ask for one of the collections. He kept the American Eagles in a small lacquered wooden chest and the Roman coins in a velvet bag, and he'd put the chest or bag on the desk and open it. He picked out special coins that he liked and arranged them, sometimes in rows, sometimes in stacks. He said touching coins that had survived through the centuries relaxed him. Sometimes he'd talk about a particular coin, tell me its age and what it was worth. He knew the value of each coin."

"Was there anything else in the safe that would attract a thief?"

"The shoe box." At Sam's frown, she continued jerkily, "Wilbur wanted cash available at any time of the day or night. He kept stacks of fifty-dollar bills in the box."

"Was the box full?"

"Yes."

"How much money was in the box?"

"I don't know. I think perhaps a hundred and fifty thousand dollars."

Sam gave a soft whistle. His eyes slid toward Hal. Hal pushed back his chair.

Susan's head swiveled to watch him cross to the huge door, push through.

A trill from a xylophone brought Susan to her feet, the chair crashing behind her on the stone floor. She scrabbled to tug her cell phone from her pocket, could scarcely stand she trembled so hard. Eyes wide and panicked, she held the phone, swiped. "Sylvie?" Her voice was half cry, half sob. "Oh, it's you, it's you— Wrong? I've been terrified. Where did they take you? Who was it? How did you get away?"

Sam heaved to his feet and Judy Weitz rose. To them, Susan's sudden distress must look like hysteria.

Susan rocked back and forth, tears streaming down her face. "Did they hurt you?" Her face suddenly changed. "Wait. Start over. . . ."

Sam frowned. "Ms. Gilbert—"

Susan held up a hand. "I have to talk to my sister." She spoke into the phone, the words rushing ahead, quick, urgent, frantic. "I thought you'd been kidnapped. I got a call last night—" She broke off, listened, her face a picture of incomprehension. "A prize?" Susan reached out, gripped the top slat in the chair, held on to it. "So it was a lie. Oh my God. But you're all right. Please stay there. I'll be home as soon as I can. Something dreadful has happened and the police are here. When I finish talking to them, I'll come home. Stay there."

She still held tight to the chair as she slid the phone into her pocket.

Sam came around the end of the long table, loomed over her, his face stern. "Who did you think was kidnapped?"

Susan stood quite still and straight. Abruptly, she lifted her chin, met his demanding stare. "I have information for you. But first I need to get something out of my car."

The big door swung in. Hal hesitated for an instant when he saw Sam and Judy standing and staring at Susan.

Sam's tone was steely. "You are not free to go until you explain that call and whatever call you received last night."

Hal closed the door behind him, stood with his hands loose at his side, feet apart, ready to block her way.

I truly revere the Precepts, including Precept Three: "Work behind the scenes without making your presence known." But as I am often forced to remind Wiggins, there are exceptions to the rule. I dropped down next to Sam, stood on tiptoe—he is much taller than I—and whispered, "Let her go to the car, Sam."

As I've said before, it's been my pleasure to assist Sam in several investigations. He has always been quite appreciative. Of course, he had no inkling I was currently in Adelaide, much less that I was present in the Fitch dining room. To say the whisper startled him put the situation quite mildly. He jerked toward the sound. "What—" he began, then broke off, clamped his lips together.

I'm afraid he almost exclaimed *What the hell!* and I was glad he caught himself. He stood like a bull pricked by a banderilla. I knew it took every bit of his iron discipline not to stare wildly about. But he knew what he'd heard. "On second thought," he said slowly, "you may go to your car. Detective Weitz will escort you, then you will return here."

I gave him an approving pat on the shoulder.

His eyes slid sideways, though he knew he wouldn't see me.

Susan showed spunk that had not been evident last night when she'd labored under extreme fear. "I have every intention of returning here." She whirled and hurried across the stone floor.

Hal held the door for Judy Weitz and Susan, then crossed to stand by Sam. "No shoe box in the safe. No bag or chest full of coins, either."

I left as Sam and Hal returned to the table. Outside, I was next to Susan when she unlocked the trunk. I was torn. Obviously, she'd decided to tell the police what had happened. Certainly, that decision was admirable. But I didn't see how this was going to end well.

Susan leaned into the trunk, grabbed the book bag. She pulled out the Reebok shoe box, dropped the bag on the floor of the trunk. She ignored the leather gloves lying on the floor of the trunk, but Judy saw them. "Gloves?" she inquired gently.

"I don't need them." Susan's tone was crisp.

I was even more uneasy when we walked into the dining room.

Sam and Hal stared at the shoe box. Sam's face was suddenly harder, his brown eyes colder. Hal's lips pursed in a silent whistle.

Susan marched directly to the end of the table, plopped the box down in front of Sam. She stood and spoke fast, starting with the ransom call. "Last night . . ."

Sam interrupted after she described the demand for a hundred thousand dollars. "You should have called the police."

Her dark brown eyes were defiant. "They said they'd kill Sylvie."

"You talk about *they*. One person? Two?"

Susan shook her head. "I don't know. It wasn't a real voice. It was high and metallic, like something out of a machine. I don't know if the caller was a man or a woman. All I know is they said they had Sylvie and I had to do exactly as ordered or she wouldn't live. I thought they had her tied up and hidden somewhere. But that didn't happen. Sylvie said—"

Sam held up a broad hand. "We'll talk to your sister. You're telling us about last night."

"Last night." She took a breath. "The voice said I had to pay a hundred thousand dollars. I said I didn't have that kind of money, couldn't get it, and the voice said, *Oh yes, you can get it. Go to Wilbur's safe and bring the box.* So I—"

Sam interrupted again. "You have the right to remain silent. Anything you say may . . ."

Susan heard him out. "I don't have anything to hide." She pointed at the box. "There's the shoe box from the safe. I intended to tell Wilbur what had happened when I got Sylvie home. I knew he'd understand. But everything's changed. Sylvie is safe. I don't have to pay ransom. There's the money. I've returned it. And here's the important part. I was in the study last night around eleven thirty. I came in through the door to the garden. The door was unlocked. The voice on the phone told me the door would be unlocked. I came inside and went to the safe. I opened the safe and took out the shoe box. Wilbur was not in the room. No one was there but me. I left through the garden and went home and waited for the kidnapper to call, but the call didn't come. It's crazy to think I got a fake call that Sylvie was kidnapped and told to get the shoe box out of the safe and there's no connection to Wilbur being found killed and the safe open. But he was not in the study when I came. He didn't enter the study while I was there. I never saw Wilbur after I left the house yesterday afternoon. Maybe this will help you." She was suddenly eager. She pulled out her phone, swiped, tapped. "Here it is. Recent Calls." She read off the number. "Maybe you can trace the phone, find out who called me, because the fake kidnapping has to be connected to Wilbur's murder."

Sam's stare was skeptical. "Why that kind of charade?"

Susan brushed back a strand of hair. "I don't know. The whole thing's crazy. Maybe the person who called me planned to kill Wilbur and thought I'd take the shoe box and keep it and somehow the police would find out and think I was guilty. But I never intended to keep the truth from Wilbur. And"—she pointed at the shoe box—"I didn't have to tell you about the box. Or return it."

Sam was emphatic. "Returning the money doesn't change the fact of theft."

"It doesn't matter."

"It matters." He sounded almost angry. "Grand theft. A felony. You can go to prison for years."

She stood on one side of the table, looked very young, very alone. She gave a huge sigh. "It doesn't matter now. Sylvie's all right. But you should listen to me. Whoever involved me must have done it to make it look like I killed Wilbur."

Sam stared at the box. "Was there anything else in your trunk?"

I knew he was inquiring about the missing coins. I was tempted to bend near and tell him Susan took only the shoe box, but that could wait until later.

"Anything else?" Susan looked blank.

Judy Weitz said quickly, "A pair of leather gloves."

Susan was impatient. "I wore the gloves when I opened the safe and held the box."

Sam was brusque. "You are in our custody for the present. I intend to obtain a search warrant—"

"A search warrant?" Susan looked shocked. "What for?"

"To search your home."

"You mean I can't see Sylvie until you get a search warrant?"

"That is correct."

"I have to see her, find out everything that happened last night."

"We will find out what happened."

"She's just a kid. She doesn't ever see bad things, doesn't believe in bad things. I have to be there when you talk to her. Look"—and now she was angry—"you can search whatever you want to. I don't care. I give you permission. Search my house and car and the garage and any place you wish, but I am going to go home and see my sister."

"We have your permission to conduct a search?"

"Yes. You can look anywhere you want."

Sam held her gaze. "In addition, you agree to remain silent when I speak with your sister."

"Yes."

Sam pushed back his chair. "Judy, interview the others who are waiting. Detach two officers to conduct a search of Ms. Gilbert's home and belongings." He leaned close to Judy, gave an instruction inaudible to us, stepped away, and looked at Hal. "Drive with Ms. Gilbert to her house."

⁂

I was comfortably seated in Sam's front passenger seat when he thumped heavily behind the wheel. He put out a hand, touched my shoulder. "I thought you might be here. As if this thing wasn't already screwy enough."

"I'm here to help."

He snapped his seat belt in place, punched the starter. The engine made an odd squealing noise.

I was startled. "What's that?"

"I've had it to three garages and they mutter about the brakes but the brakes work fine."

"The engine sounds like an eggbeater with a bent prong."

He gave a rumble of laughter. "That's good. That's what I'll tell them when I take it in next time." But the burst of good humor was quickly gone. He shot a quizzical look at the apparently empty passenger seat. "You aren't here about my car."

I went right to the point. "Everything Susan's told you is true."

A heavy sigh. "Outstanding citizen murdered. Safe rifled. Secretary comes up with wild tale about kidnapped sister and ransom money and dumps the stolen box of cash on the table. Slam dunk to arrest, charge, convict. Except for this voice— nice voice—that tells me to back off. The mayor will want an arrest ASAP. If I tell her I have it on good authority that the secretary's on the side of angels, she'll want to know, *Whose authority?* If I told her about you, I'd be in a psych ward before she could chortle, *Hurray, got rid of him at last.*"

We turned off Broadway into the area of more modest homes.

"I'd like to ignore you, pretend you aren't"—a thoughtful pause—"who you say you are. But I figured out a long time ago that the world is more than I see. Sometimes I'll go into a room and I smell gardenias and there's a shaft of light near a window and just for a heartbeat I see my sister Leah. She was killed in a car wreck. Twenty-two years old. But I see that glimmer and I know she's happy. So I know you're here. I know you are sent to help the good guys. But this time I think you've made a mistake. When did you join up with Ms. Gilbert?"

"At her house at approximately ten minutes after eleven last night. She was on the phone." I was as cogent as Della Street bringing Perry Mason up to date. "She was distraught. She begged the person she spoke to not to hurt her sister, said she couldn't get a hundred thousand dollars. She hung up, tried to call her sister. When there was no answer, she left a message." I described Sylvie's room, the discovery of her cell phone on the dresser, hearing Susan's message played back. The rush to the Fitch house, the cautious entry as the music blared, the opening of the safe—

Sam interrupted, asked for particulars, listened intently as we turned onto Susan's street. "Are you sure she took nothing from the safe except the shoe box?"

"Yes."

He nodded. As he pulled into the drive behind Susan's car, he said, "I don't have a good feeling about this one."

Chapter 5

Sylvie wriggled in Susan's tight embrace. She looked young and fetching in pink sweats. A headband with *Happy* worked in red beads against white terry cloth kept her blonde curls in check. She tried to pull free. "Hey, Susan, what's with this kidnap stuff?"

Susan held tight to her sister's arms. "You are all right. You are." Her voice shook. "Oh God, I was so frightened."

Her eyes wide as a startled doe, Sylvie looked beyond Susan at the doorway.

In the lead, burly Sam Cobb's somber face made the moment momentous. He was there with the force of law, and the law would not be denied. Hal Price, blue eyes intent, neither friendly nor hostile, watched Susan, seeking a sense of her character from her demeanor. Two uniformed officers waited a pace behind, a short middle-aged balding man with a fringe of wispy brown hair and a greyhound-lean fortyish woman with an impassive face. Their nameplates read respectively *Ofc. B. Riordan* and *Ofc. L. Malone.*

Sam turned to the officers. "You have your instructions?"

"Yes, sir." The lean woman pulled out a pair of plastic gloves. Her partner did the same.

Sylvie planted her hands on her hips. "This looks like a TV show. Big man frowning, lean sidekick, two stone-faced cops. You people need to learn how to smile."

Susan hurried to speak. "Something awful—"

Sam interrupted. "First, let's hear about last night." He moved heavily across the room, looked down. "Miss Sylvia Gilbert?"

Officers Riordan and Malone checked a bookcase, methodically pulled books out to look for any objects hidden behind.

Sylvie's hands dropped. She looked small and very young. "I'm Sylvie. Who are you?"

"Police Chief Sam Cobb."

"Police chief? Look, Susan has it all wrong. Nobody kidnapped me. You people can go away."

Sam gestured at the sofa. "Please sit down."

Sylvie looked at Susan, her blue eyes uncertain.

Susan said quietly, "Explain what happened, why you left your phone here and where you went."

The bookshelves done, the two officers moved about the room, lifting furniture.

Sylvie frowned. "What are they doing?"

Susan looked weary, resentful, grim. "They said they'd get a search warrant so I told them they can look wherever they want. I don't have anything to hide."

"What are they looking for?" Sylvie demanded.

Susan shrugged. "I don't know. But it's all right."

Sylvie fingered the neck of her pink sweatshirt. "You said there was trouble at work. Has something bad happened?"

Sam was smooth. "We'll get to that in a minute. Tell us about yesterday."

Sylvie plopped down on the sofa. Suddenly her face lightened, was eager and excited. "It was the funniest thing." She pulled off her headband, brushed her fingers through springy curls. "I went to my car after class yesterday morning and there was a bright yellow sheet tucked under the windshield wiper. I picked it up. I thought maybe it was a flyer and I'd get a discount off of something." She gave a quick grin. "I like discounts. But this was even better. I have the greatest psych prof. She comes up with fun challenges and we find out a lot about ourselves." She sounded young and earnest. "One time she had each one of us go to the animal shelter and make up a story about an animal. I picked out this huge charcoal gray cat who was missing part of one ear and—"

Sam intervened. "You found the flyer. What did it say?"

Sylvie's gaze clearly relegated Sam to the realm of old and no fun. "At the top of the sheet printed in big black letters it said: *A PSYCH TEST.* Below that in red letters it said: *Go without a cell phone or speaking to anyone for 24 hours and win two tickets to the next Blake Shelton concert.*" She paused. "Wow."

"Where is the flyer?"

"I didn't keep it. I tossed it in a trash can at McDonald's. See"—and she leaned forward—"I followed the directions. It said to put my cell phone in my bedroom. So I came home and put it on the dresser. I left Susan a note"—her glance at her sister was reproachful—"so you wouldn't worry. I told you I'd be back this morning. Anyway, I put my cell there. That was part of the instructions, everyone was to put—"

Sam held up a broad hand. "Wait a minute. Everyone?"

Officer Malone headed for the hallway and bedrooms, Officer Riordan stepped into the kitchen. There were muffled sounds from both locations as the search continued.

Sylvie was patient. "It would be our whole class. There are nine of us. The sheet said each person's phone had a GPS tracker. I don't know how she did that. Oh." Sylvie looked uncertain. "You won't put her in jail for that, will you? I know people aren't supposed to sneak trackers on people's phones, but this was for a class so that should make it all right. Academic freedom. Anyway, I got a kick out of thinking everyone in our class was busy putting their cell phones in their bedrooms. The rest of it was pretty simple. Lay low for twenty-four hours. No contact with anyone. Leave car parked where it was. The sheet said: *Transport provided. Follow map.* I did and walked ten paces west, eight paces east. There was a cute drawing of a ribbon and the instructions said *Ribbon Marks the Spot.* I followed the steps and there was a bike parked in a stand with a red, white, and blue ribbon tied to the handlebar, and it didn't have a lock so I knew I was supposed to use it. I don't know what the others did. I thought about checking in at a motel, but I didn't want to spend any money. Instead I took a sketch pad and biked to the lake."

One of the prettiest spots on campus was a small lake nestled between the fine arts building and the athletic fields.

"I sketched a heron. About five I rode the bike over to McDonald's and had supper, got a Big Mac and fries and chocolate malt. Then I rode the bike to the library and found a carrel. At closing time, I hid in a restroom, then I sacked out on a sofa in the lounge. This morning I got up and rode the bike to the cafeteria and ate breakfast. I didn't speak to anyone, so I kept my part of the bargain, and then the twenty-four hours were up. I rode the bike back to the stand across from the dorm and got in my car and came home. I decided to call Susan to tell her all about the test—"

Officer Riordan poked his head out from the kitchen. "Finished in here." He looked at Susan. "Is the garage locked?"

Susan shook her head. "We never lock up unless we're leaving town. You can lift the door. It's manual. Or go in through the side door."

"Thank you, ma'am." He moved silently away.

Sam cleared his throat, looked skeptically at Sylvie. "Did you check with your professor on this so-called test?"

Sylvie shook her head. "Doctor Rodriguez is always coming up with something different. I thought it was great fun."

"Can you text her?"

Sylvie nodded.

"Please do so. Inquire about the results of the no-cell-phone test."

Sylvie used her thumb.

I hovered behind her, read the text: *Did I win the Blake Shelton tickets?*

In only a moment, a reply pinged: *What Blake Shelton tickets?*

Sylvie's eyes widened. Quickly, her thumb moving faster than a hummingbird's wings, she sent another message.

In a moment another ping.

I read the professor's reply: *Someone played a joke on you. Sorry. If I find some Blake Shelton tickets, we can go together!*

Sylvie's eyes widened. "The test was a fake! Who—"

The back door slammed. Brisk footsteps sounded in the kitchen. Officer Riordan stepped into the living room. "Chief"— his voice was matter-of-fact, but his green eyes gleamed—"I found what we're looking for. Got photos. Objects remain in situ. You—"

Sam was already moving, Hal right behind him.

Susan stared at the retreating figures, hurried to catch up.

"Miss"—Officer Malone was in the doorway to the hall— "remain where you are."

"It's my garage. There isn't anything that could matter to the police."

She dashed across the kitchen, pushed through the screen door, clattered down the wooden steps.

The garage door was lifted, but Officer Riordan stood by a large galvanized tub near an outdoor faucet next to the back steps. Officer Riordan pointed into the tub. "The tub was bottom up. I saw some mud sticking to the rim. That stopped me. Sure, it made sense the tub was turned over to keep it from filling with rain. But I didn't like those mud fragments. They looked pretty fresh, so maybe the tub was sitting upright until, say, last night. I turned it over. Look what was there." He held a Maglite in one hand. The brilliant beam illuminated a small wooden chest and a lumpy red velvet bag.

"No." There was shock in Susan's voice, shock and utter disbelief.

I didn't need anyone to tell me that I was looking at the velvet bag and lacquered wooden chest that held Wilbur Fitch's prized rare coins.

∽

Neva Lumpkin stood with arms akimbo staring down at Sam Cobb. The mayor was a memorable figure. I think that is a kindly description. Her coronet braids were too rigid, her wide-striped orange and yellow blouse too bright, her brown slacks too tight. She was a six-foot, two-hundred-pound mass of self-regard, self-adulation, and self-aggrandizement.

She slapped her hands on the desktop. "I called twice. I texted three times. No response. I have to come to your floor and find you in a subordinate's office and, after hemming and hawing, you finally consent to speak with me. I am the mayor." The announcement was delivered in a stentorian tone. "I represent the people. One of Adelaide's shining lights has been struck down in the sanctity of his home—"

I thought sanctity was reserved for holy places, but I am always eager to learn.

"—and I pledge my sacred honor to devote myself fully to

the apprehension of his murderer." Her cheeks burned bright red. "Howie says the case is all wrapped up. The secretary broke into Wilbur's safe, absconded with cash and a rare coin collection, and the coins were actually found at her residence. I've had a dozen calls from the media. Even the *New York Times.*" A reverent pause. "I couldn't speak to them because I have not been informed."

Ah, now her fury was explained. Neva Lumpkin swayed like a cobra when the media flute played.

"Howie assures me it's only a matter of hours and an arrest will be made. I've called a press conference at noon."

Sam's face congealed at the mention of Detective Howie Harris, a sycophant the mayor would like to see named chief of police.

"According to Howie, the secretary cracked Wilbur's skull." Neva's heavy face assumed contours of sadness. "Wilbur Fitch, a town father. An example to all citizens of Adelaide, to all Oklahomans, to—"

"Yeah. All of the above."

The mayor gasped, her lips parted. Outrage lifted her penciled brows.

"I got it the first time, Neva. Damn shame about Wilbur. Agree there. We are investigating and talking to witnesses—"

She thumped the desk with a fist. "I understand the killer is in the building."

"We will interrogate a person of interest—"

"The secretary?"

"Not for publication." His voice was hard. "But," he hurried to forestall an explosion, "you are right to have the news conference. Tell reporters Wilbur Fitch was found dead in his study this morning. He suffered blunt trauma to the head. He was attacked from behind. The weapon has not been found. The ME says he was killed with a blackjack or some similar weapon. There are no witnesses to the crime. Tell reporters a shoe box filled with cash and some rare coins that were missing from his safe have been recovered. There is uncertainty as yet about the identity of his killer, but police hope to announce an arrest—" He glanced up at his clock. It was a quarter to noon. "—within forty-eight hours."

The explosion came. "Forty-eight hours! You have the killer here at this very moment."

Sam came to his feet. She was six feet tall, but he was taller. "The best of all possible worlds, Neva. You can have another press conference at noon tomorrow, spill out some more facts. I'll keep you up to date. Friday you can announce an arrest, wrap it all up with a big red bow."

Some enjoy visions of sugarplums. Neva Lumpkin's eyes glistened. Three press conferences . . .

⌁

Neva Lumpkin waved grandly at wooden straight chairs in a small room on the third floor of City Hall. She nodded at Joan Crandall from the *Gazette* and Deke Carson, a slouchy stringer for several papers, but Neva beamed at a portly newsman in a rumpled sweater and gray slacks. "You're Ted Burton, the AP bureau chief from Oklahoma City." He nodded. "I saw you at the conference of mayors."

It wouldn't have surprised me if Neva had dossiers on all Oklahoma reporters.

The room seemed full with the addition of three highly lacquered blonde TV reporters and their accompanying cameramen.

Neva gazed at each in turn. Her makeup was freshly applied, a fact apparent to any observer. She would certainly be visible on-screen, pink patches on her full cheeks and lips bright enough to rival a cherry Popsicle.

"It is with great sadness that I announce the brutal murder of Wilbur Fitch, one of Adelaide's finest citizens. Mr. Fitch was found . . ." She followed Sam's lead, concluding, ". . . intense investigation is under way and we expect to announce an arrest as soon as possible. A press conference will be held at noon tomorrow." She was too canny a politician to reveal Sam's decision to hold off on an arrest until Friday. Let the reporters assume there might be big news tomorrow.

Joan Crandall got the first question: How much money was in the shoe box?

The mayor was ready, thanks to Detective Howie Harris, her mole in the department: Approximately one hundred thousand dollars.

The AP bureau chief: How was the money recovered?

Neva was bland: Outstanding detective work. The details will be revealed when the arrest is announced.

The stringer, Deke Carson, was as unprepossessing as when

I first observed him during the murders at Silver Lake Lodge:
Is Fitch's secretary in custody?

Howie had apparently been sharing what he knew far and
wide.

Crandall and the bureau chief looked like pointers sighting
a fox.

Crandall: Who is his secretary?

Bureau Chief: Is the secretary a "person of interest"?

Neva's eyes narrowed. I suspected Howie would be instructed
that she and only she spoke with reporters. "The investigation
has not formally designated a 'person of interest.' However, I
can assure you appropriate steps are being taken. Mr. Fitch's
secretary is Susan Gilbert, and she is, along with others, being
interrogated by detectives in accordance with standard investigative practices. I assure you that—"

I rather doubted Neva would recognize an investigative practice if it joined her for morning coffee.

"—I and the Adelaide Police Department focus on the safety
of our community. Intense surveillance has been arranged, and
the public need have no fear that any danger is abroad. Thank
you very much. The next news conference will be tomorrow at
noon."

∽

I was familiar with the interrogation room at the police station.
Stark light from fluorescent bars in the ceiling illuminated the
straight wooden chair where Susan Gilbert sat. Her face was
drawn and pale. In her eyes I saw shock from the discovery of

the small wooden chest and the red velvet bag hidden beneath a tub in her backyard. She had to feel surrounded by danger, enmeshed in a trap with no way to escape. And wondering what hellish surprise might occur next.

Sam Cobb and Hal Price sat behind a wooden table. Sam's heavy face was folded in a frown. He knew what I'd told him, but Susan's guilt seemed apparent. Hal's gaze at her was cold. He'd liked Wilbur Fitch, and he obviously thought Susan was guilty.

A legal pad and pen were at each place. The table was far enough from the chair to be out of the bright fluorescent light. Sam clicked on a gooseneck lamp, twisted it to send another bright beam at Susan.

She blinked, turned a little to avoid the direct flare in her eyes.

Sam cleared his throat, repeated the Miranda warning. "You have the right to remain silent. . . ."

I bent close to Susan, whispered, "Ask him if the police have checked with neighbors about anyone seen near your house last night between one and two a.m."

She jerked to one side, slid her gaze in my direction.

Sam broke off, picked up again. ". . . the right to an attorney . . ."

I tried again. "Tell him you didn't put the coins there but obviously someone did." Susan gave a very good imitation of a rabbit mesmerized by a snake, but she did as instructed.

I said forcefully, or as forcefully as one can whisper, "The murderer was there!"

"You need to—" Susan's voice was thin.

I wished she'd stop flicking her eyes from one side to the other.

"—find out who was in my backyard after midnight. The murderer put those coins there. Not me."

"Check the neighbors." Perhaps my whisper was a little too sibilant.

Sam's face had a curious expression, a mixture of uneasiness, irritation, and resignation. Hal leaned forward and peered as if he might, if he looked hard enough, see something—or someone—who wasn't there.

"Check the neighbors," she blurted.

I scarcely heard her voice over the deep whoo of the Rescue Express. I felt a tap on my shoulder. I was being summoned. Another tap and my hand was lifted to point at the ceiling.

✍

"What a pleasant surprise." I flavored my tone with the slightest emphasis on *surprise*. I knew Wiggins had joined me on the roof. I smelled coal smoke as I sat on the two-foot coping. If I turned a bit I would have a wonderful view of downtown Adelaide and the park across from City Hall. Though the sun was high, it cast the thin warmth of November. I felt much warmer with the addition of a beautifully textured red wool jacket with a scalloped lapel. "How is everything?" Perhaps we could visit about some of his other emissaries. Perhaps I'd ask if any problems had arisen lately in Tumbulgum. There had been an occasion when he was distracted by activities in that lovely remote community in Australia.

Wiggins's deep voice was right beside me. "Quite satisfactory since Sylvie was simply the victim of a practical joke. I'm afraid I sent you on a wild-goose chase. There was no kidnapping. And Susan showed her good character when she immediately handed over the shoe box. I was a bit uncomfortable about the shoe box. Your task is done—"

The rumble of wheels was near, the whoo of the whistle deafening.

"Wiggins"—I gave up my effort at casual repartee—"my task has only begun. The 'kidnapping' was a hoax with a sinister intent." Did I sound enough like an Edwardian novel? "Susan Gilbert is the main suspect in Wilbur Fitch's murder. She returned the money but she admits to being in his study last night. The discovery of his coin collections in her backyard will be seen as proof Susan decoyed her sister and used her disappearance as a pretext for robbing the safe, was discovered in the act by Wilbur, that she killed him and this morning tried to establish her innocence by returning the shoe box, but she kept the coin collections."

Wiggins wasn't worried. "You accompanied her on her mission to the study. You saw her take only the shoe box."

My nose wrinkled as a cloud of coal smoke enveloped me. "I know she's innocent. You know she's innocent. If it were possible for us to appear and vouch for her, all would be well."

"Oh. Harrumph."

I let Wiggins digest the problem. Then I played my ace. "Chief Cobb will arrest her forty-eight hours from now unless I find the murderer. When the clock strikes twelve noon on Friday, Susan will be led to a cell."

The Rescue Express thrummed on the rails.

"Forty-eight hours." Another harrumph. "You'd better get busy."

The whoo faded in the distance. The sound of clacking wheels grew faint and was gone.

Forty-eight hours.

∽

Sam Cobb was a busy man, surrounded by officers or techs, reporting, discussing, analyzing. I didn't like the tenor of the talk. It was all Susan and nobody else. It occurred to me that I had important information. At the moment, two techs stood in front of his desk, describing the results of the investigation in Wilbur Fitch's study. They stood with their backs to an old-fashioned green blackboard with white chalk resting in the tray.

I picked up a piece of chalk.

Sam happened to be looking toward the blackboard. His gaze fastened on the slowly rising chalk.

I wrote: *Privacy, please* and drew a halo above the words. Not that I imbue my presence with any aspect of holiness, but I knew he'd understand.

Sam cleared his throat. "Good work. I have to go into a conference in a moment so you can send me the reports."

As soon as the techs departed, Sam leaned forward, clicked his intercom: "Colleen, I'm unavailable for half an hour. Call Lulu's and order salad with grilled chicken, ranch on—"

I lifted the chalk, wrote rapidly: *Cheeseburger with chili, fries, double malted.*

"—the side, iced tea. And add a chili cheeseburger, fries, and double malted."

I erased the blackboard.

His secretary's voice was amused. "Same old diet order but a little extra today?"

Sam was brisk. "I'm not straying. I may have a visitor in a while."

Colleen was bland. "Of course. Order will be placed as requested." The system clicked off.

Sam gave a morose stare in the direction of the blackboard. "Claire keeps close tabs. I've lost twelve pounds. Got eight to go. She likes to visit with Colleen. Colleen won't deliberately snitch, but she always tells the truth when asked." He was lugubrious. "A fine quality for a police chief's secretary." He sounded resigned. Then he brightened. "You probably don't want all the fries."

Lulu's single order of fries was enough for me and a grizzly. I laughed. "Happy to share."

Sam gestured at the chair in front of his desk. "Join me. I'd like to see you. Laughter issuing from the blackboard unnerves me, even though I know it's you."

Sam's office was a little chilly. A fringed lime and black plaid poncho over a lime cowl-neck sweater, black knit leggings, and black quilted boots were quite warm. I settled in the chair and crossed one leg over my knee.

Sam's face was bemused. "Sometimes I still wonder if I'm nuts. But you make my life interesting. You look like you're headed for a football game. Say"—he leaned forward—"did you ever see Roger Staubach play?"

"Bobby Mac loved the Sooners and the Cowboys." For college ball, the Oklahoma Sooners thrilled in our day, and no one was better as a pro quarterback than Roger Staubach for Dallas. "Bobby Mac and I"—I paused for emphasis—"were in the stands in Minneapolis when Roger threw The Pass."

Sam was awed. "You were there?"

"I'll tell you all about it—" The cold December day in Minneapolis (seventeen degrees with wind chill), the desperate situation, only seconds remaining in the game. "—but first"—I edged the chair nearer his desk—"I have very important information."

Sam cleared his throat. "I hate to disappoint you—"

I was suddenly apprehensive. These words rarely presage good news for a listener.

"—but you backed the wrong horse this time."

I was shocked. "Susan?" It felt like riding in an elevator that dropped without warning.

"Sorry." His gaze was kind.

"Sam, I was there. I heard her respond to the ransom call."

"Right." He pulled a legal pad close, flipped several pages. "I got it right here. She got a ransom call, thinks her sister is kidnapped, hustles off to the Fitch house, burgles the safe—"

"She took only the shoe box. Not the coins."

He was unimpressed. "Right. She took the shoe box, goes home. She waits for instructions about where to deliver the ransom. They don't come. You convince her the call is set for twelve noon tomorrow, not midnight. You pick it up from there."

I gave him a sunny smile. "True confession. I came here. I didn't think you would mind if I used your computer."

He expressed no surprise. "I turned it on after I got back from the Fitch house. I figured you'd been busy. Interesting searches." He raised an eyebrow.

"I checked out seven people. One of them"—I was emphatic—"killed Wilbur Fitch."

My grand pronouncement evoked a dismissive shrug. "Names given to you by Susan Gilbert?"

A drop in temperature, a sudden gust of wind, thin streaks of gray clouds are portents of a coming storm. Sam regretted that he was going to disappoint me, and he dismissed my offer of suspects. Two unmistakable portents. I was not only apprehensive, I was chilled, but I soldiered on. "You admit there was a ransom call?"

Sam folded his arms. "A hoax."

I was impatient. "A hoax, but that call revealed an important fact. The caller knew Susan could open the safe. How did the caller have that knowledge? At a luncheon the week before, Wilbur used his cell, called Susan, asked her to get the Roman coin collection out of the safe and bring it to the dining room."

Sam was as expressionless as a curio store stuffed alligator.

I spoke with great clarity. "Seven people heard Wilbur tell Susan to get the coins from the safe." I flicked off the names. "George Kelly, Wilbur's lawyer. Todd Garrett, chief operating officer of Fitch Enterprises. Harry Hubbard, Wilbur's stepson. Alan Douglas, a Fitch vice president. Minerva Lloyd, Wilbur's mistress. Juliet Rodriguez, a very good-looking professor who's been organizing his library. Ben Fitch, Wilbur's son. He lives in Hawaii, looks like he spends a lot of time on the beach."

Sam didn't write down a single name. That was the third portent.

A knock sounded at the door. Sam gave me a glance and I disappeared.

"Come in." He turned his swivel chair to look toward the door.

Colleen was in her fifties with a freckled open face and a kind smile. She bustled across the room. "I brought some plates from the break room. Since you expect a guest."

He was bland. "Arriving any minute." He moved aside folders for his plate, gestured to the other side of the desk for the second plate.

Colleen put two sacks between the plates. "Includes salt, pepper, ketchup. Got a couple of cups of orange sherbet as an extra. Very healthy."

As the door closed behind her, I reappeared, reached for my sack. I put the cheeseburger, chili oozing from its sides, on one side of the plate, spilled out the fries on the other. Across the desk, Sam emptied the salad with the chicken strips, looked at my serving.

I reached over, switched the plates. "What happens in your office, stays in your office." Probably the poor man's hunger pangs were distorting his judgment.

Sam hesitated perhaps a fourth of an instant, grabbed the cheeseburger, took a huge bite.

I poked a strip of chicken in the ranch dressing. I am always willing to sacrifice to seek justice. I waited until he looked as contented as a lion with an antelope carcass.

"Don't you agree that the murderer was at the luncheon?"

He used a paper napkin to wipe a smear of chili from his chin. "You have a big heart, Bailey Ruth. And I know you are sent to help someone in trouble. But maybe this isn't the first time someone in trouble makes a bad call. I understand how you got caught up in her panic about her sister. It was a pretty lousy trick, all right, to fake a kidnapping. Somebody doesn't like Susan Gilbert, and the call did result in Wilbur's murder. As for the hoax, the cell phone's a dead end. The number doesn't lead anywhere. A burner phone—somebody bought a cash card phone and they've tossed it by now. Anyway, what matters is what Susan Gilbert did. I'm getting the case ready for the DA: Somebody sets up Sylvie's disappearance, calls Susan, demands the money. Susan goes to the house, gets the box of cash, returns home. She doesn't get another call because there was never going to be another call. The joke's over. She doesn't know it's a joke so she thinks she'll get a call the next day. The caller knows she's stuck with the cash, and when her sister turns up, she'll sweat to get the box back into the safe without Wilbur knowing, and her tormentor's getting a big time kick out of her problems. Instead, here's what happened. You leave the house and come to my office. Susan's lying there, worrying about her sister, and she gets to thinking, once she turns over the ransom money she'll end up being a suspect when Wilbur looks in the safe. I don't buy this idea she was going to tell him all about it. Or maybe she thought about telling him but she got a better idea. She's already in the hole for the cash, why not grab the coin collections? She can eventually sell the coins, one way or another.

There's a market for stolen artwork, including rare coins. So she gets up and hurries back to the Fitch house. By this time the party's over. She's opening the safe and there's a noise in the hall. She darts to her little side office, hunkers behind the door. Wilbur comes in. Maybe he had a hankering for his coins. Maybe he liked to count cash in the middle of the night, found it soothing. But the painting is pulled back, the safe is open. He strides over there. She knows she's off to jail if he turns around and sees her. She still thinks she has to wait for a ransom call, rescue little sister. I checked out her office. There's a crystal paperweight. She grabs the paperweight, maybe knots it up in a scarf, comes up behind him, slam. He's down, dying. It only takes another minute to return the paperweight to her desk. She gets the coin collections, leaves by the garden door. She decides to leave the safe open and the door ajar to point to a thief from outside. She makes a detour on her way home, gets rid of the bloody scarf." He took another gobble of his cheeseburger, had only a third left.

I stared at Sam. He meant every word. He'd taken the convoluted conjoining of a fake ransom call and a rich man's murder and figured out a rationale that made sense to him. He agreed that the fake ransom call led Susan Gilbert to creep into her employer's study. He knew—because I'd been there—that she took only the shoe box. But he understood greed. He believed Susan succumbed to temptation, returned to the study for the rare coins, and was surprised by Wilbur. I was certain that she tossed and turned in restless misery, but I couldn't prove she hadn't left the house again. I was in Sam's office, checking out the guests at the luncheon where Wilbur called for the coins and, as far as I was concerned, signed his own death warrant.

Sam looked more and more content. Half the fries were gone. He grabbed a handful, finished his cheeseburger.

Unfortunately, his interpretation made lots of sense. But I tried. "The whole thing was set up to involve Susan in Wilbur's murder. If Wilbur's body had been found this morning and the ransom call never happened, the police would be checking out his family, friends, employees. Sure, you would check Susan, but without a fake kidnapping, Sylvie would have come home as usual. She would testify Susan never left the house. Instead, Sylvie was decoyed away. The killer removes her from the house and tricks Susan into opening the safe and getting the money. And this is critical, Sam, when Susan hurried to the Fitch house to get the shoe box, the study door was unlocked. She doesn't have a key. The caller told her the door would be unlocked. That means the person who killed Wilbur was in the house at that moment, possibly a guest at the party. After the party is over"— I leaned forward, tried to sound authoritative, not pleading—"the killer entices Wilbur down to the study. Maybe someone who attended the party returns, knocks on Wilbur's door, knowing Wilbur stays up late. Any excuse would do. *Hey, forgot my cell phone*, or *I misplaced my car keys.* Or *I was walking on the terrace and I thought I saw a flashlight in your study. Maybe we should go down and check.* Or if it's someone in the house, claim to have heard a funny noise in the study. The result is the same, Wilbur and his killer walk down the stairs, go to the study. Maybe the killer has pulled the painting back. That would get Wilbur's attention. He crosses to the safe, punches in the combination, the killer strikes."

Sam's broad face creased in thought.

I felt a spark of hope and speared another strip of chicken.

Sam chewed on more fries, then shook his head. "Too complicated. Why not just kill him?"

I pounced. "If you commit murder, wouldn't you want a ready-made suspect?"

Sam wiped his fingers with a paper napkin, put his trash in the paper sack. "If your take is right, this mythical killer had to know Susan could open the safe and that she had a free spirit sister who'd hide out for twenty-four hours for a couple of free Blake Shelton tickets. Plus"—he was emphatic—"that would mean the killer brought the coin collections to the Gilbert house and dallied around in the backyard for a place to hide the coins and found the tub by the back steps. You can't do that in the dark. That means a flashlight was bobbing around sometime after one o'clock in the morning. What if Susan looked out the window? What if a next-door neighbor had a toothache? A flashlight in a backyard at that time of night would get a nine-one-one call pronto. Let's keep it simple. A mean joke puts Susan Gilbert in her boss's study, but once she opens the safe and takes out the shoe box, she knows how easy it would be to get the coins."

"Who opened the study door?"

He wasn't concerned. "That's easy. The hoaxer was at the party. More than a hundred guests. I didn't say the joke wasn't well planned. Sure, it was. Susan's caller was there, all right, but had nothing to do with Wilbur's murder. That happened because she came back and Wilbur was unlucky enough to pick that moment to go into his study."

"Sam." Now I was imploring. "Susan is innocent. Why, this morning she immediately told you about the box of cash."

Sam's look was pitying. "Maybe a driveway full of cop cars scared her. Maybe she thought she would divert attention from the missing coins. She didn't say a word about the coin collections." He pushed back his chair, rose. Our conference was over. "Crimes are pretty simple, Bailey Ruth. Sex or money. I've done some checking on Susan Gilbert. Smart girl. According to most people, a nice girl. Even nice people can be tempted by big bucks. She could open the safe. She did open the safe. She admits she was there, admits she took the box full of cash. You back her up there. But she came home. No ransom call. She goes to bed. You come here. Maybe she feels like a rat in a trap, and it's always better to be a rich rat than a poor rat. She decides to go back to the Fitch house, get the coins. But her luck ran out. Or maybe I should say Wilbur Fitch's luck ran out. She's there. He finds her. She kills him."

Chapter 6

I was out in the cold. Literally. In every way. I stood on the City Hall roof, shivering. The poncho was elegant but not meant for a windchill in the forties. I added a black cashmere scarf and an ankle-length black cashmere topcoat. I no longer shivered, but I felt as bleak as an iced-over farm pond pelted by sleet. Adelaide's main street stretched below me. It was still early afternoon, but everything looked gray as thick clouds squeezed out the sun. The Christmas lights that garlanded the streetlamps did little to add cheer.

I'd never felt so alone. Before I'd always been welcome in Sam's long office with the battered desk and lumpy brown leather couch. I knew what was going on behind the scenes in an investigation. This time what I knew scared me. The investigation was over. Friday at noon Susan would be in jail, no longer a "person of interest" but held on suspicion of murder, facing an arraignment and enough evidence to convict her of first-degree murder.

Sam was focused on building the case against Susan. She probably had only a few hundred dollars in her bank account. She lived in a modest house. Likely she was paying for Sylvie's education. There could be debts, probably were debts. In his view, greed prompted her to hold on to the rare coins. Worst of all, a closed case meant Sam wasn't looking for the person who landed Susan in a murderous mess. Sam was convinced she'd succumbed to temptation when a hoax led her to open Wilbur's safe, that she decided she was already a thief so why not get something out of it for herself. Sam didn't buy my contention that the hoax was a ruse to embroil her in a murder and the plan had succeeded handsomely because she was the chief suspect. Someone with a compelling reason to want Wilbur dead created a clever diversion. Sam thought Susan had an enemy, but the real effect of the hoax was to tempt Susan and lead her to murder. I had to prove him wrong. I had to push behind the false front, find the clever mind that wanted Wilbur dead and Susan accused.

I stared down at the shadowy street, the gloom emphasized by the Christmas lights. The strands of tinsel strung across the street swayed in the sharp gusts, making an eerie rustling sound.

Adelaide, my beautiful Adelaide, no longer welcomed me. I felt as alien as any private eye walking down a mean street. Philip Marlowe and Sam Spade made those walks. So would I.

In less than forty-eight hours, I had to find Wilbur's murderer.

○○○

The grandfather clock in the corner of the living room in the Gilbert house showed the time at a quarter after two, still plenty of afternoon left to seek out suspects.

Sylvie paused to glance in the mirror above a side table. She fluffed her blonde curls. "Let's go out to dinner tonight. We need to do something fun. There's a new restaurant by the lake. Rummy's Retreat. The steaks are supposed to be great."

A drained, depleted Susan looked small in the corner of the sofa. "A last meal for the condemned?"

Sylvie whirled around, stalked across the room. "That's not funny, Susan. I just meant you and I didn't have anything to do with Mr. Fitch being killed and we need to act like everything's all right."

Susan gazed at her sister, and a smile tugged at her lips. "You look like a kitten with frizzed-up fur facing down a Doberman."

"If that awful man—"

She meant Sam.

"—was here, I'd scratch his eyes out."

Susan patted the seat beside her. "Honey, I love you. What really matters is that you're all right."

Sylvie dropped onto the cushion. "Why doesn't that police guy get it? Of course whoever called you has to be the one who killed Mr. Fitch. Why else was there a fake ransom call? It's obvious. Any idiot can see it was a clever plan to get you to go to the house and take the money."

That was my cue.

On Susan's front porch, I paused to consider my wardrobe. What should a successful private investigator wear? I didn't need a topcoat and scarf inside the house. I decided on a pale lavender merino wool basket weave cardigan over a darker purple top and matching lavender wool slacks and black leather heels. A necklace of intertwined silver links provided elegance.

I knocked firmly.

The peephole opened.

I gave a reassuring smile. I hoped my red curls didn't look too windblown.

The door opened. Susan stared at me with a mixed look of recognition, disbelief, and uncertainty.

I didn't give her a chance to derail my participation. "I came as soon as I could. I'll be glad to take on the investigation, find out the identity of Mr. Fitch's murderer." I pulled open the screen door. "If you didn't get my name earlier, I'm Private Detective G. Latham with Crown Investigations, the Dallas office." I rather liked the agency name. I thought it added a touch of class. My alias? Leslie Ford's Washington DC socialite Grace Latham often assisted Colonel John Primrose in his difficult cases. Ford's mysteries were not hard-boiled, but I enjoyed diversions into Southern mischief among the upper classes.

Susan backed away, still staring, and trying, of course, to account for my reappearance. Last night she'd dismissed me as a creation of her own distress.

Sylvie darted around her. "A private detective? That's what we need. Somebody has to find out what happened."

Susan backed into the end of the sofa.

I saw realization in her eyes. My appearance last night wasn't a product of her imagination. I could come and go. I was what I'd claimed, an emissary from Heaven. "You'll help me?" Her voice wavered.

"I will."

Sylvie clapped her hands. "What do you want us to do?"

"I'll establish some particulars first. Please make yourselves comfortable." I gestured toward the sofa. When Susan and Sylvie were side by side on the sofa, I drew a straight chair closer. I looked at Susan. "Who hates you?"

Sylvie bristled. "No one hates Susan."

Susan looked somber. "The police asked me that, too. I told them the truth. I'm a very ordinary person. I grew up here. I've known people my whole life. Lou Ann Crawford never liked me. I think it's because I was president of the student council and she wasn't. Or maybe it's because I dated her brother for a while. But Lou Ann lives in Chicago and she doesn't hate me. Not the way you mean hate. She just doesn't like me. Her brother Ted and I were engaged, but we both broke it off and he has a job in Norway. I never stole anything from anyone." A pause. "Until last night." She sounded forlorn. "Except for this week, I'm boring. I never hit anybody with a car. I'm not dating anyone right now. There are no deep, dark secrets in my life. I don't have a hidden enemy who decoyed Sylvie away just to upset me."

"It's ridiculous." Sylvie's cheeks flamed. "You can go around town and ask people. They know how good and honest and kind Susan is. And there was even a story in the *Gazette* a couple of years ago. This lady had put her purse on top of her trunk while she carried in some groceries. When she came back outside, she'd forgotten about her purse. She got in her car and drove off and the purse fell onto the street. Susan found it and took it to her house and handed it to her. Her wallet had three thousand dollars in it. To say Susan's a thief and wants something that belongs to someone else is nuts. She was desperate and she wanted to keep me safe and she was going to tell Mr. Fitch about the money and she never took those stupid coins and she would have paid him back and I would have helped."

Now Sylvie didn't look as much like a frizzed cat staring down a big dog as a Valkyrie bent on destruction.

Susan tried to keep her voice steady, but her eyes held the knowledge that she was in a desperate situation. "The police believe the ransom call wasn't meant to get money, just to upset me. The police think I went to Wilbur's house and opened the safe and took the money and later came back and got the coins. I don't know why they think I was there twice. But it doesn't much matter. I'm afraid they aren't looking at anyone but me." She reached over, picked up the newspaper lying on the coffee table. "Did you see the story in the *Gazette*? I feel like I have an X on my back."

The *Gazette* is an afternoon newspaper. This would be a story about the mayor's news conference. I held out my hand. "May I see?"

Joan Crandall had written two stories, the first straight news about the butler's discovery of the body, the ME preliminary report, death by blunt trauma by person or persons unknown, death estimated to have occurred sometime after midnight and before three a.m., a roundup of Wilbur Fitch's life and accomplishments. The quote from Sam Cobb was unrevealing. "Inquiries are being made among Mr. Fitch's acquaintances and business associates." The second story covered Neva Lumpkin's news conference. Crandall quoted the mayor's naming of Susan as among those being questioned. I understood Susan's grim expression. The story ended, "Mayor Lumpkin assured Adelaide residents there is no danger as the police are conducting around-the-clock surveillance."

"Anybody who reads about the news conference will think the police are ready to put me in jail. I guess maybe they are. And it won't help"—her voice was glum—"when they find out Wilbur left me a hundred thousand dollars. Me and a lot of people. The police will just see the will and think I wanted the money out of the safe and a bequest, too."

"A hundred thousand dollars?" Sylvie's eyes were huge.

Susan blinked away sudden tears. "He was the most generous man I've ever known. I told him I hoped the money came in when I was an old lady and I could help out my grandchildren. He clapped me on the shoulder, said if I kept saying nice things like that, he'd have to up my share to two hundred thousand. And now he's dead and he shouldn't be, and if they put me in jail I'll never fall in love and get married and maybe someday be a grandmother."

"You will," I reassured her. "I'm here."

The sisters, so strikingly different in appearance, curly-haired, blonde, incandescent Sylvie and restrained, responsible, dark-haired Susan, looked at me with a tiny burgeoning of hope.

I gave Susan a thumbs-up. "It's helpful to us that the police are focused on you. The murderer is relaxed, thinks there is no danger."

"How nice," Susan said shakily, "for the murderer."

"But I will burrow into the lives of the suspects—"

Sylvie was puzzled. "What suspects?"

"Seven people knew that Susan had the combination to Wilbur's safe."

Susan sat up straighter. "Detective Latham is talking about the lunch last week when Wilbur asked me to open the safe and bring the Roman coins. Anyone at the luncheon knew I could open the safe—"

Sylvie was excited. "So one of them made the fake ransom call knowing Susan could get pots of money." She clutched Susan's arm. "Who was there?"

"George Kelly, Wilbur's lawyer. Todd Garrett, chief operating officer of Fitch Enterprises." Susan spoke each name thoughtfully. Was she picturing that person, trying to see him or her as a stealthy figure setting a trap for her? "Alan Douglas, vice president in charge of projects and design. Wilbur's son, Ben Fitch." She stopped, shook her head. "He came out of the study last week and he was laughing. He saw me and gave me a kind of mock warning. *Dad's in the mood for a fight. Be sure and smile at him right. He's in fine form.* But he wasn't mad or irritated. And I think Ben's very nice."

"He will be a very wealthy man," I observed quietly.

She continued her defense, a spot of pink in each cheek. "Ben made a lot of money in Hawaii. Wilbur told me and he was very proud of him."

Sylvie asked quickly, "Who else was there?"

Susan was glad to move on. "Harry Hubbard, Wilbur's stepson. Minerva Lloyd—" She shot an uncomfortable look at her sister.

Sylvie was nonchalant. "Wilbur's mistress. Sis, I know about these things."

Susan managed a smile. "—his friend. And Juliet Rodriguez—"

Sylvie broke in. "Juliet's my psych prof. You know, the one I thought set up the contest. She's great. She's as nice as can be and she reminds me of champagne—"

Susan looked at her sister again.

Sylvie grinned. "I don't sit around drinking champagne out of a slipper. But that sure sounds neat. I've read all about champagne, how even one glass makes you feel like a helium balloon. That's why Juliet—she asks us to call her that—why she reminds me of champagne. Fizzy and fun. I can tell you that she never in a million years ever hurt anyone."

Being in the same room with Sylvie was exhilarating and made me feel even younger than my favored twenty-seven, the kind of young that believes in unicorns and treasure maps and happy, happy serendipity. I hoped very much that Juliet Rodriguez never disappointed Sylvie. But here was a question that needed to be answered, and Wilbur Fitch's secretary should know the answer. "Wilbur hired Juliet to catalogue his library. Did she have a background for that kind of work?"

Susan this time carefully didn't look toward Sylvie. "Juliet worked at the college library when she was an undergrad."

That scarcely met American Library Association standards for cataloguing. I continued to look inquiring.

"Well," Susan said, "he put an ad in the *Gazette*. Two librarians applied. He had some really valuable old books. I think a Shakespeare folio and at least one Gutenberg Bible. Then he met Juliet at a party. Of course"—a glance at Sylvie—"she's very charming and quite beautiful."

I persisted. "Did he make any comment to you about Ms. Rodriguez?"

That brought a quick smile. "He said she made him feel like he was sixteen again and that was a hell of a good year and he liked having her around and he didn't care if she catalogued the books in Esperanto. And that was just between us because Minerva wasn't pleased."

"Oh," Sylvie breathed. "Do you think he was interested in Juliet?"

Susan avoided looking at either Sylvie or me.

"Come on," her sister coaxed, "tell us."

Susan said reluctantly, "A couple of weeks ago, I opened the library door. He was kissing her. I closed the door and they never knew I saw them." She added hurriedly, "Minerva had no way of knowing."

I didn't dispute her conclusion, but I disagreed. A woman engaged in a long-standing affair, a woman who likely would have loved to be Mrs. Wilbur Fitch, would be highly attuned to the presence of a young and exceptionally beautiful woman in her lover's employ.

"Poor Juliet." Sylvie looked sad. "I didn't know she was interested in him like that. I mean, he was pretty old."

Susan said swiftly, "Wilbur wasn't old. He was only forty-eight. He married when he was just nineteen. The first time. He packed more into one life than most people could in a dozen. He played racquetball and climbed mountains and liked to hang glide. And a lot of women like older men."

Especially, I thought, if they were worth mega millions. But if Juliet and Wilbur were on kissing terms in the last couple of weeks, likely she had no motive for killing him. The same could not be said of Minerva.

Susan jammed her fingers together. "It's awful to try and imagine someone killing Wilbur. Minerva's smart and intriguing and hardworking. Her shop is a great success."

Her defense of Minerva meant she could indeed imagine that Minerva might struggle with jealousy.

"One of seven is guilty," I reminded her. "Give me Wilbur's last comments about each one of them."

She looked like I'd asked her to throw a lobster into boiling water. I didn't doubt that she'd march the creature right back into the sea.

"Pretend you're a reporter. A day in the life of a tycoon. Am I right that Wilbur didn't mince words when he locked horns with people and he spent a lot of time locking horns?"

"He made a lot of noise. But he didn't hold grudges. He

wasn't mean. He just said what he thought." Again a wisp of a smile. "Loudly."

"I want to know what he thought about the guests at that luncheon. Start with Ben Fitch."

Susan took a little while to answer, then said in a rush, "Wilbur was excited to have Ben visiting. He told me he thought Ben had a great future. I think he wanted him to stay in Adelaide." But she didn't meet my gaze.

"George Kelly?" I remembered a photograph in the society page, big lanky guy, broad imposing face with a high forehead, bright blue eyes, bold nose, jutting chin. Easy to picture him wrestling down a calf or striding up and down in front of a jury, long arms gesturing.

"Bigger than life. I was surprised he and Wilbur got along as well as they did. But George always remembered who paid the bills. They did have a dustup a couple of weeks ago. George lost a lawsuit in Shawnee, and Wilbur was furious. He told George maybe it was time he found a new lawyer, that he thought he had a bull in the courtroom but it turned out to be a steer." She looked at me questioningly.

My uncle had a cattle ranch. A steer is a neutered bull. I gave a low whistle. "But George came to the luncheon."

"A luncheon invitation was a command performance." She hesitated. "I overheard part of a call. I think he was talking to George. He was pretty rough. He said . . . *out of patience. We're going to have a talk.* He slammed the phone down. I had just come up to the desk with a folder. He looked at me. *Susan, let me give you a piece of advice. I think you'll go far*—Wilbur knew I'd been working on a greeting card business and he encouraged me—*and you need to remember: If the work isn't good, move on.*" I suppose I looked blank. He laughed, that big booming laugh. *In other words, if you hire an artist who turns in lousy designs, it won't matter how well the artist plays golf or how nicely she smiles at you, it's out the door. Slam. Bang.*"

Susan was likely right that Wilbur had been talking to George, but the golf reference interested me. Perhaps Wilbur was dissatisfied with his easygoing and likely unproductive stepson.

"How about Todd Garrett? I assume he runs the company day to day."

"No." The reply was quick and definite.

I was surprised. "Isn't he the chief operating officer?"

"Todd and Wilbur were in high school together. Todd was a big deal then. Quarterback of the football team."

I needed no explanation of the status that conferred in Adelaide.

"Wilbur was an ungainly nerdy guy from the wrong side of the tracks. A lot of the kids made fun of him or ignored him, but Todd was nice to Wilbur. Todd, well, I don't think he's very smart. To tell the truth, he was a figurehead. Wilbur made all the decisions for the business. Todd's job was to speak at civic events and glad-hand everybody. Of course, Todd didn't see it that way. Wilbur talked over everything with him, and the ideas were Wilbur's, but he let Todd make announcements, send out directives. Sometimes Todd went out on a limb, made promises he shouldn't have. Usually Wilbur could work things out, and he never embarrassed Todd or complained. Maybe Todd got to thinking he really was running the business. Anyway, the day before the luncheon I was coming back from an errand and I opened the study door, then I stopped. Wilbur was shouting. He said he damn well knew Fitch Enterprises was a tech company and nobody knew more about tech than he did and he didn't need Todd telling him a SIMPLE Car wasn't high-tech because that was the damn point and Todd making fun of Alan's idea at the Kiwanis supper was disloyal to the company and he hadn't made up his mind yet about the car but it was still a possibility and Todd better walk back any criticism he'd made, ASAP. I shut the door and went to the end of the hall. Todd came out. I guess I've never seen him without a grin. His face was red and he had his fists clenched and he stomped out the front door. Now"—and the words came quickly—"Todd was at the luncheon and he was being really charming to Juliet when I came in with the coins. Wilbur never held a grudge, so I guess everything was worked out."

"Harry Hubbard?"

Her face lightened. "Harry's the exception to the rule that you're supposed to resent your stepfather. Wilbur loved golf, and Harry was always ready to play. I think Wilbur put Harry on the payroll—he's in the PR office—mainly so he'd always have a game. Harry has the ambition of a sloth but buckets of charm. Even when Wilbur drew the line at buying him a Maserati, he managed to keep on Wilbur's good side. Wilbur told me Harry gave him a salute and said, *I know you have a big soft spot so I tried for a big one.* Wilbur laughed and said, *Harry never gives up.* On his way out, he stopped at the door, grinned, and said, *On my Christmas wish list, Pops.* Wilbur thought that was priceless."

Sylvie's tone was admiring. "Harry's cute. He wouldn't hurt anyone. Can you imagine Harry figuring out a complicated way of killing Wilbur? He's way too laid back to do something like that."

Susan blinked in surprise. "How do you know Harry?"

Sylvie looked a little embarrassed. "Oh"—very offhandedly—"I met him one time when I came to see you and you were busy. We had Shirley Temples out in the garden. Last summer." A mischievous grin. "I think his had gin in it."

Susan's face assumed a big-sister look.

Sylvie wriggled a little on the sofa. "I've seen him a time or two. He drops by the campus and we go for a Coke in the student center." She sat up straight. "Now don't tell me he's too old for me. I'm eighteen." She spoke as if an aged sophisticate.

"Harry's too old for you." Rather sternly. Then more equably, "But I agree that casting Harry as a villain is silly."

I didn't ruin this moment of agreement by suggesting that charm was no guarantee of innocence. More to the point was Harry's obvious lust for the fine and the fancy, and he likely knew quite well that Pops wouldn't put the keys to a Maserati in his Christmas stocking. Harry sounded like a first-class mess, but I wouldn't be surprised if I, too, found him charming. What is it about good-looking men who make no secret of their indolence and expectation of pleasure?

I ended the diversion. "Alan Douglas?"

Susan was quiet for a moment. "I don't know." She spoke

slowly. "Once Wilbur told me he admired Alan because Alan was like a bear trap, once he got an idea in his mind, he never let go, and that could be good. But you always had to remember with a one-track mind that you better both be on the same track or something would smash up."

"Juliet Rodriguez?"

"Wilbur liked beauty. She's beautiful. He talked to her on the phone that last day about flying to Dallas, and he was smiling."

"Minerva Lloyd?"

Susan looked miserable. "I don't like talking about people like this."

Sylvie patted her shoulder, gave me a swift look. "Susan's the biggest softy in the world. She never says anything bad about anyone. But"—and she was emphatic, her young voice high—"it isn't mean to tell the truth. You always say, *Tell the truth and you'll never have any regrets.* So you tell Ms. Latham and me everything you know about the people at the lunch, and if they are innocent, well, no harm done. But maybe something you say will help Ms. Latham find out who killed Wilbur. That's what matters."

Susan took her sister's hand. "You're right. After all"—she glanced at me—"you aren't the police. What I tell you won't get someone else in trouble. So"—she drew a breath—"I'll tell you about Minerva."

"Last week, I think it was Wednesday or Thursday, there was a knock on the study door. I got up to go see and the door opened. Minerva came in. She was her usual spectacular self, wearing a soft green wool dress and a pearl necklace and tall green heels with gold buckles. She looked like a *Vogue* model. She turned her eyes on me, and that's when I knew something was up. Her eyes kind of burned with fury. She spoke nicely enough, *I'd like a latte, Susan.* I started for the door. Wilbur barked, *I have staff. Sit down, Susan.* Minerva walked up to his desk. *Wilbur dear, some words are not meant for employees. Susan will run right along.* I looked at Wilbur. His face was getting red. I thought it was better if I left, so I murmured something about a morning break and headed for the hall. I heard Minerva say, *Are you taking Juliet to Dallas next*— as I closed the door. She was terribly angry."

"Ooh." Sylvie practically bounced on the cushion. "You have to call that big man, tell him. Minerva is smart enough to plan anything. She probably knows all about you and me from Wilbur."

Susan looked skeptical. "Somehow I doubt Wilbur regaled Minerva with tidbits about his secretary and her sister. Anyway"—Susan shook her head—"the police can't arrest Minerva because she had a spat with Wilbur."

Sylvie said darkly, "A mad mistress is a good place to start." She looked at me. "You'll go after Minerva, won't you?"

"Minerva. And the other six luncheon guests."

As Sam Cobb tartly observed, *Crimes are pretty simple, Bailey Ruth. Sex or money.*

I decided to start with sex.

Chapter 7

Juliet Rodriguez opened her apartment door on the third knock. Instead of G. Latham, Private Eye, I was equipped with a lovely leather folder containing a police ID for Detective Sergeant G. Latham. Happily I could remain in street clothes for both the Crown investigator and the Adelaide homicide detective.

She was, as Susan said, drop-dead gorgeous, hair the color of wheat in sunlight, huge dark brown eyes. I am not a connoisseur of women's figures, but my husband had a word for women like Juliet: *stacked*. The fawn sweater was molded to her and a nice foil for scarlet slacks.

She beamed at me, a bright, engaging smile. She was clearly eager to meet the unknown redhead at her threshold, an attitude that likely had opened many doors for her. People like smiles.

I spoke quickly as I flashed my badge. "Detective Sergeant G. Latham. If you have a moment, Ms. Rodriguez, I hope you can assist the police department in the investigation into the murder of Mr. Wilbur Fitch." In the past, I'd sometimes appeared as Officer M. Loy, a tribute to Myrna Loy in her role as Nora to William Powell's Nick Charles in the film version of Dashiell Hammett's *The Thin Man*. To pursue Wilbur's killer, I awarded myself a promotion.

Her smile was replaced by a moue of distress. "It's so awful about Wilbur." Her eyes filled with tears. "He was the nicest man. I didn't know until I went to the house after my class." She held the door, welcoming me inside. "I've been cataloguing Wilbur's library. I can't believe someone killed him. And I saw the police"—her brown eyes were huge—"take Susan Gilbert away. I suppose they needed information from her." She gestured toward an easy chair, took her place opposite me on a rattan sofa. The decor was inexpensive, bright travel posters and everyday furniture likely picked up secondhand, but a comfortable room in a small apartment. "Susan's sister, Sylvie, is in one of my classes." Juliet was a luncheon guest who knew enough about Susan and Sylvie to make the fake ransom call. Ditto Harry Hubbard, the charming ne'er-do-well stepson. But what of the others? It was time to test out my theory. "I understand you were among Mr. Fitch's guests at a luncheon last week."

Juliet brushed back a tangle of honey-colored hair, looked young and appealing. "It makes me so sad that Wilbur's gone. He laughed and boomed and kept everything fun. He loved sharing. It could be an eagle feather he found on a camping trip or a 1929 stock certificate. That was one of his most appealing qualities. He was always himself and he loved having people for lunch and showing off his things."

"I understand he asked his secretary to open the safe and bring some coins."

Juliet nodded eagerly. "They were gorgeous. I love old coins. They make me think of castles and dusty roads and caravans. Susan brought them to the table in a red velvet bag. That was so Wilbur. Red velvet. Susan placed the bag on the table and said, *Here you are, sir.* As I told everyone after she left, she could be the perfect secretary in a TV show, and it just goes to show how different siblings can be. I told them all about Sylvie and how she's always game to try anything and how she didn't tell Susan when she and Harry, you know, he's Wilbur's stepson, went out to the airport and went up and parachuted into a field and there was a bull and, golly, it was a near thing. But she and Harry grabbed up their chutes and shook them and that distracted the bull and they got over a fence and she'd never ever tell Susan because Susan was always so cautious. Harry laughed and said I had to promise not to tell Susan because she still didn't know, and I was right, Sylvie was the closest thing he'd ever known to a human glider, just going whichever way the wind blew and loving every minute of it."

Juliet's lovely face was open and cheerful and quite disarming. I wondered if I was being played by an imaginative and clever killer. In any event, I now could be sure that everyone at the luncheon was well equipped to place the ransom call. Including Juliet.

I looked at her pleasantly. "I understand you and Mr. Fitch had travel plans."

A slight flush stained her cheeks, and her dark brows drew down in a frown. "He was taking me to Dallas to go shopping. He said it was a bonus for making his library a fun place. I can't believe how Minerva Lloyd acted. Everyone knows they've been having an affair for years, but she's certainly not a very nice person. She told Wilbur I was a little gold digger just because he gave me a fancy necklace for my birthday. Well, it was his idea. He asked me what I liked and I told him I just loved pretty emeralds and I had no idea he would go right out and buy me this gorgeous necklace."

I maintained a pleasant expression, but I saw a gleam of satisfaction in those dark chocolate eyes, whether at the acquisition of a fine necklace or the pleasure of denigrating Minerva. "Perhaps Mr. Fitch was interested in you as a companion."

She tossed her head, such an exquisitely feminine—and revealing—gesture. "That's what *she* was afraid of. He told me he'd settled her down, made it clear he'd take me to Dallas if he wanted to." A sigh. "He was fun. I hate it that someone hurt him." And perhaps hated it more that a wealthy man was no longer eager to please her with baubles far beyond what she could ever afford. I had a sudden hunch. Susan mentioned her bequest and how that added to the police conclusion that she murdered Wilbur for money. Obviously Wilbur had told Susan about her inclusion in his will. Did he tell other beneficiaries? That seemed in character. Wilbur Fitch was outspoken, impulsive, fast-moving. He'd only known Juliet for a short while, but obviously she attracted him.

"I know you appreciate the bequest to you in his will."

Her glance at me was quick, revealing. There was knowledge in her eyes, calculation, decision. She clapped her hands together. "A bequest? Oh, how wonderful. I didn't know."

Of course she did.

⌯

Yellow curtains added a cheerful accent to the pale gray walls in Minerva's shop. The lighting was bright enough to enhance the texture and color of the clothing, muted enough to create an atmosphere of relaxation. Several pieces of a sectional sofa upholstered in yellow and gray offered islands of comfort near tall mirrors angled for privacy. No customers were present. I paused to admire a pencil skirt in a rich faille fabric and varying shades of blue in a dramatic floral print. Very nice.

I found Minerva in her office at a small French provincial desk. She was on the phone. Her tone was imperious. ". . . no excuse. If the shipment isn't here by ten a.m. tomorrow the order is canceled." She didn't wait for an answer, hung up. She was classically beautiful, waves of golden hair, violet eyes, patrician features. With no one present (so far as she knew), her quite lovely face held more than a trace of petulance. She was impeccably attired in a pink Shetland wool blazer with gold buttons over a matching pink turtleneck sweater, gray slacks, and rose pebbled leather flats.

She replaced the phone in the receiver, a faux antique gold-plated phone. The expression of irritation faded. She slumped a little in the chair, and suddenly her face was vulnerable, her eyes held pain and sadness.

I returned to the front of the shop, stepped behind a manne-quin. In an instant I was there. I took a moment in front of a mirror to smooth my hair and straighten the hang of my cardi-gan. I moved to the front door, opened and closed it. A muted bell sang.

Minerva stepped out from the back corridor with the automatic smile and careful scrutiny of a shopkeeper alone in her business. There was an imperceptible brightening and relaxation. The good quality of my sweater and slacks had been duly noted. And I was a distraction from the emotion she'd felt sitting alone at her desk with only her thoughts—and memories—for company.

I moved confidently forward, my hand out with an oblong leather case open to display an ID. "Detective Sergeant G. Latham, Adelaide Police Department. If you can spare a few minutes, ma'am, I'm here about the investigation into the mur-der of Mr. Wilbur Fitch."

"Wilbur." She took a breath and for an instant her lovely face looked older, bereft. "It's terrible. Unbelievable." Her voice was low and soft. "His stepson called me this morning."

I gestured toward a sofa. "If we might sit down, ma'am."

She sat across from me, laced her fingers around one knee as she leaned forward, her gaze demanding. "Harry said the police took his secretary in for questioning."

I shook my head in a chiding manner. "There are always

misunderstandings in every investigation. The police requested the assistance of the secretary and she was glad to be helpful. Now the investigation is expanding. We understand you and Mr. Fitch were very close."

"He was my good friend." Her husky voice was forlorn. "My best friend."

"Perhaps more than friends?"

"We were friends." She spoke with finality.

"There's information that you and he quarreled recently."

She sat immobile, expressionless. "We were on very good terms. In fact, last night I served as his hostess at the anniversary party for the company."

"Did you often stay all night at his home?"

Her shoulders lifted and fell in a slight shrug. "Sometimes."

"Last night?"

"No."

"Why not?"

"I chose not to do so." For an instant, the veneer that protected her cracked. "Oh, I wish I had. I almost did. If I'd been there, he might not have been killed." She stared at me. "Do you know why he went downstairs?"

I had no idea what Harry Hubbard had told Minerva in his call. "Mr. Fitch was found in his study. He may have discovered a theft in progress. Or there is a possibility that someone he knew came to his door, said there was a light in the study and perhaps they should investigate. If that is what happened, he went downstairs with another person and was struck down from behind when standing near the safe."

Her gaze bored into me. "The police think he knew who killed him."

"Yes."

"Wilbur dead is horrible, but to think someone he knew killed him is truly awful." Her hands came together in a tight grip. The eyes staring at me were dark with pain.

"What was Mr. Fitch's demeanor when you said good night?"

For an instant, she pressed her lips together, finally managed a slight smile. "Wilbur had a grand time at the party. He was proud of the company. Proud of himself and he deserved to be proud. He did so much and he did it all by himself. He was so happy. He certainly didn't expect someone to kill him. I still can't believe it's true."

"Do you live alone?"

"Yes." She gave her address, a nice area in an older section of town. "The party ended a little after midnight. I said good night to Wilbur, drove home. I was just leaving for the store this morning when Harry called me."

"Did you return to the mansion at"—I gave it a guess—"around one a.m.?"

"No."

I nodded and rose. "Thank you for your assistance, Ms. Lloyd." She rose, too.

At the door I turned as if struck by a final thought. "I understand you were displeased that Mr. Fitch planned to take a holiday with a Ms. Juliet Rodriguez."

Her reply was sharp. "That's not accurate. Wilbur was always too kind to employees. She heard him talking about a flight down to Dallas on business and persuaded him to invite her. He flew his own plane. I doubt she's ever been on a private plane." Her tone was dismissive. She, of course, was quite accustomed to private planes. "She's rather a greedy young woman. She persuaded him to buy her some emeralds." Minerva's eyes were hard. "He would have found out soon enough that she was taking advantage of him."

"You and Mr. Fitch quarreled?"

"Wilbur and I never quarreled." A confident stare.

"You were overheard."

She raised a sleek eyebrow. "Those who eavesdrop often mishear. Wilbur assured me she'd asked for a ride to Dallas and he was going to be quite busy but he didn't mind if she came along." A negligent wave of one hand with scarlet-tipped nails. "It wasn't important."

"If it wasn't important, I'm surprised you brought the matter up with him."

She made no reply.

"How much money did Wilbur leave you in his will?"

"I fail to see why you ask."

"It's important to establish who profits from his death."

Her cheekbones looked sharp. "That is offensive. Wilbur was well and strong and should have lived to be eighty. I never expected to inherit anything from him."

"How much was the bequest?"

She took her time answering. Should she claim lack of knowledge? Should she refuse to answer? Finally, she said brusquely, "Wilbur loved to joke about being worth more dead than alive to his good friends. He counted me as a good friend. If I remember correctly I believe he said I would someday inherit five hundred thousand dollars."

I rather thought she remembered the sum with great clarity.

Perhaps with Minerva the crime, if she were the killer, came down to both sex and money.

§

I hoped Minerva Lloyd truly mourned her lover. She could be a clever murderess playing a role, but I hoped that wasn't the case. We all need love and I hoped Wilbur Fitch had known love. The young woman who made him feel sixteen again regretted his demise, but there was no sense of grief. Both the woman with whom he'd shared passion and the charming young professor were quite aware that they would soon be much better off financially than they'd been before. Especially perhaps Minerva. Was her hostility to Juliet based more on the feeling that Wilbur's interest in Juliet meant Minerva would not be the third Mrs. Fitch? That might have caused not only jealously and anger, but a determination to get money while the getting was good.

Wilbur Fitch was very rich. Now it was time to find out who else benefitted from his death.

In one of my previous excursions to Adelaide, I spent some time in the offices of a well-heeled law firm. I realized immediately that the offices of Kelly and Wallis on the second floor of a frame building near a midtown shopping area were second tier. The waiting area contained two leather sofas, three plastic-covered chairs, and a secretary's metal desk. A thin, harried-looking woman punched buttons on a copy machine. She had fine brown hair in a bun, a slender gentle face, and a worried expression. "I'll call the computer service department again. I can't get it to collate."

A balding, stork-like man with long shoulders and long arms loomed over her. "That brief has to be filed this afternoon. Take it to a copy shop."

I found George Kelly in a corner office with windows overlooking the end of a strip mall and a parking lot. Several folders were stacked on one side of a cherrywood desk. The office itself was nicely furnished with dark brown drapes at the windows. I admired framed photographs of desert scenes and a branding iron mounted on a slab of weathered wood on the wall opposite his desk. Two comfortable armchairs faced the desk. A well-worn cowboy hat rested atop a coat-tree. A suit jacket hung from one hook.

George was absorbed in skimming a document and making occasional notations on a legal pad. He wore horn-rimmed glasses. I hovered behind him, discovered the files all pertained to the estate of Wilbur Fitch. Very good.

In the hallway outside the law firm, I checked to be sure no one was near before I appeared. I was ready to open the door when the panel jerked inward and the secretary bolted out and collided with me. "Oh. Sorry, so sorry." A folder dropped to the floor and sheets of paper slewed out. She gave a hunted look over her shoulder, then bent to scrabble the papers into a stack. I reached past her to close the door. I recognized that look for what it was, a defensive, don't-shout-at-me, panicked stare of a person accustomed to abuse.

"Here, let me help." In an instant, I had the numbered sheets back in order and held them out to her.

"I have to hurry. He gets mad if I make mistakes. It isn't my fault the copier won't collate."

"I'm sure it's not. I'll walk along with you. I'm with the Adelaide police and I have a few questions."

We were already downstairs at the main entrance. She opened the door. "I'll be glad to help if I can." Her reply was vague. "There's a copy shop across the street." She was focused on her task and the impatient lawyer.

I kept up with her as she darted across the intersection and wended past parked cars to the copy shop. I waited until the pages were slapping out of a copy machine, four copies collating neatly, and offered a soothing smile. "I know you are a great success at what you do and I'm sure you can help me. I'm Detective Sergeant G. Latham, Adelaide Police, and Mr. Kelly is assisting us with our investigation into the death of Mr. Wilbur Fitch."

She scarcely glanced at my ID card. "Oh." Her voice was a soft stricken coo. "I'm so sorry." Her eyes were shiny. "He was the nicest man in the world. He heard about the time that awful dog got my cat and she was in surgery for hours and then intensive care and the vet bills were over a thousand dollars and I didn't see any way in the world I could pay, and Mr. Fitch took care of the bill. Every Christmas I sent him a picture of Cleo, that's my cat's name, Cleopatra, she's very elegant, and he always sent me a lovely gift card and said I should buy Cleopatra a pretty nightgown. It was our joke. I always used every bit of the gift card for her." Her voice was earnest. "Her food and shots and things."

Susan told me Wilbur Fitch was generous. There is a special place in Heaven for those who care for "the least of these." I wasn't privy to Wilbur's arrival and welcome, but I knew the angels sang.

She was carefully lifting out the sheets in order. "If I can help you with Mr. Fitch, I will do everything I can. I know Mr. Kelly's going to be really busy."

"Mr. Kelly is taking care of the estate. I suppose that will require quite a bit of work."

"Oh yes," she breathed. A little frown tugged at her lips. "I heard Mr. Wallis—"

Wallis would be the tall stork-like man who very likely shouted at the secretary when he was irritated.

"—this morning after the police left. They came just before lunch and talked to Mr. Kelly because he was Mr. Fitch's lawyer. They stayed about fifteen minutes. After they left, Mr. Wallis went to Mr. Kelly's office. He left the door open so I heard them, and Mr. Wallis was, well, it isn't nice to say, but he was super excited. *Talk about a bonanza. What is the estate? Forty mil? Fifty? You can rack up a half million before that one's through.* Mr. Kelly told him that was no way to talk, that Mr. Fitch was not only a client but a friend and he for one wasn't thinking about fees now. He said there was too much to do to help the son get everything in order, that the estate was very complicated. He'd be working nights and weekends for a long time. Mr. Wallis laughed and said, *Ka-ching, ka-ching*. I didn't think that was very nice, and I'm glad Mr. Kelly doesn't feel that way.'"

We were quite friendly as we walked back across the street, and she immediately punched her intercom after she settled at her desk. "Mr. Kelly, a police detective is here to see you."

He came to his door and waved me inside. His height made the desk look small, and I definitely looked up at him. He exuded masculinity. There might be a suit jacket on the coat-tree, but he wore a western shirt and a black string tie. True to Susan's description, his gaze was a little too familiar. I was willing to guess his wife divorced him because he was too interested in other women.

I was pleasant, matter-of-fact. "I'm following up on our inquiries this morning. Could you give me the particulars of Mr. Fitch's estate?"

He was just this side of rude. "I listed the beneficiaries this morning."

"I know, sir." It was no surprise that Sam Cobb had already gained this information. I hoped to skate past the obvious overlap. "This is simply a confirmation with a focus on beneficiaries currently in Adelaide. We are aware of course that the business and the greater portion of the estate will pass to Ben Fitch. Please give me an estimate of his inheritance."

Obviously irritated, he gestured at a chair, took his place behind his desk. "As I told the officers earlier, Ben Fitch will have sole control of Fitch Enterprises, a privately held company, as well as approximately twenty-four limited liability companies, considerable real estate holdings in Oklahoma, Texas, and Montana, oil and gas leases in those states and several others, and a cattle ranch."

"The estimated worth of Ben Fitch's inheritance."

George leaned back in his chair, looked expansive. "There are tax ramifications and the process of evaluations and appraisals and possibly some contested matters. I would not be comfortable enunciating a figure. There is much work to be done."

I persisted. "Enunciate an estimate. Thirty million?"

He shook his head.

"Your turn." I gave him a sweet smile.

That elicited a boom of laughter. "Wilbur and you would have got on like a house afire. He never minced words. I'll act like Wilbur, not his lawyer. I think he'd approve. I won't be surprised if the ultimate worth of the estate to Ben might be in excess of fifty million dollars."

"What are the bequests to Adelaide residents?"

He raised an inquiring eyebrow. "Why are the police interested in bequests to local residents?"

I said carefully, "In a murder investigation, it's important to establish who profits from a death."

His broad face re-formed in an expression of surprise. He gave a sharp whistle. "Now you have my attention, Detective. This morning I had the clear impression that the investigation was centered on Susan Gilbert. I understood there was a matter of money missing from the safe though she'd offered it back. I don't know how that worked out. The police gave me a receipt for Wilbur's money box and two coin collections. I told Wilbur that box of money was going to get him in trouble, but he blew me off, said he didn't know anybody big enough to wrestle it away from him. I was afraid somebody would hear about the money and hold him up. I guess that's what happened. As for Susan, she receives a bequest of one hundred thousand dollars. Why do the other bequests matter?"

"This investigation is no longer centered on Ms. Gilbert. In fact"—I took pleasure in the announcement—"she has been very helpful to the police as a witness. The focus has shifted. The other bequests, please."

He drummed the fingers of his right hand on his desk. "Hell of a deal. I was shocked to hear Susan was a suspect, but I figured the police had some evidence implicating her." He stared at me.

My expression was bland. "As I said, the investigation now is wide open."

His large face squeezed in thought. "Since Wilbur was killed in his study, do you figure he knew the person who killed him? But he knew a lot of people. Why are you focusing on those listed in his will? Maybe he'd made somebody mad. Maybe he threatened someone."

"We are looking at everyone, including those who will benefit."

He nodded. "Wilbur was generous. Even to his ex-wives. I ragged him about that. I wouldn't give a dime to mine. But his exes don't live here. Local beneficiaries are Harry Hubbard, five hundred thousand dollars; Minerva Lloyd, five hundred thousand; Todd Garrett, five hundred thousand; Susan Gilbert, one hundred thousand; and Juliet Rodriguez, one hundred thousand. Fifty thousand each to his butler, Carl Ross; housekeeper, Rosalind Millbrook; and cook, Marta Jones."

The sums weren't huge to a very wealthy man, but they surely amounted to a small fortune to the recipients. I glanced at an ornate bronze clock on a side table. A quarter after four. Wednesday was spinning past, as time always does when it is limited. I had less than forty-eight hours to find a murderer and forestall Susan's arrest. I was glad I didn't need to add the butler, cook, and housekeeper to my list of suspects. They could scarcely be aware of Susan's sister, Sylvie, much less know that Susan could open Wilbur's safe.

"That covers the bequests." He gestured at the stack of folders on his desk. "If that's all you need, I'll get back to work."

I rose. "Thank you for your assistance. I imagine the estate will consume most of your time now."

"Yes. I'm honored that Wilbur entrusted the matter to me." He exuded satisfaction.

"What is your hourly rate?" From my contact with a law firm on a previous mission to Adelaide, I now understood that lawyers usually bill for time spent on a project.

"Three hundred dollars an hour. Five hundred for exceptionally complicated matters."

I expected settling the Fitch estate would make that category. "How long do you think it will take?"

"That depends upon many factors."

"Will you make five hundred thousand dollars in fees?"

"Perhaps." There was arrogance in his gaze. He knew a police salary was modest. "I'm good at what I do. Ben Fitch will be pleased. I'm confident he and I will be working together for a long time after the estate is settled."

At the door, I looked back. "Information received indicates Wilbur Fitch intended to fire you as his lawyer. His death is rather opportune for you." I gave him a steady look, closed the door quietly behind me, though not before I saw his face flatten a little in shock. He had been quite relaxed when I spoke of the profit motive for others. It wasn't quite so pleasant when it became personal.

Chapter 8

I disappeared in the hallway outside the law offices and wished myself to the broad front steps of the Fitch home. The police cars and forensic van were gone. A single modest black sedan remained. The huge Mediterranean-style home looked dull in the late-afternoon gloom beneath heavy clouds.

I hovered in the great entry hall, looked through an archway into the majestic formal living room, where the occupants of the house waited to be interrogated by the police this morning. Straight ahead rose a sweeping double staircase to the second and third floors.

I wanted a better sense of the layout of the mansion. I stepped through the archway to my left into a long hallway and explored the rooms in turn, a magnificent library, a narrow office with files and a computer and printer, and, finally, near the end of the hall, the study where Wilbur met his death. The study had an empty feel to it. It had been restored to order, the floor scrubbed where blood had seeped, the painting again flush against the wall, covering the now closed safe, the door to the garden shut.

At the end of the hall, I looked toward a central back portion of the house with a view of the terrace. Here was the informal living and dining area, intended for family use, comfortable chairs and sofas, a game area, a small dining table, small in the sense it would seat eight instead of the twenty or so in the baronial dining hall. Stairs at either end led to the second floor.

In the west wing upstairs I found Wilbur's suite. I admired the living area, noted an open book splayed pages down on a mahogany coffee table. I looked at the title: *Hillbilly Elegy.*

I heard familiar voices. I found Detectives Judy Weitz and Don Smith in a huge masculine bedroom that overlooked the terrace and lake. The view was chilling this late November afternoon, scudding clouds, the lake slate gray.

Don gave an impatient glance at his watch. "Okay, you wanted one more look at the rich guy's bedroom. Now can we call it a day?"

Judy was pointing at the bed. "Kind of like a fancy hotel. The covers are turned back, a Godiva chocolate bar on the pillow. The drapes closed. Look at those curtains. I'll bet they weigh a couple of hundred pounds. Somebody pulled those shut every night, pulled them open in the morning. They're thick enough to make this place blacker than a pot of fresh asphalt when he turned off the lights. Can you imagine if somebody turned your covers back and brought you chocolates and closed the curtains every night?"

Don was amused. "You sound like a disapproving Puritan. Hey, I could live with it. Like Fitzgerald said, 'They are different.' He was talking about the very rich."

Judy was precise. "Fitzgerald thought the rich believed they were better than everybody else. I don't think that was true of Wilbur Fitch. Maybe because he made those millions all by himself. Anyway, being rich wasn't lucky for him. That's why he's dead. But the real point is the drapes were closed. You can bet he didn't do that. We can check and see."

"So the drapes are closed." Don sounded bored.

For an answer, she opened the door into the sitting area, pointed at the book on the coffee table. "The butler says Fitch often stayed up late, only needed four or five hours' sleep a night. So he has the big party, everybody finally leaves. It's probably a little past midnight and he's relaxing, reading a book. What happens next? Here's how I see it. He's in his private place. This house has massive walls. He wouldn't hear anything from downstairs. Look at the cushion on the sofa. Still kind of depressed. Fitch was seated, reading. He wasn't looking outside and the drapes are drawn in here, too. Anyway, it's absurd to think that someone burglarizing the study would turn on the lights to spill out into the garden. Why not throw in a brass band? So, why does Fitch go downstairs?"

Don shrugged. "Maybe he wanted a different book."

She pointed at a bookcase that filled one wall.

"Okay, maybe he wanted a pastrami sandwich."

"Maybe"—her voice was silky—"somebody knocked on his door. Then the door opens. Someone he knows—and trusts— pokes a head in, says, oh, there are a lot of different ways it could have happened, but I'm betting the visitor said something like, *I walked out on the terrace tonight and sat down to make a call and left my phone on a table. I came back a few minutes ago to get it. I was walking down the sidewalk by the west wing and the door to the study was open. I knocked, but there was no answer. I thought this was odd so I stepped inside and turned on a light. There's a painting that's been pulled back against the wall. Maybe we should go down and you can check and make sure everything's okay."*

Don folded his arms, looked combative. "Or Fitch decided he wanted another book, schlepped downstairs, saw a light beneath the study door, wondered what the hell, went in. The secretary's back for her second go at it. She hears the knob turn, darts across the room, hides behind a sofa. He comes in, sees the open safe, charges toward it. She moves like a flash, and whack, he's down and dead."

Weitz was equally combative. "It doesn't compute. Think about it, Don. She gets a ransom call and hightails it here and takes the cash box. She gets away with it. Takes the stuff to her house. Why would she come back, take another chance of being caught?"

"Greed." His somber stare held memories of years in law enforcement.

Judy was impatient. "If I have the timing right, and I'm sure I do, she would no more than have reached her house than she would have had to start back."

Don shrugged. "It's kind of nuts. You ever know any nutty crooks?"

She waved the sardonic query aside. "I don't buy it. Fitch went into that study with someone he knows. He wasn't attacked by a burglar. No bruises. Nothing but the bash on the back of his head. He was a big man. Maybe a burglar could use a gun, force him to open a safe, but I don't think so. I don't think he was expecting trouble. From the way he fell, he was standing at the safe. I don't think the safe was open. I think Fitch saw the painting ajar and opened the safe to check and see if everything was in place. If that's the setup, then the secretary's claim she was framed adds up. Somebody arranged for her to sneak in, get the cash box. Why would she come back? If she wanted those coins that were hidden beneath a tub in her backyard, she would have taken them when she got the cash box. Instead someone at the party and/or somebody who lives in the house came to Wilbur's door and persuaded him to come downstairs. He had to be killed in the study because that's where the secretary came. Somebody is a hell of a chess player, but this time the pieces are other people's lives. Somebody wanted Fitch dead and made sure the secretary took the rap. It was never about taking what was in the safe. The killer took the coins and hotfooted it to the secretary's house and tucked them under a tub. The secretary's not that stupid. She's being framed."

Don had a supercilious male expression. "Just because you know Gilbert at church, you're spinning her a way out."

Judy glared at him. "I do not spin. I look at facts." With that she stalked toward the door.

I regret to say Don slouched after her with a smirk on his face.

I felt sure Judy's take was right. The murderer attended the party, was familiar with the layout of the house and the location of Wilbur's suite, knew Wilbur stayed up late. During the party, the murderer at some point slipped downstairs and into the study to unlock the garden door for Susan. The murderer likely was in the hallway near a window, waited until Susan left, then went back into the study. Instead of returning to the party, the murderer may have remained in the study, possibly sitting in darkness, waiting for guests to leave and the house to fall silent. Finally, sure no one was about, it was time to open the door into the garden, turn on a light, pull the painting away from the safe. Now there was a breath-catching ascent up the private family stairs near the informal living area to the second floor. Another cautious survey, a dash to Wilbur's door, a knock. Wilbur opened the door, saw a familiar face, and the sands of time began to rush away for him.

When Judy Weitz and Don Smith stepped into the hallway, I waited until the door closed and then I appeared. I was in a hurry but I gave them time to reach the stairs. I eased the door open. The hallway was quiet. The police, of course, had interviewed everyone present in the house. But I doubted they had the same goals.

I continued to explore, and my search was rewarded on the third floor of the west wing. Two doors contained nameplates: *Rosalind Millbrook, Housekeeper. Carl Ross, Butler.* I knocked on the butler's door, then twisted the knob. He stood at the windows overlooking the garden. He turned as I stepped inside. His crisp white shirt, red tie, black trousers, and leather shoes had the look of a uniform. He projected an aura of toughness, a burly man who could hold his own in any confrontation. He had shaved since I glimpsed him this morning in the formal living room.

I held out my leather ID folder. "Glad I caught you, Mr. Ross. We have a few more questions."

He glanced at the clock on a metal desk. A quarter to five. "All right."

"Were you on your way home?"

He jerked a thumb over his shoulder. "I live above the garages. One of the perks. No rent."

He didn't offer me a seat. He remained standing so I did as well.

"Mr. Ross, please describe your normal evening duties."

He had a heavy face beneath the balding head, a fleshy nose, thin lips. His eyes were flint gray, observant, cold. His muscular shoulders lifted in a shrug, fell. "Depended. A regular night Mr. Fitch ate dinner around seven, maybe worked in his study. Sometimes he played pool with me or we did some skeet shooting. He has an indoor range on the other side of the lake. But he usually went upstairs around eleven. Some nights he was out all evening with Ms. Lloyd. When he spent the night at home, he had a glass of milk and peanut butter cookies in his suite around midnight."

"And chocolate on the bed as well?"

"Yeah." A slight quirk to those thin lips. "He liked money, women, and food in that order."

"Who was in charge of locking up the house at night?"

"Me."

"How about last night?"

"I checked the ground floor doors except for the kitchen and the main entrance. The caterer was responsible for closing up after the cleanup. I closed the front door at half past twelve and I was done."

"What time did you check the door from the garden into the study?"

"Nine o'clock."

"The door was closed and locked?"

"Right."

Likely the ransom caller waited until around eleven to slip downstairs and into the study to unlock the door.

"You arranged Mr. Fitch's room last night?"

"Right." He was matter-of-fact. Nothing in his impassive face reflected the reality that he would never perform those duties again.

"You worked long hours."

"My time didn't start until four in the afternoon, weekends off. I like working nights. The cook served breakfast and lunch unless there were guests, then she brought in some girls from the college to wait the table."

"How about last night?"

"I brought the milk and cookies about twenty after twelve.

He was sitting on his sofa, gave me a wave, asked what I thought about the music. He was kidding me. I don't like the kind of stuff they play now. I stopped going to a bar that started playing all this squealy stuff. I like rock 'n' roll. I told him it sure sounded like he had a pig farm in the ballroom. He slapped his hand on his knee, said, *I like that. I can see it now. A bunch of pigs in tuxes and gowns.* He was still laughing when I went out." The heavy face squeezed a little. "That's the last time I saw him."

"When you stepped out in the hall did you see anyone?" It must have been near the time that someone knocked on Wilbur's door.

He raised an eyebrow. "Like who would I see? The house was shut down for the night."

"Wilbur went downstairs."

"Yeah." A considering tone. "Funny."

"Unusual?"

"Yes." He folded his powerful arms across his front.

That had been his posture in the living room this morning as he waited to be seen by the police. I wondered if this was his pose when he was deep in thought.

I remembered Don Smith's comment to Judy Weitz. "Do you think he might have gone to the library for a book?"

The thin lips curled in a wry smile. "The library was a showpiece. Classics. Rare books. The books he read were in his living area."

"Some work he'd forgotten?"

The cold gray eyes were dismissive. "He never forgot anything. Whatever he intended to do yesterday, he'd done."

"Possibly he heard a noise downstairs—"

"No noise in his suite."

"If he looked outside would he see a light shining from the windows of the study?"

"The curtains were drawn. Besides"—he was more animated—"I get the idea some stuff was taken from the safe. I don't think a burglar would be stupid enough to turn on a light."

Nor did I.

"So you have no idea what led Wilbur to go down to the study after you said good night to him."

He turned up two beefy palms, a physical display of puzzlement, but he looked like a man who had his own thoughts.

"If you know anything, it's important to tell the police."

His fish gray eyes told me he had little respect for either authorities or women. "What would I know?" His tone was just this side of insolent.

⁓

Following Ross's directions, I returned to the second floor and walked up the west wing to another massive oak door, knocked.

In a moment, the door swung inward. I held out my ID folder, introduced myself.

"Come in." Ben Fitch was very young to look so bleak. He gestured toward a cream leather couch next to a fireplace. The suite wasn't quite as large as his father's, but it was very nice indeed, expensive comfortable furnishings, bright paintings on the walls. An open door in one wall likely led to a bedroom and bath.

Ben Fitch was pale beneath his Hawaiian tan. His curly dark hair needed a comb, and his cheeks were heavily shadowed. He looked like a young man who'd been the life of the party and suddenly the party was over. I noted his red-rimmed eyes and that he looked at me expectantly. "Any—" He broke off, pressed his lips together. How hard would it be to ask about the murder of your father?

I liked him. I reminded myself that the person who killed Wilbur would make an intense effort to appear appropriately concerned. Still my voice was gentle after I settled on the couch. "You've not been back in town long."

He flung himself into a massive red leather chair, jammed a hand through his thick dark hair, stared at flames dancing among crackling logs. "Too long." His face ridged. "But not long enough." He gazed at me and there was misery in his young face. "Dad—he was bigger than big. Always in command. We were like fireworks and somebody drops a match. We couldn't ever be in the same room for long without all hell breaking loose. I should have left last week, but he wanted me to stay. Dammit, he wanted me here, wanted me in the business, but I knew it would never work. You know"—and now there was a shine in his blue eyes—"he really was proud of what I did in Hawaii. I took a little surf shop and now I've got shops on all the islands and business tripled last year. He liked that, said I was a natural, then yesterday I told him he needed to dump Todd

Garrett—he's the COO—and it was like old times, he was hot and mad and telling me I was a wet-nosed kid and what the hell did I know about Todd and I should spend a year working for Todd and maybe figure out how to get along with people and find out what a chief operating officer does. We were both shouting—"

I now understood why Susan spoke so carefully when I'd first asked her about Ben Fitch. No doubt she heard this quarrel, but was convinced—or wanted to believe—that this was simply Wilbur being Wilbur.

"—and I slammed out of his room and yelled I'd get back to the islands and maybe next year I'd see him again." He looked at me and the shine was clearly tears. "Now my stepbrother and I are arranging his funeral. Got Mom and Hayley, that's Harry's mom, on their way. Next Monday. The First Baptist Church. I closed down the offices and the sorting sheds today. Dad would say get on with it. But not today. I couldn't have everything going on like it always was. We'll close Monday. Any more than that and he'd probably be yelling from the hereafter. Yelling . . . I told Dad next year. I yelled *next year* at him. Now I won't ever see him again." He hunched forward. "Look, are you getting anywhere? I can't figure out how it happened. They told me the door to the garden was open. And that the painting was pulled back and the safe was wide open. Why would Dad open the safe? It must have been the middle of the night. The party didn't end until around midnight. I didn't spend much time in the ballroom. I was up here"—he gestured with his hand—"getting my stuff packed." There was a backpack leaning against one wall and a chock-full duffel bag. "I was going to drive down to Dallas and get a flight out. And now—"

"Will you stay in Adelaide?"

He squinted at me as if I spoke Portuguese. "I can't leave. That would break Dad's heart. Todd couldn't run a bake sale. They were old buddies. Dad let Todd run around town, act like a COO, be a big deal, but Dad ran everything. If I left, Fitch Enterprises would crack up. I don't have a choice. I'll stay and I'll make Dad proud of me." His voice broke a little. "I'll run it like a son of a bitch."

"Will you get rid of Todd Garrett?"

An impatient wave of his hand. "I'll keep him on, let him pretend to be a big deal. Just like Dad did. He was Dad's oldest friend. Maybe sometimes we can talk about Dad."

"How about Alan Douglas and the SIMPLE Car?"

He leaned back in the leather chair, his expression thoughtful. "Dad had good instincts. He saw the appeal. A lot of people want the world to be open again, not tethered to a device twenty-four/seven. That's the kind who end up in Hawaii and they want to see orchids and ride boogie boards and throw rocks in a volcano. But he agreed after we talked about it. SIMPLE isn't the way of the future. Look what Amazon's done with Alexa. That's the future. Everything connected everywhere all the time. I'd already—"

The prospect sounded hideous to me, but happily in Heaven everything is personal. You think of someone and you are with them. There's no need for cogs and wheels or chips. Joy and love satisfy hearts and souls. Who needs anything else? If you have a question in your mind, the answer comes. No need for Alexa or Siri.

"—told Dad going back isn't going forward. He was still tempted. I think he just wanted an old-fashioned car for the fun of it. But the concept wasn't right for Fitch Enterprises. He talked to Alan yesterday."

Ben spoke as if this was no big deal. A business decision. I wondered how big a deal it was to Alan Douglas.

"Did you see your father after the party?"

"I didn't see him." Sharp. Definitive. Sorrowful.

"Were you in the study last night?"

"No."

"Do you have any idea who might have gone to the study with your father?"

"Gone to the study with him?" He looked puzzled. "I thought the idea was that Dad surprised someone there. I got kind of a garbled story, something about Susan Gilbert getting a threatening call and rushing over here and taking the cash box out of the safe and for some reason coming back later to get the coins. But I understand she explained what happened and returned the cash box and she says she didn't take the coins. She's not a crook. She wouldn't hurt Dad." He spoke emphatically.

I looked at him in surprise.

There was an odd expression on his face. "Dad thought the world of Susan. I can tell I will, too. I've got a knack for people. Just like Dad did."

Ben Fitch was not lacking in confidence.

He gave me a long stare. "Just like I can look at you and know you wouldn't hurt anyone. Neither would Susan."

Since I was a counterfeit police detective, I could speak honestly. "I agree, Mr. Fitch."

But his quick mind had already moved on. He frowned again. "If you think Dad went to the study with someone, that changes everything. There wasn't any reason for Dad to be in the study that late."

I said quietly, "It seems possible that someone came to your father's door and knocked and persuaded him to go down."

Ben's face squeezed in thought. "That person must have known him well enough to go to his bedroom and been confident Dad wouldn't be shocked at his appearance. That clears Susan Gilbert right there. He would have been astounded if she knocked on his door. Someone who knew Dad well . . . That explains why Susan was tricked into coming here last night." He thumped a fist into his opposite palm. "I got it. The murderer set the study up to look like a robbery, maybe turned on the light, opened the garden door, pulled back the painting, then knocked on Dad's door, told him it looks like something's up in the study. Dad came downstairs, opened the safe, and the murderer hit him. But how did anyone get into the house that late at night?"

"Perhaps a key. Perhaps someone who attended the party slipped into the study and opened the garden door."

He came to his feet. "I'm going to go see Susan Gilbert."

I rose, too. "I appreciate your time." When we were out in

the hall, I murmured, "I have a few more rooms to check." He nodded but he was no longer focused on me. He walked swiftly to the stairs. I waited until he was out of sight. As the clatter of his steps receded, I disappeared.

I wasn't finished with Detective Sergeant G. Latham's interviews. Charming stepson Harry Hubbard, bumbling executive Todd Garrett, and hopeful inventor Alan Douglas were still on my list. But I wanted to talk to them at work. The offices would be open tomorrow. For now I was finished with my police inquiries.

I had an important stop to make before treating myself to a chicken-fried steak, cream gravy, and mashed potatoes at Lulu's. As my mama always told us, "Don't let the sun set on a man's misperceptions or they'll harden like concrete."

⌒

Sam Cobb's office was fully lighted, but he wasn't in his desk chair. Perhaps he would return soon. I felt a little stab of disappointment. I thought Sam would still be at work. The murder of a leading citizen demanded all-out effort.

Unless the case was considered solved.

I glanced at the round clock on the wall. A quarter to six. For an instant, my stomach squeezed. You know the feeling. You wake up at eight fifteen and the final started at eight. You had a good tight hold on someone's hand as floodwaters swirled and suddenly your hand is empty. You are alone in the house at midnight and there's a heavy step in the upper hall. I fought down a crest of panic, spoke firmly to myself. "Steady, Bailey Ruth. You'll save Susan." I took five deep breaths and moved to the chalkboard. I picked up a piece of chalk.

"A voice with no visible source, deep breaths, and airborne chalk are unnerving. How about spinning yourself here."

I whirled to see Sam Cobb lumbering up from the sofa, staring this way.

"Sam. You're here!"

"Where do you think I'd be? This is Claire's bridge night. I was thinking." He pointed at the sofa. "I think better staring at the ceiling."

I like being present. After all, as I once explained to Wiggins when he complained that I was overeager to appear, it is always my sincere wish to make everyone comfortable. I didn't add that I was including myself. What was the joy in a fashionable ensemble if I couldn't see it? I appeared and smoothed the sleeve of the lavender cardigan, loving the texture of the cable design. I felt my spirits lift as I settled on the couch beside Sam.

Sam's big face was a mixture of amusement and, I am glad to say, affection. He smiled at me. "Besides, I was hanging around because I had a feeling Officer Loy might drop by."

"Actually, Detective Sergeant G. Latham." I pulled out my leather police ID holder.

Sam took the holder in a huge hand. "Kind of spooky. Right down to the last detail." He returned the ID. "Wonder if that thing holds fingerprints." Sam obviously didn't want any connection to a fake police ID.

"Not to worry. It disappears right along with me. But speaking of fingerprints." I looked at him urgently. "Did you have prints lifted from Wilbur's suite door?"

"He was killed in his study." Sam's gravelly voice was patient.

"That doesn't answer my question."

"You sound like my first grade teacher. Okay, okay. Forensic evidence was taken only from the scene of the crime."

"Sam, please send the techs out first thing in the morning. Take prints from the suite door. The killer knocked. There might be DNA traces, too."

"DNA's expensive."

I ignored the comment. "Here's what the killer did last night. Attended the party. At some point slipped downstairs and into the study. Probably had gloves in a purse or pocket. Put them on. Unlocked the garden door so Susan could get in. Maybe went back upstairs, maybe not. Probably called Susan from the study, then went into the hall and looked out a window, watched her arrive. Susan leaves. The watcher returns to the study. After the guests depart and the house is quiet, it was time to turn on the light in the study, open the door to the garden, pull the painting back from the safe, then slip upstairs to knock on Wilbur's door. No gloves there. Wilbur might not have sensed danger from someone he knew well, but gloves would look very odd."

Sam leaned back against the leather cushion. "According to you, the visitor was a guest from the party who claimed he/she had returned for something, saw a light in the study, found the door open, yada yada."

"Do you have a better idea why Wilbur went downstairs?" I spoke pleasantly.

His brown eyes awarded me a point. "Maybe he wanted to check something in his office."

"Weak."

Sam shrugged. "There could be a reason."

"Let's say you're right. Wilbur decides to go down to his study and it happens to be just at the moment when Susan returns to get the coins? It's always been a stretch that she came back a second time."

He was still skeptical. "Instead of a party guest gone rogue, how about Susan Gilbert unlocked the garden door of the study before she quit work yesterday."

I countered. "She didn't know she was going to get a fake ransom call."

A slight nod as my score increased. "Maybe she'd already decided to burgle the safe."

"And she got a call demanding one hundred thousand in cash and Wilbur's safe is mentioned? Lame, Sam. Besides the door was locked at nine p.m."

He raised an eyebrow. "Who says?"

"The butler. Carl Ross checked the ground-floor doors. That door was shut and locked when he made his rounds at nine."

Sam's heavy face folded in a frown. Then he shrugged. "She had a key."

There I was on safe ground. "She did not have a key to the house, neither to the front door nor to the study door. She told the caller she couldn't get into the study, but the caller assured her the door to the study would be unlocked. I was with her and she went as instructed to the garden door of the study and it definitely wasn't locked."

There was silence. Sam rubbed the knuckles of one hand along the side of his five-o'clock shadow. I could hear the faint tick of the wall clock. I avoided looking triumphant. As Mama always told us, "A man won't change his mind if you embarrass him."

"Garden door locked at nine p.m." His voice held a considering tone. "And Gilbert wasn't at the party."

"Do you have the guest list?"

He nodded, pushed up from the couch. In a moment he was back with a folder. He handed it to me as he sat down, shook his head. "A hundred and five guests. Catering crew of nine."

"Only seven names matter." I opened the folder, found a pen in my cardigan jacket. Heaven provides. It took me only a moment to scan and check seven names. I returned the sheets.

He took a quick look. "You're still singing the same song."

"Who knew Susan could open the safe? These seven."

"I've looked at them."

I was surprised.

"Gilbert is heavy odds guilty, but I do my job. Per your intelligence, I checked out all seven. The disgruntled mistress. The pretty young thing who charmed herself into his will. The son who will now be Adelaide's richest citizen. The laid-back stepson who can buy a lot of fancy golf clubs and maybe never show up at the office. The vice president who has a great idea but Wilbur said no. In that regard, we have to wonder if the idea for a

SIMPLE Car might be considered a Fitch work product and not belong to Alan Douglas. The old football hero who might be on the outs with his boss. The lawyer who will rack up huge fees as he settles one of the biggest estates in Adelaide's history."

"Sam, you're wonderful." I meant the compliment sincerely.

"Gilbert's not home free," he said firmly, "but maybe she's halfway between second and third. I had another visitor just before you came. Judy Weitz has a linear mind, and she says it doesn't add up for Gilbert to be the perp. Too many holes. A fake kidnapping unconnected to a murder is just a bridge too far. Judy believes the hoax was set up to put Gilbert on the spot. Judy says it's nuts to think Gilbert was at the house twice. She also says if Gilbert hid the coins, intending to keep them, she would also have kept the box of cash. Plus she says her brother went to school with Gilbert and she was valedictorian of her class and only a terminally stupid thief would have hidden the coins beneath that tub in the garden knowing, if she killed Fitch, that she would be a suspect and her house and yard would be searched when the items from the safe were missed. Finally, Judy says it's obvious the coins were planted and the only person who could have planted them was Fitch's murderer."

The stress from the day melted away. An honest police chief and a good detective weren't closing the book yet.

"And," his deep voice continued, "to put a little whipping cream on your sundae—"

Sam had good ideas. I added a sundae to my soon-to-be order at Lulu's.

"—Ben Fitch called a few minutes ago, said he talked to

Susan and she explained everything about the ransom call and he's sure she was set up by someone to take the fall. He wanted me to know he'd get a private detective on the case ASAP if the police didn't do a complete investigation. He said Susan has a private eye from Dallas looking around." His gaze was steady. "A redhead. Name of G. Latham."

I smiled serenely.

"Private eyes who use fake cop IDs can get in a heap of trouble."

"Fancy that," I observed.

"Shameless," he growled. "Back to Fitch, he wanted to know if we'd canvassed the neighbors about anyone skulking in her yard around one thirty in the morning to hide the coins."

"So tomorrow you'll get the prints and maybe DNA from the Fitch house and talk to Susan's neighbors."

"And try to get Neva to back off an immediate arrest."

I beamed at him.

He shook his head. "The odds are still good Gilbert's guilty. But I'll keep looking."

⁊

I enjoyed every bit of my celebratory dinner at Lulu's, and the cherry atop the sundae was a tart delight. I felt nostalgic. I love Adelaide. It is different now than it was in my day but still the same kind of people, a waitress who called me hon and moved with skill and energy, fellow diners relaxing after a busy day of work. Soon I would climb aboard the Rescue Express, my mission done. But I wasn't through quite yet.

I was tempted to drop by Susan's house, but decided to wait and give her a complete report tomorrow after Detective Sergeant G. Latham spoke to Harry Hubbard, Todd Garrett, and Alan Douglas. I would again visit Sam and discover the results of the tech check of Wilbur's suite door and inquiries with neighbors about late Tuesday night.

After I paid my bill, I strolled out into the chilly night and disappeared. In a moment, I was at Rose Bower and in the room I'd used this morning for a luxurious shower. It was almost eight.

I found a collection of Browning's poems and settled on a chaise longue. I always feel very Marie Antoinette-ish on a chaise longue, as if I should have curls piled high above my head, wear a low-cut satin gown, and hold a delicate fan to flutter coquettishly. I savored the elegance and grace of his poetry. Time passed slowly. My eyes wandered to the clock. Almost ten.

It was very silent in the huge old mansion. Perhaps the total absence of sound, no doors opening and closing, no voices, no one about, or the size of the high-ceilinged room or a memory of Mayor Lumpkin's choleric face plucked at my sense of well-being.

I put the book on my lap, frowned. Perhaps I should be out and about, checking on the activities of the seven. No one, of course, would wear a placard announcing *MURDERER*. I felt restless, uneasy. Was I taking too much for granted? Sam intended to look beyond Susan tomorrow, but—

The deep whoo of the Rescue Express thrummed against my ears. I jumped to my feet, the book sliding to the floor. Coal smoke swirled around me. The thunder of the wheels clacking on the rails seemed to echo from the walls.

Wiggins stood before me in his usual white shirt, black suspenders, black wool trousers, and black shoes. This was his attire in his office that overlooked the curving silver tracks at his station. For Wiggins to abruptly appear in a silent room at Rose Bower shocked me.

His spaniel brown eyes were wide with distress. "There's no hope for Susan now."

Chapter 9

Susan stood rigid, arms raised. "Don't shoot. I don't have a gun. I don't!" Her brown eyes were wide with shock. She stood with her back to the sink in a wet bar. The water was running. Her hands were wet and the cuffs of her sleeves were wet. A sopping dish towel lay partially in the sink.

A young police officer, his face pale, his cheeks taut, gripped a service revolver with both hands, aimed the muzzle directly at Susan. He was tall and thin, not long past a teenager. "Don't move." His voice was a little too high and it wobbled.

A muscular officer in his forties, thinning blond hair, a tired face, eased from behind the younger man. He ordered in a deep voice, "Cover me, Porter. I'll handcuff her." He moved toward Susan, a pair of handcuffs dangling from his left hand. His right hand hovered near his holster. Even with the backup of his partner, he kept an unwavering stare on Susan, ready for any movement.

I felt a squeeze on my arm, a signal that Wiggins was leaving me here to do my best. The scent of coal smoke diminished. The sound of the wheels faded. The departure of the Rescue Express wasn't heard by the three people—four, if you counted the dead man on the floor—in the rustically furnished living room of the cabin near the Fitch lake.

"Take two steps forward. Put your hands behind your back." The officer's order was brusque.

"Will he stop pointing that gun at me?" Susan's voice wavered.

"When I snap the cuffs, he'll put the gun away." The words were quick, cold.

Her eyes never moving from the muzzle of the gun, Susan slowly took two steps forward, stopped, lowered her arms, put her hands behind her.

The bigger man moved fast, swung behind Susan. Click.

Officer Porter's eyelids fluttered. He took several breaths, slowly lowered the gun, eased it into the leather holster.

I had a sense he was struggling to keep his hands from shaking.

Susan watched as he slid the gun into the holster, then she, too, drew deep breaths. Susan would have been lovely in a tan long-sleeved blouse and midcalf navy flannel skirt if it weren't for a face slack with shock and a smear of blood on one of her tan suede wedge heels. She looked bewildered and stricken. "I tried to see if he was alive. I got blood on my hands." There was horror in her voice. "I came over here to wash my hands so I could call for help."

The older policeman—his nameplate read *D. Warren*—gave her a hard level stare. "No hurry for him." He lifted his phone, punched, spoke loudly. "No longer active shooter scene. One-eight-seven. Male. DOA. Cabin on Fitch estate approximately half mile from house. Apparent gunshot to chest. Forty to fifty years old. Five foot ten to six feet tall. Weight around one eighty. Possible suspect in custody. Female. Name Susan Gilbert. No weapon visible. No search has been made." A pause. He stood a little straighter. "Yes, sir." He repeated the information. "We have everything under control."

Porter's eyes scanned the floor. He knew better than to disturb the body until death was officially proclaimed by the medical examiner. "I'll look around." He made a slow circuit of the room, looking behind furniture.

Susan stared at Officer Warren. "How do you know my name?" She was grappling with the fact that he knew her. How could he know her? And how was it that the police were here?

I knew she'd read the *Gazette* story, but obviously she'd not focused on the mayor's announcement about around-the-clock surveillance. I'd paid no attention, either. The killer, who well knew that Susan must be of intense interest to the police, didn't miss that information. The killer knew the police likely would follow Susan wherever she went. How about decoying her to the murder scene, waiting for her arrival, then, as a clever finishing touch, shooting the gun and knowing there would be cops to hear the shot.

Susan tried again. "I just got here." Her voice was thin. "I found him—"

Warren made a sharp chopping motion with his left hand.

Susan broke off.

Warren listened. "That's right, Chief. Susan Gilbert. Porter and I were staked out at the Gilbert house tonight. She exited her back door at approximately four minutes before ten. She departed her driveway at two minutes before ten. She drove to the back entrance to the Fitch property, turned in at three minutes after ten. We parked on street at four minutes after ten, proceeded on foot. Came in view of cabin at six minutes after ten. Gilbert's car was parked in front of cabin. The cabin porch light was on and the front windows were lighted. We were approximately a hundred yards from the porch when a shot was fired. We ducked into the shadows, called for backup—"

Sirens wailed. Homicide and the forensic van were arriving. It isn't far from the police station in City Hall to the homes high on a hill in the best part of town.

"—and worked our way up to the cabin. All remained quiet. We moved from shadow to shadow, reached the porch at maybe eleven after ten. Porter got here first. He asked me to cover him. He went up on the porch from one side, hugged the wall, moved to the door. The door, no screen, was ajar. He yelled, 'Police. Hands up,' kicked the door open, went in sideways like he was supposed to, had his gun out." There was an admiring tone in Warren's voice. He thought the young cop passed a tough test. "I was right behind him. Gilbert was over at a sink. The water was running. She swung around and looked toward the door.

Porter ordered Gilbert to get her hands up. She did. She's handcuffed—"

The shrill sirens abruptly cut off. Doors slammed. Feet thudded outside on the wooden porch. Sam Cobb was first through the door, Detective Sergeant Hal Price close behind. Sam was holding his cell phone. He had obviously moved quickly from his car, but there was no struggle for breath as he surveyed the room: Susan. His officers. The dead man.

In less than a minute, Sam had the scene under control, everyone outside on the porch to await the arrival of the medical examiner. As he spoke with Porter and Warren, a lean intense figure approached the cars and whirling lights. Joan Crandall as always held a notebook and pencil. No doubt access was barred from the street, but Joan likely nodded when she was prohibited from entering then walked far enough away to slip into the woods and find a way to the cabin road. Joan stood a few feet away from the porch and scanned the waiting figures. Her gaze settled on Susan. She began to write.

Susan tried to speak, "I knew he was hurt and—"

Sam shot her a hard look. "We'll get to it in time, Miss Gilbert. For now you're in custody as a material witness. I want to warn you that anything you say—"

Susan listened to the Miranda warning. "I didn't shoot him."

Sam was brusque. "You can have your say later. We have a body to deal with." He jerked a thumb at a redheaded officer. "Understand she was washing her hands." He looked around, gestured for a tech. "Put some adhesive tabs on her right hand to check for gunshot residue. Put them in an evidence bag." He turned back to the big redhead. "When that's done, check her in at the jail. She gets one phone call. Impound the car. Get a search warrant."

I was on the porch next to Susan when headlights swept over the parked cars and the knot of officers on the porch. The red-headed officer moved Susan toward the steps, a large hand gripping her upper left arm. A familiar red sports car squealed to a stop behind the forensic van. The door swung out and Jacob Brandt was on his feet and moving fast toward the cabin. He looked snazzy tonight in a blue sport coat, red pullover sweater, and navy slacks. He carried a leather satchel. "Hell of a time to get a call." He looked glum. "She's too damn pretty to sit there by herself for long. Where's the body? Inside?" And he was through the door.

Susan and the officer were at the foot of the stairs, turning toward a cruiser. I hovered next to Susan, bent near, whispered, "I'll come see you as soon as I can."

She jerked to a stop, looked wildly to her right.

I kept close. "Get Megan Wynn for your lawyer. Tell her Jimmy's redheaded friend wants her to help you."

Susan said blankly, "Redheaded friend?"

The officer was brusque. "Knock it off."

Susan glared at him. "I'm not talking to you."

"Who are you talking to then?"

Susan took a deep breath. "That's a good question. But I have an answer. Jimmy's redheaded friend."

The officer's grip tightened. "Like I said, knock it off. Acting nuts won't save you, either."

Susan tried to shake free. "Let go of me. I'll walk to the car. I'm not nuts. You people are nuts. I come here and find a body and nobody listens to me. I didn't shoot Carl Ross. I'm here because he called and said he knew something that could help me and I believed him. He would have seen Wilbur Fitch after the party, made sure he didn't want anything else that night. But I didn't shoot Carl. I don't have a gun. I've never had a gun. I've never shot a gun. I came to meet him and I found him on the floor. I tried to help him and then I heard a shot—"

The officer, face expressionless, grip still tight on her arm, urged her forward. They reached the first cruiser. He opened the back door, none too gently pushed her in.

"—and all of sudden the police are shouting and one of them points a gun at—"

The door slammed.

Joan Crandall was a few feet away, writing furiously.

I hated watching the cruiser pull away. I hoped Susan wasn't ordered to don an orange jail jumpsuit. Perhaps a material witness was permitted to remain in street clothes. She was already shaken and upset, finding Wilbur's butler in a pool of blood, trying to help, staining a shoe. The fact that the police had followed her, had been assigned to watch her, indicated how tenuous was her hold on freedom. And now she was found standing by a dead man. She must feel that the ordinary world had disappeared and she was plunged into a nightmare that didn't end. But for now I needed to stay here and learn what I could about the death of Carl Ross.

I moved back into the cabin. The overhead light in the living

169

room was a chandelier shaped like a wagon wheel with lights that looked like old-fashioned lamps. The room was designed for comfort, several rustic sofas in a cheery maple with cushions upholstered in blue denim, a large wet bar against one wall, a bridge table with a checkerboard, a pool table with cues in a nearby rack, the balls contained within their triangle on the green felt. A ceiling-to-floor plate glass window would offer a clear view of the lake in daytime. Now there was only darkness beyond.

Jacob Brandt knelt by the body. He stripped off a plastic glove, touched the dead man's cheek. He pulled off the other glove, balled them in his left hand, and pushed up from the floor. "Gunshot oblique angle. Left front to right back, struck the heart. Shooter was standing, victim seated. That accounts for the angle. Death instantaneous. No exit wound. Bullet may be lodged in the spinal cord. I'll get it to you. Tomorrow."

"Tonight," Sam said mildly.

"If she's still at the table, I want to make nice for a couple more hours. I'll take a look for it around midnight. I hope not any earlier. Otherwise"—he was stuffing plastic gloves in his jacket pocket—"no other apparent trauma." He started for the door. "Room isn't overheated, maybe sixty-eight degrees. I'll do an incision, poke a thermometer into the liver when I do the autopsy. But I think I can get pretty close right now. Dead at least an hour, absolute max two hours." He glanced at a watch with enough dials and hands to navigate the Bosporus. "Ten forty-five now. Roughly he was shot between eight forty-five and nine forty-five at the latest. My best estimate is around nine thirty. That's all for now." He made it to the door and through faster than a greyhound chasing a lure.

As the door closed behind the medical examiner, Hal murmured to Sam, "She must be a knockout." Outside the sports car engine roared.

As the forensic team began its careful work, I looked down on the scene. I recognized Carl Ross's gray sweats and sneakers, perhaps his costume of choice when not working. His eyes stared sightlessly at the ceiling. His sweatshirt was soggy with blood. The blood had welled onto the floor. There was a smear and what looked like a partial footprint. Susan said she'd tried to see if she could help him. Perhaps she hurried across the room and as she bent over she stepped into a pool of blood.

Lights flashed as photos were taken. One tech held a camera, filmed the body and the surrounding area.

I scanned the room for a clock. The film would record not only the scene but the time the video was made. Ross lay a little on one side. One long arm splayed out. I moved close, carefully turned the wrist so I could read the time. Ten minutes to eleven.

"Hey."

Faces turned. Sam's heavy face was inquiring.

The tech clutched the camera close to her chest. She retreated one step, another. "Hey, somebody take a look. His arm moved."

Sam strode nearer. "Maybe rigor mortis." He was soothing. "He's dead. The ME said so. And so do I."

The tech swallowed. "I don't care what anybody says, his right arm turned. Like he was going to look at his watch." The last words quivered.

"Uh." Sam glanced around. "Not to worry. Maybe there was a little quake. Shook his arm. You know we have them all the time." His voice was still soothing. But his brown eyes continued to check out the room. "Alert of you to notice, Roberts. Continue to film."

Slowly the videocam was lifted.

"Speaking of time"—Sam continued to think out loud, looked at Porter and Warren—"tell me again when you left the Gilbert house?"

Warren pulled a small notebook from his pocket, repeated the times he'd relayed in his call to the dispatcher.

Sam looked thoughtful. "Shot fired at about seven minutes after ten?"

Warren nodded. "Yes, sir."

Sam and Hal exchanged a glance. They moved out of the way of the filming tech, stood near the pool table with a good view of the overstuffed chair and the body that lay at an angle to it. I was close enough to hear their low-voiced conversation.

"Screwy." Hal stood with his hands pushed deep into the pockets of well-worn chinos. He was as remarkably handsome as the first time I glimpsed him, tall, lean, a blue-eyed blond with regular features and a mouth that could spread in a generous grin. Then he'd been an attractive bachelor. Now he was married to Deirdre Davenport, a young woman I'd assisted when her fingerprints were found on a murder weapon.

"Screwy sums it up." Sam rubbed his chin with the knuckles of his right hand. "Jake is good at his job. If he thinks Ross was dead by nine forty-five at the outside limit, the timing of the shot is an anomaly."

"You sound like Deirdre." Hal's wife was a writer and teacher. "Anomaly's above my pay grade. How about, Why was a shot fired if he was already dead? And who fired a gun?"

Sam heaved an irritated sigh. "Coincidence sucks, but maybe somebody was out in the woods and shot off a gun."

"Once?"

"Seems so."

Hal persisted. "Right next to a cabin where a guy's been shot?"

"That," Sam said ironically, "is the coincidence."

"Okay." Hal was equable. "For now let's skip the seven minutes past ten shot. Whether it killed him or not, he was definitely shot here tonight within the last couple of hours."

"And the woman we think killed her boss is right on the scene." Sam's gaze settled on the chair and the body. "Here's how I read it. He was sitting in that chair. Jake said he was shot by somebody standing while he was sitting. That correlates with the body slumping off the chair onto the floor." His gaze flickered to a sofa to the right of the chair. "The sofa is at a right angle to the chair. I picture Ross and a guest, both seated. They had a talk. I'd like to have heard that talk. We can figure that Ross knew something that made him a danger to Wilbur Fitch's murderer. Ross was used to staying up late, seeing if his boss wanted anything. That was probably true unless Minerva Lloyd was spending the night. I imagine Wilbur gave him those evenings off. Otherwise, he's on duty until Wilbur sends him away. What happened last night?"

Hal was right with him. "Ross saw something or someone that he linked to Wilbur's murder. Maybe he was in that cross hallway, about to call it a night, when he heard a knock on Wilbur's door. Maybe he looked around a corner, saw someone he knew. The visitor didn't alarm him. Instead, Ross decides he's off duty and goes downstairs and out to the garage apartment. Or maybe he was on his way to the garage apartment and saw someone in the garden. The person was known to him so he didn't raise an alarm. He saw someone somewhere. This morning he finds out Wilbur was bludgeoned to death in his study sometime after midnight. He figures the late-night visitor is the killer."

"He didn't call us." There was a note of finality in Sam's voice. "Instead Ross saw himself riding a gravy train. He knew something, could tell the police something, prove someone was with Wilbur after the party, and no one has admitted seeing Wilbur after midnight. He called Wilbur's late-night visitor, said something like we have a matter to discuss, like where you were at so many minutes after midnight last night. The police would find that information interesting. But maybe we can work out a deal. I'll forget all about what I saw for, say, fifty thousand dollars. I'll take a down payment. Bring five thousand to the lake cabin at, depending on who shot him, either a little before ten if Gilbert's the perp or a quarter past nine if somebody set her up. After Ross made the demand, he hung up."

Hal was curious. "Why a quarter past nine?"

The crime techs continued their work, one creating a meticulous drawing to scale of the room and its contents, including Ross's body, another dusting for fingerprints. A low hum of conversation.

Sam tapped his wristwatch. "Jake pegs him as dead by nine forty-five. If he's right, the killer probably got here around nine thirty. I doubt they talked long. The killer had already decided Ross had to die. Besides, if Bai—" He caught himself. "—if Gilbert isn't the perp, the killer had to have time to get her here and then hang around long enough for her to arrive, shoot the gun, get the hell away. Tomorrow I want the woods searched for a gun. And a cartridge. And any traces a car was parked off the road."

"If the killer isn't Gilbert"—there was definite doubt in Hal's voice—"you're talking a heavy-duty planner."

"If the killer isn't Gilbert"—Sam was grim—"somebody did a lot of planning, starting with a fake ransom call to get her to the Fitch study Tuesday night and some kind of call to get her over here tonight."

"Without leaving a trace anywhere?" Hal was dubious.

"A call to get her here tonight . . ." There was a musing tone in Sam's voice. He looked at a plump tech with unlikely purple hair and green harlequin glasses. "Abbott, check the phone receiver for prints."

She nodded, gestured at a table a few feet from her where a landline telephone sat. "That's next, sir. Almost finished here."

Hal squinted at the body. "I talked to Ross earlier today. Pretty big guy. Strong. Seemed smart. Pretty stupid to think he could handle a murderer."

"Terminal mistake." There was no commiseration in Sam's voice. Sam didn't like killers or blackmailers.

Abbott dusted fingerprint powder on the arm of the sofa that sat at a right angle to the chair near the body. She stared at the arm, then pushed her glasses higher on her nose as she turned to look at Sam. She pointed at the sofa. "The armrest doesn't have a single print. No prints. No smudges. Somebody polished the wood clean."

Sam looked satisfied. "Alert us if you find any other clean areas."

"Like you said." Hal's gaze was impressed. "Ross in the chair, killer on the sofa."

Sam pointed at the sofa. "Ross's guest stood up, walked toward him, reached into a purse or jacket, pulled out a gun, pulled the trigger. That doesn't square with Gilbert as the perp. She didn't have time to sit down and have a chat before Warren and Porter heard a shot."

Hal shrugged. "Maybe she blew in through the door and Ross stayed in the chair, too cool to get up. As for the armrest, maybe somebody started dusting the place and only did the sofa arm."

Sam gestured at the room, now more than three-fourths vetted. "Warren and Porter were in here like June bugs on an oak leaf. Where's the gun?"

An officer stepped in from an adjoining room. "Got an open window in a bedroom, Chief."

Hal glanced from the chair to the bedroom door. "She was fast if she got to a window in the bedroom and was back in here by the time Porter came in. She could have managed it. They were approaching a cabin with a live shooter, so they took a few minutes."

Sam's stare was thoughtful. "They found her at the sink. She said she was washing blood off her hands. Maybe she was washing away gunshot residue."

⁓

The door to Carl Ross's garage apartment was unlocked. That wasn't surprising. He'd gone to the cabin intending to return soon. The upstairs apartment was behind a mansion in a fine neighborhood, not a likely target for a stray thief.

A lamp on a side table was turned on. The living room was spacious, the walls painted a light blue, a braided gray and blue oval rug on the floor, a leather sofa, two easy chairs, a huge wall TV screen. No books. No magazines. A whisky glass sat on a coffee table in front of the sofa. I bent near, sniffed. Scotch. The ice had melted. There was nothing dropped casually on a chair. The neatness was almost regimental.

I moved around the room, stopped in a corner next to a treadmill that faced a wall of framed photographs and memorabilia. Ross in fatigues, Ross in a Marine uniform, a bronze medal with an eagle in the center hanging from a dark green ribbon with a narrow stripe of white near each edge, Sergeant Ross receiving commendation as a drill instructor, Ross standing in front of a brick wall with a Marine symbol to the right of large letters:

177

CAMP LEJUEUNE
HOME OF
EXPEDITIONARY
FORCES IN RESIDENCE

I understood why Ross didn't worry about meeting Wilbur's murderer. Wilbur had been caught from behind, unaware. Ross had no intention of turning his back on his guest at the cabin, and he likely figured he could physically handle the murderer. I slid over the possibilities in my mind, that short list from Wilbur's luncheon where he displayed the Roman coins: Ben Fitch, Alan Douglas, Harry Hubbard, George Kelly, Todd Garrett, Minerva Lloyd, Juliet Rodriguez. Certainly the butler/ former DI had no fear of either woman. Ben Fitch was lighter than Ross but he was lean, wiry, and young. Alan Douglas was tall and weedy. Harry Hubbard looked like the guy who would melt into the distance when a badass slammed through the saloon door. The lawyer appeared in good shape for a middle-aged man and was taller and heavier, but no match for Ross. Todd Garrett was an old football player, but he was thirty years past his playing days and flab had replaced muscle.

Ross was counting on his strength and combat training. He forgot only one point. If the other guy has the firepower, you're a dead man.

I was at the door, making one last survey, when a car horn blared. The sound was piercing, strident. In an instant, I was outside on the landing next to the second-floor apartment door.

The huge house loomed between me and the squall of the horn. Abruptly the horn beeped four times in succession, then once again was pressed and held.

I came over the top of the three-story house.

The front porch was dark, but night-lights flared every few feet along the rim of the third floor. An ornate iron lamppost spread a golden glow near the front steps. Sylvie Gilbert, blonde curls stirred by the wind, stood next to her Camry. The motor was running. The driver door was open, and she leaned inside to hold the car horn down. The Camry headlights threw a harsh white light across the front of the house.

As I dropped down beside her, the front porch lights were turned on and the door opened.

Sylvie's young face looked frantic. She jerked away from the horn, and in the sudden silence her shoes thudded as she shot up the stone steps.

A scowling, barefoot Ben Fitch in a sweater and jeans met her at the top of the steps. His face changed abruptly. Shock and concern replaced the scowl when he recognized her. "You're Susan's sister. What's wrong?"

A police cruiser screeched into the drive, slammed to a stop behind the Camry. Two familiar officers climbed out. Both looked wary and approached cautiously. Officer Porter's hand hovered near his holster. Officer Warren's gaze flicked in every direction. Both men obviously had an indelible memory of the man who had been shot to death not more than a quarter mile distant.

Sylvie glanced at them, but it was as if they were background figures, unimportant to her. Instead she took a step nearer Ben, gripped his arm. "Where's Susan? She said she was coming here. She got a phone call, and I wanted to come with her, but she said she had to come by herself. She left a few minutes before ten and now it's almost eleven." Sylvie's voice quivered.

"Here?" Ben repeated blankly.

Officer Warren reached them, looked from Ben to Sylvie, demanded, "Who honked the horn? What's going on?"

Sylvie whirled to him. "Why are you here?"

Warren's broad face was impassive. "Who honked the horn?"

Sylvie poked her hands on her hips. "Nobody answered the door. So I honked. I'm looking for my sister, Susan Gilbert. She got a call and she told me she was going to the Fitch place. I'm not leaving here until I find her." Sylvie wasn't far from tears.

I felt a sinking sensation. I was sure Susan said the Fitch place instead of the Fitch cabin because of the cabin's remote location. Susan wanted to forestall Sylvie demanding to accompany her. Now this discrepancy would likely be used against Susan: *Why did you lie to your sister, Ms. Gilbert?*

"You looking for her here?" Warren took a step nearer, his blue eyes intent. "Maybe I can help. Start from the first, miss. Your name."

Susan was a person of interest now en route to the jail to be held as a material witness so, of course, she had been read her Miranda rights. Sylvie, so far as the police knew, was not involved with the murder at the cabin, but she was seeking Susan not far from the site of the murder. Warren was as alert as a coon dog on a hunt.

"Sylvie Gilbert." She swung toward Ben. "Are you sure she's not here? She was coming here."

"Now, miss." Warren was as charming as only a cop scenting pay dirt can be. "Let's calm down. I'll be glad to help if you'll just tell me what happened. When did you last see your sister?"

"A little before ten. The phone rang and I answered and this man asked for Susan so I gave the phone to her. . . ."

I had a dire sense that Sylvie might be digging Susan a very deep hole. But there was nothing I could do to stop Sylvie's well-meant revelations.

∽

I was familiar with the long hall of cells in the Adelaide City Jail. The door between the police department and the jail required the correct code punched into a keypad to gain entry. Not, of course, an impediment for me. Cells lined both sides of a long hallway. Stark fluorescent ceiling lights burned day and night.

Susan was in the cell nearest the door. She was lying on the bunk attached to the back wall. A toilet and washbasin were in one corner. In the light from in the hallway, I could see that her eyes were open. I was pleased that she still wore the tan sweater and long skirt. One suede shoe sat on the floor next to the bunk. The other likely was in an evidence bag and would be tested to see if the bloodstain matched Carl Ross's blood. A thin cotton blanket covered her feet. The air in the cellblock was dry and the temperature warm.

I stood next to the bunk, whispered, "Did you contact Megan Wynn?"

She stiffened. Her gaze jerked toward me but, of course, she saw only empty space.

"It's all right. I'm here beside you."

She swung her legs over the edge of the bunk, sat up. "I told Megan you were Jimmy's redheaded friend. She said, *Tell her Blaine and I are getting married next month. Thanks to her.* I told Megan everything. She said I was to decline to answer any questions and that she'd be back to see me tomorrow. You know what she didn't tell me?"

"What?"

"She didn't tell me I was a done duck, but I watched her face. I think that's what I'd look like if somebody unshackled a bear in front of me and told me the bear was my problem. But she said when this was all over, we'd have lunch and she'd tell me things she'd never told anyone, and she bet I had some interesting experiences, too. So if I'm crazy, she's crazy, too, and she doesn't seem at all crazy. I know she'll do her best, and I appreciate your trying to help, but I don't think anything anyone does will matter now. Megan tried to sound encouraging. She said miracles happen. I thought about it after she left. You have any miracles tucked in your purse?"

"Saint Jude is in charge of miracles."

At her blank look I continued hurriedly, "Tell me what happened tonight."

She sighed. "Dumb me. I should have known better. I was feeling kind of upbeat after you left this afternoon. You seemed so certain that a luncheon guest killed Wilbur that I thought maybe the police would realize a bunch of people had motives and I was a kind of innocent bystander. Of course it didn't help matters that I filched the money box from the safe even though I thought I had to. Cops take safecracking seriously. But still I thought maybe everything would work out. Sylvie and I went to the new steak place and it was nice." A sudden smile. "The waiter was probably nineteen and he talked in a stilted voice. *I am Jacques and it is my pleasure to serve you.* I could tell Sylvie thought he was cute. The steaks cost a fortune, and I can fix a better one for half the price, but the music was cheerful, show tunes, and for a little while I didn't feel like a face on a wanted poster. We'd only been home a few minutes when my cell rang. I'd dropped it with my purse on the table by the door. Sylvie popped up and answered. She covered the receiver and whispered, *It's a guy and he's calling from the Fitch house. Maybe it's that cute Ben.* Ben Fitch came over to the house this afternoon—"

"I spoke with him."

"—and I guess I think he's cute, too, because I was kind of excited. I took the phone and—"

I interrupted again. "Try to repeat exactly what was said."

"A man's voice. Very low, quiet. He said, *Miss Gilbert?* I said, *Yes.* He said, *Carl Ross. I know something that may help you with the police, but I don't want to get involved. Come to the cabin at* *ten. I'll be watching. If anyone's with you, I won't show up.* He hung up. Of course Sylvie was looking at me and she knew from my face that the call was something odd, something disturbing. I told her I needed to talk to someone about the murder. She wanted to know who called and I told her it was Wilbur's butler, that he knew something but he didn't want to get involved with the police and I was going to go over to the Fitch place for a few minutes. She would have insisted on coming with me if I told her I was going to the cabin. She wanted to come with me anyway, but I told her I had to go by myself, he wouldn't show up unless I was alone. I told her I'd be back soon and made her promise she'd stay home. Does she know where I am? She'll be panicked."

"She went to the Fitch house. No one answered the door so she leaned on her horn until Ben Fitch came out. I expect she may know you are here by now." I didn't doubt Officer Warren alerted Sam Cobb. "I'm sure she will try to see you tomorrow." Not tomorrow now, actually today.

Susan sat up straighter. "I don't want her to come to the jail. Please, tell her not to worry, that everything will be all right, that I want her to stay home."

"She's tougher than you think."

"She's eighteen years old. She shouldn't have to see me here. Please, will you talk to her?"

"I will." I remembered Sylvie's fierce attack on the front steps of the Fitch house. I had confidence in Sylvie. She might always see the world in a different way, but she was nobody's pushover.

"I can't bear seeing Sylvie here."

I heard tears in her voice.

"In that event, let's get busy and get you out of here. Did you recognize Carl Ross's voice?"

"The caller said he was Carl Ross. I thought he was speaking quietly because he didn't want to be overheard. Could the caller have been Carl? Yes. Was it Carl? I don't know. I rarely spoke with him. Carl had a very soft voice. That always seemed odd for such a tough-looking man. He made me think of a cotton-mouth slipping through water, dangerous if you got in his way. Maybe I thought that because I knew he was a Marine. Tonight the voice was—" She pressed fingertips against each temple, then her hands fell and she sighed. "I don't know. Low. Soft. Almost a whisper."

"Could the caller have been a woman?"

"It was definitely a man. But it may not have been Carl."

"I don't think the caller was Carl." I was frank. "Carl was already dead and the killer called you, wanted you to come."

"Is that why there was a gunshot after I went into the cabin?"

"Exactly." My eyes were grainy with fatigue. There was something about the cabin. . . . Oh yes. "When was the last time you visited the cabin?"

"Never. I worked up at the house. I don't even know if the cabin was used much. Anyway, I never had occasion to be down there."

It was as energizing as a jolt of Mountain Dew. "Describe what you did when you got out of your car at the cabin. Everything."

"The cabin lights were on. That was reassuring, meant he was already there. I parked in front. When I got out of the car, I remember thinking it was awfully quiet. An owl whooed. I'm scared of owls. They're so big and they swoop so fast. I hoped the owl wasn't coming my way. Anyway, it was very quiet. It sounded loud when I went up the steps. The door was ajar. I called out, *Carl?* No answer. I went up to the door—"

"Did you touch the knob?"

She frowned. "I knocked and the door swung in. There isn't a screen door, just this big wooden door. I looked inside and didn't see anyone. I called out again. It was very quiet. I almost didn't go inside, but I thought he was in the woods watching me to make sure I was alone, so I decided to go in and wait for him. When I stepped inside, I saw him. I ran across the room and reached down." She shuddered. "That's when I got blood on my hand. I heard a shot outside and that was terrifying. I knew I needed to get help. I went over to the sink and I was washing my hands so I could call and then somebody yelled, *Police*, and the door banged open and he shouted at me to get my hands up."

"Did you touch anything?"

"The cold-water handle at the sink. Nothing else. I never had a chance. That gun was pointed at me and I had to raise my arms and then the other policeman put those handcuffs on me." She sagged back against the plastered wall.

"You heard the shot. Where did it sound like it came from?"

"Outside." Her answer was quick and definite. "Someplace outside. Maybe closer to the lake. I was afraid someone was going to shoot me. I kept thinking I had to get the blood off my hands and call for help, but the door banged back against the wall. I whirled around and a policeman was aiming a gun at me and shouting. And now no one will listen to me. What am I going to do?" She was scared, could foresee arrest, a trial, prison. Perhaps worse.

I would have been scared, too. I made my voice warm and relaxed. "Everything will be fine."

I hoped Saint Jude was listening. I was beginning to feel like it would definitely take a miracle to free Susan.

Chapter 10

I would not want to be seen as a complainer. I simply state that arduous activity, both physical and mental, is as wearing on an earthly visitor as for anyone else. In other words, a ghost—excuse me, Wiggins prefers *emissary*—knows when it is three o'clock in the morning and the next day is a final chance to accomplish a mission that looks doomed to failure. I needed energy, but I had one more task before I could snatch a bit of rest.

Sam's office, of course, was dim and quiet. The password was unchanged. I skimmed the reports labeled *re: Fitch/Ross homicides*, made several notes. As I read, I felt as cheerless as an OU booster leaving the stone-quiet stadium after the Irish trounced the Sooners 7–0 on November 16, 1957, ending OU's forty-seven-game winning streak. In essence, the reports could be summed up: Gilbert, Gilbert, Gilbert. I was pleased by one sentence in

Sam's cogent conclusions: *If Ross dead at nine forty-five, Gilbert innocent and shot heard by Porter/Warren an anomaly.* Unfortunately, the very next sentence was a sobering qualification: *ETD (estimated time of death) is notoriously unreliable, so it's possible Gilbert shot Ross immediately upon arrival at the cabin.*

I went to the blackboard, printed the initial sentence. I underlined *innocent* three times, then squeezed my tired face in thought, forced myself to concentrate. I needed Sam's help. As Mama always told us kids, "If you want someone to join your parade, play the trombone like you're Tommy Dorsey."

SUSAN GILBERT NOT GUILTY

Check for Susan Gilbert's prints in the cabin.

Confirm Susan Gilbert not a gun owner, has never shot a gun.

Gunshot at seven past ten occurred outside cabin, near lake. Ask Officers Porter and Warren to describe shot. If the gun went off inside cabin, the sound should have been muffled, less distinct.

Person who called Susan Gilbert to arrange meeting at the cabin was male.

Wilbur Fitch's murderer attended luncheon where Wilbur called Susan and asked her to open the safe and bring the Roman coins and Juliet Rodriguez talked about Susan's ditzy sister, Sylvie. Five men attended the luncheon in addition to the host. Those men are Ben Fitch, George Kelly, Alan Douglas, Harry Hubbard, and Todd Garrett. One of them killed Wilbur

Fitch and Carl Ross. It is important to determine their where-abouts last night between nine and ten thirty p.m. Do not ap-proach them directly. Ascertain their activities from other sources.

⌒

I was at Lulu's at six a.m. Thursday when the lights flashed on and the door was unlocked. As I stepped inside, I glanced at the mirror behind the counter. I take special care in choosing my ensemble for a challenging day. I admired my choices, a pale blue blouse with dark blue cotton dots, white wool slacks, and blue moccasin flats with silver metallic beads. But when I slid onto a red leather stool, my gaze went straight from the image to the round clock. One minute past six. At noon, if the schedule still held, there would be a press conference at the mayor's office starring Neva Lumpkin. The mayor would likely be eager to announce that Susan Gilbert was being held as a material wit-ness, that she had been found at the scene of yet another murder. This would be a stellar press day for Neva Lumpkin. Would she be content to settle for Susan as a material witness or would she press for an arrest today?

The stool beside me creaked. Sam Cobb looked weary in the mirror, face somber, brown suit wrinkled, likely the same one he'd worn yesterday. "Claire stayed up 'til I got home. I told her to sleep in, I'd pick up a bite at Lulu's. Thought you'd be here." He looked up at the waitress. "The lady and I are together." He ordered for both of us and included all my favorites: sausage, grits, fried eggs, waffles, and Texas toast.

The waitress gave him a bright smile. "Coming right up, hon."

Sam waited until she moved away before he gave me a level stare. "I went by the office first. The DA will ask me if I believe in unicorns if I try to convince him Gilbert's not the perp because of some leeway on the ETD."

As Mama always said, "When you disagree with a man, say it like you think he's wonderful."

I gave him an admiring look. "Of course we all know"—I put us in the same lifeboat—"ETDs can be questionable. Lots of variability. But when the ME arrives on the scene so soon after death, isn't the estimate more likely to be accurate?"

"Hmmm."

Our orders arrived. Sam put honey on his toast, I plopped butter in the grits. We spoke between bites.

"Cell phones register when calls occur, so the fact that Susan received the call a little before ten won't be in dispute. Moreover, her sister can testify the call was received in their living room." I indulged myself and pooled a little honey on my plate. Sausage and honey are scrumptious.

Sam ate stolidly. "Hmmm."

"Of course"—I beamed at him—"Jacob Brandt was cautious, he always is, but he clearly thought Carl Ross had been dead for at least an hour, probably longer. In fact," and now, as per Mama, I spoke with pleasant certainty, "it's likely Ross was shot at nine thirty. That gave the killer time to use the phone in the cabin and call Susan's cell." I looked at him inquiringly. "Did the tech find fingerprints on the telephone?"

Sam was halfway through his waffle. I decided it would not be tactful to inquire if waffles were included in his diet. He looked like he was enjoying his breakfast, if not the conversation. "Indeterminate."

"What does that mean?"

"No clear prints."

I felt a surge of satisfaction. "As if perhaps the last person to hold the cradle did so with a gloved hand."

"Could be put that way."

"And where were Susan's prints found?"

"At the sink. On the cold-water handle."

"Anywhere else?"

"No."

"Back to the telephone with smudged prints. A call from the cabin would show Wilbur Fitch on caller ID. Sylvie told Susan the call was from the Fitch house. Susan said the caller spoke very softly. If the killer made that call, Ross was already dead, so Brandt likely was right that he died around nine thirty."

"Yeah." Sam wasn't too concerned. "A defense attorney can spin the time, get Brandt on the stand, but Brandt will be the first to hem and haw, say ETDs are variable, yes he could have been shot a few minutes after ten, and then the DA points out with great drama that two officers arriving on the scene heard a shot at seven past ten and found Carl Ross dead upon entering the cabin and the defendant there with Ross's blood on her shoe."

"Just for a moment let's say I'm right and that shot was intended to convict Susan."

Sam's broad face was suddenly pleased. "Bingo. The logical fallacy. Why do we know there was a shot at seven past ten?"

"It was heard by Susan and by your officers."

"If Porter and Warren weren't following Gilbert, they would not have heard the shot, and it's their testimony that will convict her. How did this mythical murderer know there would be anyone to hear a shot purportedly fired to incriminate Gilbert?"

I relaxed. For a moment I'd feared we were engaged in the if-a-tree-falls-in-the-woods-and-no-one-is-present-is-there-a-sound debate, and I've never done well with that. As far as I'm concerned of course there is a sound. It's only that no one heard it. "You need to read yesterday afternoon's *Gazette*. Joan Crandall covered the mayor's press conference and informed *Gazette* readers that surveillance was in place, and the story makes it clear that surveillance was linked to Susan."

Sam's good humor evaporated. "Neva strikes again."

"Now, as I was saying, let's assume Susan did not shoot a gun at seven past ten."

He balanced some scrambled eggs on a bite of waffle.

I spoke a little louder. "If the killer was out in the woods and shot the gun after Susan arrived, that means the call to Susan was not made by Carl Ross. Wilbur's murderer called her after killing Ross. Susan was called by a man, just as it was a man who made the fake ransom call. There are five men who had the knowledge to set up the web that entangled Susan. Do you agree?"

"If I accept your premise."

I reached across the table, put my hand atop his broad strong hand. "You'll find out where the five men were last night when Ross was shot."

Sam was resistant. "Ah, the famous five. You put them on a list because they are men and the caller was male. The odds are like ninety-nine percent that the male caller was Carl Ross and he said she'd better hike over to see him or he'd go to the police because he saw something that would send her to prison. Maybe he saw her sneaking out of the study with a blackjack in her hand. Maybe he followed her and knows where the weapon is." His voice had a touch of bluster.

I shook my head. "The caller didn't threaten her. The content was clever. The caller acted reluctant to be involved, and you know a lot of people don't want to get involved with the police. The caller enticed her by saying he knew something that could help clear her."

Sam raised a grizzled eyebrow. "So that's what Gilbert claims. Of course that's what she'd say." He balled his napkin in a wad, finally, grudgingly, said, "There's a couple of points in her favor. The test for gunshot residue showed her right hand clean. Of course she'd just washed it. She claims because of blood."

"Would Susan even know about gunshot residue?"

He shrugged. "Maybe she just thought her hand felt greasy. Whatever. No residue. Another maybe positive point is a next-door neighbor thought she saw a flashlight in the Gilbert back-yard around one fifteen a.m., but by the time she got out on her back porch, everything was quiet so she decided she'd made a mistake. Of course, Gilbert would have used a flashlight, too.

But there's a boost for your five-men theory. Minerva Lloyd showed up at the station yesterday, asked to see Detective Sergeant G. Latham. They called me from downstairs. I told them to send her up. One good-looking broad. I told her Detective Sergeant Latham wasn't available but I would be glad to help her. The upshot was she'd seen the story in the *Gazette* and thought we ought to know that Wilbur told her, it was the Saturday night before the anniversary dance, that he was going to make some big changes at Fitch Enterprises, starting the day after the party. She said, *Wilbur had on his buccaneer face, said he wanted the best for the company. He looked at me and said he always surrounded himself with the best, like me.* Then she started to cry."

"Big changes." I was emphatic. "Like firing someone. He wouldn't be talking about his secretary."

A heavy sigh. Sam speared the last scrap of waffle, ate. "I'll check out where the five were last night."

"Don't alert them. Talk to neighbors, secretaries, people around them."

He frowned. "That requires a lot more man power. Why the heavy emphasis on no direct approach?"

I avoided his gaze, poured both of us fresh coffee, lifted my cup.

He lifted his cup, took a deep swallow. "Maybe I don't want to know?"

I gave him another approving smile. It would be awkward, possibly result in irate calls to the station, even to the mayor, if upright citizens were besieged by multiple police detectives and Detective Sergeant G. Latham had her own agenda.

His large mouth spread in a lopsided grin. "What I don't know can't hurt me, right?"

⬄

The porch light flashed on and the peephole opened. Sylvie flung open the front door. She was dressed in a fuzzy orange angora sweater, shamrock green tights, and feathery blue mukluks. Even so, she was appealing and quite pretty. She burst out, "Where have you been? They put Susan in jail—"

"I've spoken to Susan. She's fine." As fine as a terrified woman confined behind bars could be, but Susan desperately wanted Sylvie reassured.

Sylvie led the way across the living room, stood by the sofa. Her intense, defiant face broke. For an instant, there was heartbreak and a small child's terror at abandonment. "She—" Her voice quivered. Sylvie gulped for air, then her chin jutted. "They can't do this to Susan. Ben Fitch agrees with me. He's really nice and he thinks Susan's not being treated right." Sylvie dropped onto the sofa, patted the seat next to her.

I gave her a positive smile. "Megan Wynn, a very good lawyer, is representing Susan. The firm of Smith and Wynn." I spoke as if the young firm was Adelaide's finest, which I was sure someday it would be. "Moreover, I have narrowed the list of suspects."

Sylvie's eyes bored into mine. "Narrowed the list? How?"

"A man called Susan last night. I'm sure the caller was the murderer."

"Why?"

She had a future as a reporter or lawyer. It would do no harm to offer information that would reassure her. "The medical examiner firmly believes Carl was dead by nine forty-five at the latest. Susan didn't get there until right after ten."

"Then why are they holding Susan in jail?"

"Because the police following her heard a shot and found Susan standing by the body."

"If there was a shot," Sylvie thought out loud, "it must have been the murderer trying to get Susan in trouble. The murderer . . . He has to be one of the men at the luncheon, right?"

I looked at her with respect. She'd listened and listened well when Susan and I discussed how the original crime was planned and that the planner had to know that Susan could open Wilbur's safe.

"Exactly. I am continuing my investigation." Susan's arrest for homicide would be announced tomorrow at noon. As I glanced at the grandfather clock, the minute hand moved. That black hand would move and move and move. I had so little time. I knew the murderer was one of five men, but which one was guilty?

Sylvie clenched her fists. "I called the jail. The soonest I can see her is at one this afternoon. Ben will come with me."

I said quietly, "Susan doesn't want you to see her at the jail."

Sylvie's eyes were bright. "She loves me. She's always tried to keep me from knowing about bad things. But I have to see her. I'll tell her I know you're working hard for her."

I didn't try to discourage her. Seeing Sylvie would be a boost for Susan, and I rather thought Ben would be a welcome addition. "I don't know about the jail rules, but it would be nice if you took her some clean clothes and a pair of shoes." I remembered the single suede loafer on the cement floor below the bunk.

"Shoes?"

"When she tried to help Mr. Ross, one of her shoes became stained."

There was a flash of horror in Sylvie's blue eyes. Violent death became terribly real when she pictured blood on her sister's shoe. "That's awful. I'll take her everything fresh." A pause and now her eyes glinted with anger. "I'm surprised there wasn't a picture of that shoe in the newspaper. There was sure plenty of bad stuff about Susan in the paper yesterday. I talked to the reporter at the *Gazette*."

I must have looked surprised.

Sylvie nodded eagerly. "I called the *Gazette* and talked to that woman who wrote the story that made it sound like Susan was involved. She was kind of gruff but nice. She said all she does is report the facts and those were the facts released at the mayor's news conference and if the facts changed, she'd change her story and there was a news conference at noon today. And all I can say is, if they're going to say things about Susan, they're going to hear from me."

༄

Five men. I'd spoken to George Kelly, who would surely soak up big fees as he closed the estate, and Wilbur's son, Ben, who shouted at his dad but now looked quite ready to take over a multimillion-dollar business. That was a profiteering pair. Were the others a three of a kind? I'd find out. Detective Sergeant G. Latham had some questions for Alan Douglas, the vice president with big ideas; Todd Garrett, the ostensible COO who wasn't a savvy businessman; and Harry Hubbard, the charming stepson with expensive tastes.

Fitch Enterprises occupied several acres of land on Highway 3 near the city limits. Perhaps two hundred cars were parked in asphalt lots adjoining a one-story brick main office building and two warehouse-sized galvanized steel buildings. I checked out the nearest large structure. I'd never had any experience with a factory or assembly line. There was a subdued atmosphere that I attributed to the deaths of Wilbur Fitch and Carl Ross. I suspected on an ordinary day not marred by loss there would be cheerful conversations. The huge ground floor was open to sunlight through skylights in the ceiling. Today there was no brightness because of thick cloud cover. Stairs led up to a row of offices and a walkway that overlooked the floor. Bars of fluorescent light offered excellent illumination. The temperature was comfortable. Employees, either standing or seated, worked at long wooden tables. Some dismantled electronic devices, some sorted components, some worked with intricate wiring, some used magnifying glasses to pluck out computer chips. Workers wore everything from dressy casual attire to cowboy shirts with string ties, well-worn jeans, and cowboy boots.

I took a last look from the second-floor walkway, impressed by Wilbur Fitch's achievements. I hoped his son would do as well and that jobs, good jobs, would continue to be created. As

Mama told us kids, "Work is the stuffing in the Raggedy Ann." It didn't take long for me to understand what she meant. Doing a good job and having a good job to do gives you pride, and we all need to be proud. Wilbur Fitch gave his workers a lot more than a paycheck. Wilbur gave his workers pride.

Now it was time to find out whether a man he knew well— his son, his stepson, his lawyer, or a top employee—knocked on his bedroom door after the party.

Still invisible, I arrived in Harry Hubbard's office in the public relations department in the main office building. Why was I not surprised to find the overhead light off, the room unoccupied? I doubted Harry was punctilious in observing office hours. The decor was cheerful if bland, cream-colored walls, green curtains at the windows, a nicely polished parquet floor. The desk was unpretentious metal. There were several folders in an in-box, nothing in the out-box.

I settled behind the desk in a very comfortable leather chair and turned to the computer. I used the mouse, tapped. Company policy might dictate closing down a computer every evening, but perhaps Harry thought that was another rule that didn't apply to him. I checked the most recent Google searches. Long-term rentals in Aruba and Tahiti.

The office door opened. Harry was as attractive as always, his sleek blond hair artfully brushed, model-perfect features relaxed. A yellow cashmere pullover, blue shirt, gray wool trousers, expensive Italian loafers with a flash of yellow socks.

I was out of his chair by the time he strolled across the room. In the hall I made sure no one was near and appeared. I gave a quick knock, opened the door, and stepped inside with a confident smile. I held my leather ID case in my right hand. "Detective Sergeant G. Latham. I understand from Wilbur Fitch's son, Ben"—I was walking across the room as I spoke—"that his father had great confidence in you, and I'm hoping you can give me some insights about Mr. Fitch's business activities."

My intention was to reassure a possible murderer that he was not under suspicion by the police. That was the main reason I wanted Sam to discover the location of each man last night. A relaxed adversary doesn't expect an attack. If—I had that sudden empty feeling that precedes a step into space—I ever learned enough to mount an attack. I pushed away the negative thought and a shocking feeling of helplessness. Probably that's what it would be like to skydive. As an emissary, I enjoy swooping without fear through space, but on earth I'd had a careful regard for heights. I could see very well, thank you, standing back a good ten feet from the rim of the Grand Canyon. But the sensation of hollowness reminded me how little time I had to find a murderer.

I saw an admiring glint in Harry's eyes as he gestured for me to take the chair in front of his desk. I reminded myself that I wasn't here to bask in his admiration for redheads and I would be on guard against his undeniable charm.

"I'll be glad to help." His expressive face was suddenly grave. "I saw on TV that somebody shot Carl Ross. What the hell's going on?"

"That's what we're trying to determine. To be frank"—a phrase that almost always precedes a carefully worded hook for an opponent—"we have received information from a confidential informant that suggests Mr. Fitch and Mr. Ross were murdered by a Fitch Enterprises employee. To be specific, and I assure you anything you say will be held in total confidence as part of an investigation, we are interested in two employees." I leaned forward, dropped my voice. "Alan Douglas and Todd Garrett."

Harry's handsome face crinkled in thought. Abruptly he shook his head. "You got a bum steer. Alan's this kind of nerdy nice guy who lives, eats, and breathes Fitch business plans. I don't think he ever does anything but figure how to maximize profits or start something new that nobody else has thought about. And he's"—an awkward pause—"he's not a rugged guy. I mean, I don't think he ever played a sport. He's, well, he's kind of girly. And Todd is a good old boy. He might shoot you if you ran over his dog or messed with his girlfriend, but he wouldn't sneak up behind Wilbur and whack him on the back of his head."

⁊

Not surprisingly, Alan Douglas's office was up the stairs in the galvanized steel structure. When I knocked and opened the door, he looked blank for an instant, his mind clearly involved in the papers before him, then he saw me and rose.

I didn't think Harry's estimation of Alan as girly was quite fair. He had excellent manners and hurried to pull out a chair for me in front of his desk. He was tall and thin and unpretentious in a blue work shirt and khakis and tan boots. His shortcut brown hair was neatly combed. He had a diffident way of speaking. "I want to help. It's awful what's happened. Wilbur and Carl. I can't believe someone could kill Carl." There was recognition in his eyes of a macho man, recognition and a flash of dislike.

I used the same approach, but this time I named Harry Hubbard and Todd Garrett.

Alan sat very precisely behind his desk, hands folded on the wooden top. Suddenly his lips spread in a swift smile. "Harry bashing Wilbur and shooting Carl would be like a lazy house cat suddenly turning ferocious. Harry's too much into being comfortable and safe and indulged. He never stirs if it's raining. He's fastidious about his clothes. Sure he likes money. But Wilbur gave him a job and all Harry had to do was play golf a couple of times a week. Harry"—his pale blue eyes narrowed—"doesn't take chances. And I think he was scared of Carl. Of course, he'll be even more comfortable with what he inherits from Wilbur, but he's not a risk-taker."

I looked at him curiously. "Are you a risk-taker?"

He was abruptly thoughtful. "I guess I'll find out soon. There was a business deal—"

I knew he referred to SIMPLE Cars.

"—I hoped Wilbur might finance, but he decided against it. He told me I was free to take my idea and build my own company. I may just try it unless Ben is interested."

"Did Wilbur sign a waiver that the company agreed to forego its proprietary interest in your plan since you developed it as a Fitch Enterprises employee?"

For an instant his sensitive face was utterly blank. He stared at me. "Wilbur told me it was all right. Ben will honor his father's promise."

But there was nothing in writing.

He gave a negligent wave with one hand. "But that's not why you came to see me. You said two employees are under suspicion because of a confidential informant."

"Yes."

"I understood Susan Gilbert was, how do you put it, a 'person of interest.'"

"Investigations often take a different turn."

"That's good news for Susan and I think very sensible. She's not that kind of person. I don't know who's feeding you information, but I don't think much of the claims. Todd and Wilbur yelled at each other a lot. It didn't mean a thing. Todd thought Wilbur was a great man."

"Does Todd know how to shoot a gun?"

Alan laughed out loud. "Proves you've never met Todd. He's a good old boy. By definition in Adelaide, a good old boy played football, drinks Bud, wears boots, goes hunting. But"—he leaned forward—"a good old boy will give you the shirt off his back and carry a woman across a puddle and eat ribs with his fingers and not worry about the sauce. Todd never hurt Wilbur." Alan's blue eyes were cold and intent. "If you people are looking for somebody who had it in for Wilbur, check out his lawyer. I was in Wilbur's office last week and I heard him tell George Kelly he was out the door."

⁓

Todd Garrett's office in the brick one-story building was similar to Harry's though larger, the same cream walls and parquet flooring, but there was a Persian throw rug in front of a more imposing desk. Folders were stacked on the desk, on the floor next to the desk, and tucked in a bookcase. A leather sofa faced the desk. Two easy chairs sat opposite each other on either side of the sofa.

Todd stood at a window with the venetian blinds raised. He looked out at a field with dun-colored grass cut short. A massive bull appeared to be the only occupant of the pasture. The bull had his back to the building. His tail twitched, but otherwise he stood motionless.

Todd's posture was forlorn, slumped shoulders, hands jammed in his trouser pockets. Scraggly brown hair curled a bit on the back of his neck. He would have benefitted from a trim.

I left the office, ready to appear as Detective Sergeant Latham. In the hallway, a coffee cart was stopped two doors up. The attendant, curly dark hair, a cheerful round face, knocked, called out, "Coffee. Tea. Donuts. Pastries." As she poked her head inside the office, I appeared, twisted the knob of Todd's door, and stepped inside.

He turned as I walked toward him, hand outstretched with my leather ID folder. "Detective Sergeant G. Latham."

Todd was somber, his stare morose. "Hell of a deal. Wilbur. Now Carl." He waved toward one of the easy chairs.

I found the chair very comfortable but noted a worn spot on one arm.

He sat down on the leather sofa. He looked older than forty-eight, as if he carried each year on his back. His voice was dull, weary. "I go back a long way with Wilbur. When I came in this morning, the whole place felt like it was empty. He filled everything up. But I think you people have it wrong." He leaned forward. "The story in the *Gazette* made it sound like Susan Gilbert's under suspicion. I don't believe that for a minute."

"Ms. Gilbert is being very helpful to the authorities." I was glad the *Gazette* was an afternoon newspaper. Wait until he saw Joan Crandall's lead story today when Susan was reported to be in custody as a material witness. "I will definitely notify my superiors of your support of her. You have a unique perspective as COO of the company. In fact, I am here because we received confidential information about two Fitch employees that requires investigation. We understand Mr. Fitch recently had harsh words with"—I drew a small notebook from my purse and turned a page as if checking my information—"a Mr. Harry Hubbard and a Mr. Alan Douglas."

Todd's somber look was replaced with a flash of genuine amusement. "Somebody told you Wilbur yelled at them, right?"

"That's right."

His pudgy face re-formed in a smile that held a trace of sadness and nostalgia. "You got to understand"—he was earnest—"Wilbur yelled at everybody. Wilbur could hardly talk without yelling. He reamed out Harry about a bill he ran up at a ritzy hotel in Dallas, told him he was like a leech and if somebody stepped on a leech it squished blood but Harry would squish money, Wilbur's money. Wilbur liked to hassle Harry. Harry always gave him a day or two to cool off then he'd call and say, *Pops, how about I eat at your place tonight. I'm hungry for sautéed leeches*, and Wilbur would boom out a laugh and everything would be okay."

I studied the man sitting on the sofa. His blue eyes didn't look very intelligent, but they looked open and honest. Those guileless eyes were suddenly narrowed and spiteful. "I didn't hear Wilbur yell at Alan Douglas. Maybe if he'd yelled, Alan wouldn't have looked like a whipped dog on Tuesday. See"—he hunched forward—"Alan had this stupid idea about making a car that nobody but a geezer would buy. Tuesday I was in the hall at the house and I started to open the door to the study—"

I looked at him blandly, pictured a jealous, insecure man turning the knob, hearing the voices, listening, then slipping away after the conversation ended.

"—and I heard Alan and Wilbur. Alan was saying something like maybe Wilbur could give it some more thought. Wilbur was nice enough but he told Alan no deal, nothing more to talk about. I'd told Wilbur last week it was a dumb idea. I told everybody it was stupid and it came up at the Kiwanis luncheon and I knocked the idea flat and that made Wilbur mad because he hadn't made up his mind. He yelled at me. But Wilbur always thought things over. I hadn't seen him since he'd unloaded about Kiwanis. I stood there and realized he'd followed my advice." There was definite satisfaction in Todd's voice. "But he always liked to think everything was his own idea, so I left and didn't try to talk to him. And that night at the party, Wilbur was having a great time. I'm glad I had a chance to tell him what a great party it was. He gave me a thumbs-up."

Wilbur berated Todd for disloyalty, but now Todd insisted Wilbur's displeasure was always fleeting. Perhaps this time Wilbur's anger wasn't appeased.

I closed my notebook. "Will you be staying with Fitch Enterprises, Mr. Garrett?"

He blinked those uncertain blue eyes. "I'll stay long enough to help Ben sort everything out. I keep good records." He was proud. "Wilbur always figured out what to do, but I kept everything in order. I'm not"—he was suddenly humble—"the brightest guy about business. But I'm careful. Wilbur appreciated me. I'll do what I can to help Ben but then—" There was a flash of eagerness, of youthfulness. I had a sense of what he looked like when he was young and the crowd roared as he fell back and cocked his arm to send a football spiraling though the air on a crisp fall day. "—I've got a little cabin down on Lake Texoma and a boat. See, Wilbur left me a lot of money—"

I recalled George Kelly's dry recitation: *Todd Garrett, five hundred thousand.*

"—and it's enough for me to live there. I've met a few people in Madill. There's a gal at the catfish cafe. She's real nice. I can live in my cabin and fish and do a little hunting."

And no one would yell at him again.

Chapter 11

George Kelly looked like a man quite pleased with himself and his world. A cigar smoldered in an oversize bronze ashtray. He hummed a toneless little tune as his fingers raced over a calculator. He looked at the sum, nodded, picked up the receiver, punched numbers. "Calling Les Timmons. . . . Hey, Les, that car I talked to you about, the Lexus sports car. I want it in red. . . . Houston? Yeah. Tell you what, I'll fly down there next week, pick it up. Since it's going to be my work car"—a small laugh—"I can deduct the trip expense if I drive it up here. Right. Sure thing."

Life apparently was good for Mr. Kelly at the moment.

The hallway was unoccupied. I appeared and stepped into the outer office.

The secretary greeted me as an old friend. "Do you want

to see Mr. Kelly? He's here." She reached out to touch the intercom.

I said quickly, "Don't announce me. I'll pop in."

At her look of concern, I said, "Since no one was here, perhaps you were gone to the ladies' room, I showed myself in." She was up and stepping into the hall before I reached Kelly's office door.

Kelly turned at the sound of the opening door. His pleased expression was replaced with a frown. "I'm expecting a conference call—"

"The secretary must be on break. I only have a few minutes so I didn't wait. I know you are eager to be helpful in the investigations. Some questions have arisen about two Fitch employees."

He didn't want to deal with me, but he was the attorney for the executor of the estate, and whatever affected Fitch Enterprises was within his purview. He listened to what was by now my almost rote recitation. When I concluded, he made a dismissive gesture. "I suppose the police have to pay attention to anonymous tips, but this is nonsense. Todd Garrett and Alan Douglas were loyal to Wilbur. They knew a shout today would be a backslap tomorrow. Why"—and now he leaned back in his desk chair, was relaxed, expansive—"Wilbur fired me more times than I can count. We had a dustup last week. Of course nothing came of it. Wilbur being Wilbur. So, you can"—he smiled—"chalk this up to somebody with a gripe."

I was still standing. I asked politely, "Who do you think committed the murders?"

He put his fingertips together, looked judicious, used the sonorous voice suitable for a jury. "I am confident the investigation will solve the crimes." A head shake. "Shame about Carl Ross. If he had any information he should have taken it directly to the police. But perhaps he was uncertain, willing to give someone a chance to explain."

I looked inquiring.

Kelly turned his hands over, palms up. "Wilbur always insisted that women be treated with utmost respect. Perhaps that influenced Carl."

"The only woman who has been mentioned publicly in regard to the investigation is Mr. Fitch's secretary. Are you referring to her?"

He was bland. "I make no claims. I simply know what I read in the *Gazette*. It sounds as though an arrest is imminent. Is it?"

It was my turn to make a disclaimer. "The investigation continues."

Kelly stood, looked at his watch. "If that's all, I have an important call to make."

"I appreciate your cooperation." At the door I turned and looked back as if struck by a thought. "One more thing. Did Mr. Fitch ever apologize about his remark?"

"Remark?"

"When he told you he thought he had a bull in the courtroom but you turned out to be a steer."

Kelly's face for an instant was hard with antagonism. For me? Or at the memory of Fitch's steer slur? Then he gave a wry laugh. "Wilbur at his worst. He could be a sore loser. I told him the suit was a long shot but he insisted we try it. He had to blame somebody when we lost."

～

Neva Lumpkin's azure blue pants suit would be attractive on a willowy model. Suffice to say the too-tight jacket and slacks emphasized an operatic bosom and matching hips.

Almost every chair was taken in the third-floor meeting room. I had an equally good view of both the podium and the audience from my vantage point along one wall.

Sam Cobb stood to one side of the lectern, a foot or so behind the mayor. His broad face beneath grizzled dark hair was impassive. A blue suit today but as wrinkled as usual. He held a yellow legal pad.

The regulars were in the front row, Joan Crandall of the *Gazette*, lean as a greyhound and poised to run; Ted Burton, the AP bureau chief with a plump man's cheerful countenance but slate blue eyes that didn't like anybody very much; counterculture representative Deke Carson flaunting a necklace with dangling brass knuckles, a sweatshirt with an obscene expletive, and tattered Bermuda shorts. I suspected his knees were cold when he stepped outside, but a man will do what he must to be different from the norm. I counted six blonde TV reporters and their nearby cameramen.

My gaze stopped on the third row. Sylvie Gilbert's orange sweater and vivid green pants seemed even brighter in contrast to Ben Fitch's subdued gray cashmere pullover and navy slacks.

Sylvie would always attract attention. Several of the TV cameramen glanced her way as men do when women, young or old, have a special magic. Even in a room filled with attractive blondes she was noticeable, her curls shining, fresh, obviously untouched by chemicals. Her blue eyes appraised Neva and Sam, and there was cool judgment in her gaze: *Lady, you're fake, mister, I don't like you but you look strong.* Ben Fitch seemed an unlikely companion with the air of a man more at home at the country club grill.

I glanced at the lectern. The mayor was checking off the attendees. Her gaze stopped for an instant at Sylvie and Ben, moved on. She would have no reason to know Susan Gilbert's sister, and Ben had not been in town long enough to be recognized as the owner of Fitch Enterprises. She likely assumed they were reporters from around the state. But Sam knew who they were, and his stare was speculative.

Neva cleared her throat, stepped forward. In the small venue she had no need for a microphone. "I am Neva Lumpkin, mayor of Adelaide. I am joined today by Sam Cobb, our chief of police. Chief Cobb is directing the investigation into the murder Tuesday night of revered Adelaide business leader Wilbur Fitch and the murder last night of Carl Ross, Mr. Fitch's butler." She picked up several sheets of paper, read aloud, "The body of Wilbur Fitch was discovered Wednesday morning by his butler, Mr. Ross. Mr. Fitch died of massive head trauma in the study of his home. No weapon was found at the scene. No weapon has been recovered. The medical examiner estimates that death occurred after midnight Tuesday and before three a.m. Wednesday. The motive for his murder isn't known, but a safe normally hidden behind a painting was found open and the painting swung back against the wall. The door to the garden was open. Coins taken from the safe were found in the yard of Mr. Fitch's secretary, Susan Gilbert. Ms. Gilbert disclaims any knowledge of the coins and insists they were placed there by another party."

"What's with the dead butler?" Deke Carson sounded supremely bored. He lounged back on the straight chair, feet poked out straight in front of him.

Neva ignored him, turned a page. "Ms. Gilbert, though not named as a 'person of interest,' was under police surveillance yesterday." The tone of her voice indicated she certainly saw Susan as a "person of interest."

There was a sudden intensity in the reporters' posture. Pens scratched. Fingers flew over keyboards. Microphones were held up to capture her voice. "At shortly before ten p.m. last night Ms. Gilbert received a phone call and departed her house. Two officers followed her. She arrived at a cabin on the Fitch property at a few minutes after ten. She entered the cabin. Officers approaching the cabin heard a gunshot at seven past ten. Officers Warren and Porter proceeded to the cabin and found Ms. Gilbert in the act of washing blood from her hands—"

Chair legs scraped. Sylvie jumped to her feet. She was a picture of youthful fury, blonde curls quivering, heart-shaped face flushed. "I'm Sylvia Gilbert. I've got something to say. Those people"—she pointed at Neva and Sam—"aren't telling you everything. Susan went inside the cabin just after ten p.m., pay attention to that time, that's when Susan got there. I was with her all evening until she left the house because she got a phone call from a man who said he was Carl Ross but now we know it was the man who killed Mr. Fitch and decided to kill Carl Ross probably because Carl asked for money to keep quiet about what happened Tuesday night when Mr. Fitch was killed—"

The reporters were all standing and turned toward her. The cameramen were jockeying for good shots. The blonde TV reporters were worming nearer, thrusting their microphones at Sylvie.

"—and so the man who murdered Mr. Fitch killed Carl Ross and then he called Susan and said he was Carl Ross and talked really nice to her and persuaded her to come to the cabin, but what you need to know—"

Neva Lumpkin slammed her hand on the lectern. "Hush. Get that person out of here. It's against the law to interrupt an official public proceeding—"

Sylvie simply raised her voice. "—is that the medical examiner states Carl Ross was dead probably by nine thirty and not later than nine forty-five, and at nine thirty Susan and I were getting into her car at that new restaurant out by the lake. So a shot heard by the police after ten o'clock was the killer trying to make it look like Susan killed Mr. Ross. Write it down. Carl Ross was dead at the latest by nine forty-five. A shot at seven past ten was fake because—"

Ben Fitch was a little apart from Sylvie now, reporters squeezing between him and Sylvie. He already had an air of command about him, the confident expression of a man who mattered. He looked like the young scion of a wealthy family, dark hair nicely brushed, handsome features, expensive sweater and slacks. He watched Sylvie with an expression of amazement tinged with delight. Once he clapped.

"—Susan didn't leave our house until almost ten and the police were watching her so she's proved innocent. And more than that, we hired a private investigator—"

Uh-oh. It hadn't occurred to me to ask Sylvie not to mention G. Latham.

"—and she knows who murdered Mr. Fitch and Mr. Ross and—"

Joan Crandall, shaggy brown hair swooping low on her cheeks, used a sharp elbow to butt her way in front of Deke Carson. "Who's the murderer?" Her thin face had the intensity of a fox on the prowl.

Questions zinged at Sylvie. "Who'd you hire? Where can we contact her? Phone number? Have you informed the police?"

Sylvie realized she was the center of attention. She spoke even more loudly. "That's what I'm doing right now. The murderer is a man. And he was at a lunch last week at the Fitch house when Susan was asked to open the safe and bring some coins to the dining room, and that's how it all started because she had to open the safe Tuesday night to borrow some money because she got a call from a man who said he'd kidnapped me and Susan didn't know it was all a plan to get her to go to the house the night the man planned to kill Mr. Fitch."

"Your sister took money from the safe Tuesday night, the night Fitch was killed?" The AP reporter looked like a man trying to sort out what mattered in a welter of information.

"She was going to tell Mr. Fitch the next morning, but he was dead and—"

Ben interrupted. "I'm Ben Fitch, Wilbur's son. Susan Gilbert returned the money when she realized the kidnapping was set up to put her in an incriminating position."

Deke Carson gave a hoot. "She sneaks in the house, opens the safe, takes a hundred grand, and now claims it was all a mistake?"

Ben Fitch was firm. "My father would definitely have understood that Susan had no intention of profiting personally, that she was in an impossible position and took the cash only to secure her sister's safety. In fact, and the police can confirm this, Susan Gilbert returned the cash of her own volition Wednesday morning. My father had the utmost confidence in Ms. Gilbert, and I do, too. I am here with her sister to try and prevent a grave miscarriage of justice."

Joan Crandall hadn't moved an inch away from Sylvie. She was like iron to a magnet. "Who killed Mr. Fitch?"

Deke Carson yelled, "What ransom call? When?"

A TV blonde implored, "Look this way, Sylvie. Tell us about you and your sister."

Neva Lumpkin's face was mottled with rage and frustration. She banged again and again on the lectern, then abruptly turned and stomped from the room.

*

The noon timing of the press conference had precluded lunch. Thankfully, I was aware of Sam's store of M&M'S in the lower left drawer of his desk. I was pouring another handful when his office door opened.

He stepped inside, closed the door, stared. "Mobile M&M'S. That might be a great TV ad. *When the spirit moves you, M&M'S are at the ready.* How about I ask Colleen to order from Lulu's?"

"A perfect solution."

"Same order as yesterday?" He didn't meet my gaze.

"Of course." As Mama wisely instructed: "Don't embarrass a man if you want him to cooperate."

I was in the chair facing his desk when he flicked off the intercom. He leaned back in his chair and began to laugh. "Did you see Neva's face? And then Joan Crandall got the girl off in a corner and put on her best sob sister routine. I can see this afternoon's *Gazette*. 'A Sister's Passionate Defense. Questions Raised about Police Investigation. What Happens When a Medical Examiner Won't Play Ball?' Neva's already sent out a memo demanding to know who leaked the ME timing to the kid. I like the kid, by the way. That's the kind of family to have. Maybe the unkindest cut of all was when Ben Fitch introduced himself and said that his father had the highest confidence in Susan Gilbert and would certainly have understood about the ransom money and then"—Sam's gaze was amazed and admiring—"he complimented authorities for their decision to protect Susan Gilbert by holding her as a material witness since she had the unfortunate experience of walking into a trap set by his father's murderer and that it was despicable of the murderer to use the closeness of a family to direct suspicion at an innocent woman." He started to reach for the M&M'S drawer.

"Lunch will be here soon. Perhaps you don't want to ruin your appetite." Unsaid was the prospect of responding honestly when Claire inquired about his lunch. As for lunch, he could honestly report that he'd ordered the diet plate for himself and a cheeseburger for a visitor. It wouldn't be necessary to say who ate what. We gazed at each other in mutual understanding, and he picked up a pen, did a drum tap on the desktop. "Ben Fitch is smart. Did you notice how he interrupted Sylvie to prevent her naming the men who were at the luncheon? She could have ended up with a defamation suit if she'd named the five."

A knock on the door. I disappeared as Colleen brought in two sacks from Lulu's. Sam took the sacks, put them on opposite sides of his desk. "Expecting a visitor ASAP. No calls for half an hour." As the door closed behind her, he switched the sacks without comment, ripped his down one side. He wolfed a good third of the cheeseburger in a first bite.

I reappeared, lifted out my salad, splashed the greens and grilled chicken with ranch dressing.

"I told Colleen to switch all calls for me to Hal and alerted him to explain the investigations into the murders of Fitch and Ross are active and therefore the department has no comment about a report that five men are considered suspects and that an announcement would be made at a press conference at noon tomorrow. Got a text from Hal asking what did I know about a private detective named Latham. I told him"—Sam's face radiated innocence—"that the department was unaware of the activities of any private detective."

They say confession is good for the soul. I reached over, took one of Sam's french fries, poked it in the ranch dressing, mumbled, "Those five men were interviewed by Adelaide Police Department Detective Sergeant G. Latham."

"It's a pretty serious offense for a private eye to pretend to be a cop. Looks like that's what happened here." Sam didn't sound disturbed. "The department will, of course, make it clear that there is no detective of that name employed by the Adelaide police. I suppose Joan Crandall will write a story about the elusive G. Latham when she discovers there is no private eye of that name and no police detective of that name. Being a good reporter, she'll get a description, red hair, narrow face, green eyes, freckles, five foot five inches, weight approximately one hundred and twenty——"

"One sixteen."

"Well dressed. I like that top. It'd look good on Claire. Nifty with white slacks."

He wiped a smear of chili from his fingers. "So Detective Sergeant Latham talked to the five. What did she get?"

I put down my fork. "There wasn't a gotcha moment." I remembered them, George Kelly seeing dollar signs, Todd Garrett looking forward to a future at the lake, Harry Hubbard too charming for his own good, Alan Douglas diffident and disarming, Ben Fitch at home in a mansion. "Do you know where they were last night between nine and ten thirty?" I leaned forward, hoping that routine careful police work could point me in the right direction.

Sam used two napkins to wipe his hands, turned to his computer screen, clicked a couple of times. "Judy Weitz handled this.

She went to the public library, slipped upstairs, found an unlocked office, and used the phone. She claimed to be Monica Holman and said her car was swiped by a car in the grocery parking lot last night. Another shopper got the license plate and she wanted to know where he, whichever of the five she had on the phone, was around nine twenty. Lots of back and forth. At the end she read off a license plate number. She had the numbers for their cars including one of the Fitch cars, and in each instance her number was one digit off the correct number, so apologies and thank-yous all around. By that time she had the information she wanted. Ben Fitch said he was home reading. No way to confirm. No staff in the house at night so he wouldn't have any trouble slipping out. George Kelly says he was in his office, had a lot of work to do, death of a major client. Checked the area around his office. Woman in a little house next to the parking lot said she'd complained before about his office light shining into her bedroom and he'd forgotten again to draw his curtains. Todd Garrett was actually in the parking lot at the grocery, insisted he never sideswiped anybody's car and if he had sideswiped a car he sure would have left a note. Alan Douglas was in his garage, making some changes to his model for a SIMPLE Car. Neither of his next-door neighbors was home last night. Alan could have been in his garage or he could have been at the Fitch cabin."

I was thoughtful. "Garrett says he was at the grocery?"

Sam shrugged. "He could have been there, fudged on the time. Nobody charts customers at a supermarket. Maybe he had groceries stashed in his trunk before he went to the cabin to meet Ross. If he did meet him."

I suppose my disappointment was evident. I'd hoped at least one or more of them might be crossed off the list if a concrete alibi existed. There was no alibi for any one of my five.

"But"—Sam's voice was upbeat—"I have some good news for you. Don Smith has covered Susan Gilbert's past like Madame Curie peering at radium. Gilbert does not have a license for a gun. Gilbert has never purchased a gun. Gilbert, according to friends, has never shot a gun. Neither of her parents ever owned a gun. Her father was not a hunter. In fact, she grew up in an anti-gun household, wants to see laws enacted that prohibit the sale of assault weapons. Moreover, her house and car were thoroughly searched Wednesday and no gun was found in the house, garage, yard, or car." He looked to me for approval.

"That's great." I tried to sound enthusiastic. Susan's lack of access to a weapon was great material for her defense attorney, but I knew she was innocent. "Is the lack of gun and fingerprints enough to keep her from being charged tomorrow?"

"If I were calling the shots, I would keep the investigation open. Neva has the bit in her teeth."

Bit in her teeth is Oklahoma-speak for a runaway horse.

"Bailey Ruth, I'll continue to look for facts even after Susan's charged. But"—he turned his big hands up in a gesture of resignation—"I have to tell you I don't have anything yet that points at a different person."

∽

Susan was transformed in a sweater as vivid as holly berries and gray wool slacks. She was no longer barefoot, wore gray leather flats and ribbed gray socks with flecks of red. Nice. I'd observed her in moments of stress, her dark brown eyes filled with terror and despair and fear, her angular face pale with the cheekbones too prominent, the generous mouth kept from trembling by huge effort. Now she looked young and almost carefree and this despite the somber silence that pressed against her in the solitary cell. There were no other occupants in any of the cells. That was likely to the good. A jail cell can never be a place of joy.

This small cell might be the exception.

Susan was sitting as comfortably as possible, her back against one end of the bunk, one leg crossed over the other. Her eyes held a glow, the kind of radiance that shines from good memories, a kind word, a smile, and from anticipation that no matter how dark the sky there is a sliver of light on the horizon and faith that the light will grow and grow and soon there will be an explosion of brightness.

"Susan."

Her face turned toward the bars and the corridor. I stood between the bunk and the bars, and had I been present she would have looked at me directly. Her gaze wasn't startled or distressed. "I thought you might come. Thank you for telling Sylvie about my shoes. She brought fresh clothes, too. She and Ben told me how she made the police look silly today. Ben said everything will be much better in the newspapers tomorrow, that he and Sylvie were behind me a hundred percent." Her voice was soft. "I can't believe how nice Ben is. He knows I didn't hurt his dad. But to come with Sylvie to see me." Her voice held wonder. She looked toward me with those luminous eyes. "That's special, isn't it?"

"Very special." Special enough to fill this steel-barred concrete space with light and joy and hope.

"Ben," she said softly. And then she seemed to bring herself fully present. She moved to swing her legs over the edge of the bunk. She came to her feet, eager, excited. "Do you know yet?" Only four little words, but they meant life and freedom and a future for her. I'd told Susan and Sylvie I was sure the murderer was one of five men and I would bring to justice the man who had put her in such danger. I would find him and convince the police and the cell door would swing open and she would walk free. I, Bailey Ruth Raeburn (aka G. Latham), had promised.

One of five, one of five, one of . . . I didn't know which one.

But I couldn't bear to dim her radiance. "By noon tomorrow everything will be wonderful."

Five men . . .

Chapter 12

I'd gathered a great deal of information about the men who would be affected by a big change at Fitch Enterprises. I'd felt even more confident I was on the right path when Sam Cobb reported the visit from Minerva Lloyd. I pictured the interchange between Wilbur and Minerva, a domineering man enjoying a show of power—I'm making a big change—with an admiring woman as his audience, a buck pawing the ground near a doe. Obviously Wilbur enjoyed women, liked beauty, wouldn't hesitate to emphasize his strength. But I didn't feel an iota nearer knowing which of the five was a killer, even after speaking with each of them. Time was running out. There was one more possible source of information.

Juliet Rodriguez evidently never met a stranger. She beamed at me as she opened her apartment door. "Detective, come right in." She waved me to the sofa, closed the door, and hurried to join me. "I'm so glad to see you. It's as if it's meant to be." Her gaze was now earnest. "I saw in the paper—"

The *Gazette* would be pleased to know it was so widely read.

"—that Susan is trying to help you, and I thought we all should be trying to help, and I've thought and thought and I hate to say it"—and now her lovely face drooped—"but Wilbur was so mad. I talked to him Tuesday afternoon. He came in the library and he was just beside himself. I don't want to cause trouble for anyone, but what's true is true. I wasn't going to say anything but here you are." And now she clearly struggled. "I hate to say anything because I liked him. So handsome. Not anything like his father with that dark hair and those blue eyes. But Wilbur said he was going to wipe his name off of every-thing, drop him from the will. He said there was nothing worse than a son who thought he was better than everyone else."

⁂

Rose Bower was bequeathed to Goddard College by Charles Marlow. The Marlows were great supporters of the college, and his wife Lorraine's portrait hangs in the library on the first-floor landing of a double stairway. Light shone cheerfully through the ornate rose window above the front entrance. I moved inside and was pleased to see that the stately rooms be-yond the huge marble foyer lay in darkness except for lavalieres on the side of each archway. To my right the chairs behind a magnificent rosewood desk were empty. The college used this expansive structure to host grand events and also to provide on the second floor elegant rooms for visiting dignitaries. If an event were planned or guests expected, the desk would be staffed.

I was ready to go upstairs when I noticed a stack of newspapers on one side of the desk. I was there in an instant. I picked up the *Gazette* and scanned the headlines:

SECOND MURDER ON FITCH ESTATE; BUTLER FATALLY SHOT IN LAKE CABIN

SUSPECT'S SISTER CLAIMS FITCH SECRETARY FRAMED

TIME OF DEATH IN QUESTION; WAS 10:07 GUNSHOT RELEVANT?

I went straight to Joan Crandall's breathless depiction of Sylvie Gilbert (gallant and determined) and how she single-handedly disrupted Mayor Neva Lumpkin's noon press conference about the murder of Wilbur Fitch early Wednesday morning and the murder of his butler, Carl Ross, Wednesday night.

I loved Joan's lead.

Official Adelaide was no match Thursday for a sister on a missi—

"Hey"—the voice was high and uncertain—"how are you doing that? Buddy, where are you? How'd you make the paper hang in the air like somebody's reading it?" A few feet away a slender girl with auburn hair and a sweet face stood by the desk. Although she and her apparent coworker Buddy (In the men's room? At the soda machine? Outside on his cell phone lining up a date?) were absent when I arrived, she was now on the scene.

I had been too absorbed to hear her approach. I looked at the *Gazette*, and of course it looked like someone was holding the newspaper at eye level and reading because I was holding the newspaper at eye level and reading. As clever people, the kind who take physics, would be the first to agree, newspapers do not suspend themselves in the air. Regretfully, I let the sheets slip from my hands and flutter to the floor.

The girl watched the descending newsprint much the way she might have observed an upside-down car driving by.

I very much wanted to read the stories about the investigation, but I would have to return at a later time and cautiously filch a *Gazette*.

From the second-floor landing I looked down.

The girl was approaching the scattered sheets stealthily.

I suspected that when she gathered up the sheets and found no evidence of an elaborate mechanism to account for a newspaper hanging in the air before suddenly descending to the floor, she would devise a reassuring explanation: The newspaper on the desk was blown into the air by an inexplicable gust—the door opened or the heating system hiccupped—and she'd only imagined that it was being held as though being read because, of course, no one was standing there. She could be sure of the latter. She'd seen it with her own eyes.

It would never occur to her that a ghost held the paper and that excused my inadvertent transgression of Precept Six: "Make every effort not to alarm earthly creatures."

Last night I'd stayed in the Red Room. A fine porcelain nameplate is attached to the door of each guest room. What would I choose tonight? I bypassed Scholar, Cardinal's Nest, Gusher, paused at Will.

Shakespeare is always good company: *Strong reasons make strong actions.* Murder is a strong action that springs from a powerful motive. When I knew which motive mattered, I would see the face of a murderer.

Inside I realized my mistake. I should have known when a pattern of lariats bordered the nameplate. The lariat motif was continued around the borders of framed quotations from Will Rogers. Rogers is perhaps Oklahoma's most famous native son, rodeo star, movie actor, comedian, political commentator, author, and a whiz at lassoing livestock. The quotes were embroidered in bright red letters against a dust-colored background. I read all the quotations, returned to four.

> *This would be a great world to dance in if we didn't have to pay the fiddler.*

> *Diplomacy is the art of saying "Nice doggie" until you can find a rock.*

We are here just for a spell and then we pass on. So get a few laughs and do the best you can. Live your life so that whenever you lose it, you are ahead.

Why not go out on a limb? That's where the fruit is.

The decor was bunkhouse comfortable with lots of leather and maple and the aura of don't-be-the-last-to-saddle-up. I settled in a green leather easy chair. How could I be in a room suffused with the exuberance of Will Rogers and not succeed at my task? It was a matter of judgment. I had the information. Instead of a wide-open search for a double murderer, I knew with certainty that one of five men was guilty. I had spoken with each of them. So what were the anomalies?

The Tiffany lamp on the table next to my chair shone on a spiral notebook and a pencil. I picked up the notebook, the kind my students used in long-ago classes, and the soft-leaded pencil. I flipped open the notebook, wrote.

Ben Fitch

Motive:

> *Wealth. Power. His last encounter with his father ended in a shouting match. Ben appears to be grieving. If he killed his father he would act the part of a bereft son. In his defense, he supports Sylvie Gilbert's effort to weaken the case against Susan.*

I liked Ben Fitch and, face it, he was hugely appealing to women, that curly dark hair and those blue eyes and air of the islands with his tanned skin. But what could appear more innocent than to rush to the defense of the woman he'd set up so nicely to take the blame first for his father's murder and then for the man foolish enough to attempt blackmail. The pencil moved swiftly.

Points against Ben:

He profited hugely.

Juliet said Wilbur was going to disinherit him, was "beside himself" with fury. He was staying in the house and could easily knock on his father's door after the party Tuesday night. His father would have had no reason to fear him.

He could use any phone in the house to call Susan's cell Wednesday night.

He grew up in the mansion, knew the surroundings, would be comfortable standing in the shadows by the lake to shoot the gun to implicate Susan after her arrival at the cabin.

He was young and strong, would have had no fear of dealing with Carl Ross.

He was smart, quick thinking. Was it quick thinking that prompted him to lay out the scenario that must have occurred, a knock on his father's door, a familiar face, a claim the study light was on, the safe exposed, a suggestion they

*go down to see, a quick rush downstairs, the
decision to open the safe and check its contents, a
jarring blow from behind?*

Points in Ben's favor:
    *Red-rimmed eyes and difficulty talking about the
        murder of his father.*
    *Successful businessman on his own and no apparent
        hunger to run the Fitch empire, instead
        accepting his role as CEO as a duty.*
    Attracted to Susan Gilbert.
    *Standing by Sylvie at the press conference, offering
        the weight of the family name.*

George Kelly

Motive:
    *Money. A client like Ben Fitch would have absorbed
        most of Kelly's time. How would he fare as a
        lawyer if Ben Fitch meant what he said, that Kelly
        was on his way out as the attorney for Fitch
        Enterprises? Now Kelly would continue to fatten
        on the Fitch money as he settled the estate for big
        fees and Ben Fitch would have no reason to fire
        him as the company lawyer.*
    *Pride—Kelly lost a case Wilbur thought he
        should have won, and no man in Oklahoma
        wants to be described as a steer, i.e., an
        emasculated bull.*

Nothing succeeds like success and nothing is more damaging to a professional's stature as the loss of a big client. Being dumped as Wilbur's lawyer would likely have been devastating both financially and professionally.

Points against George:
If fired by Fitch, Kelly faced severe financial loss.
Fees for estate work will be substantial, perhaps a half million dollars.
A tough dude. Would have felt capable of dealing with Carl Ross.
Exhibited surprise to learn there was some doubt about Susan's involvement.

Points in George's favor:
Dismissed company employees as possible suspects. May have been negative about Susan because she turned him down for dates.
Appears relaxed and confident.
Was known to have combative relationship with Wilbur yet remained his lawyer. Likely Wilbur admired his attack-dog response to confrontation. Lawyers thrive on conflict. That's what they do.

Harry Hubbard

Motive:
Greed. Harry Hubbard lived a soft and comfortable life. He worked for his stepfather but apparently

his main duty was to serve as a golf companion.
He never minded asking Wilbur for expensive
gifts, used charm and good humor to inveigle
indulgences. He inherited enough money to
provide a great many luxuries.

Wilbur and his stepson were apparently on good terms with no suggestion of a quarrel or disagreement. Harry's easy charm made it difficult to imagine him committing murder. In very different ways, Harry Hubbard and Ben Fitch were appealing and likable.

Points against Harry:
He wanted a lifestyle that exceeded his income.
He was knowledgeable about both Susan and Sylvie
*   Gilbert.*
He checked out long-term rentals for pricey
*   condos in Aruba and Tahiti. Was this winter*
*   dreaming or making plans for a soon-to-come*
*   inheritance?*
Inherits five hundred thousand dollars, which will
*   buy a lot of expensive pleasures he couldn't*
*   afford on his salary.*
Didn't have his usual affable expression in the FB
*   photo with the poker players. Those were not the*
*   kind of dudes to owe money to. Could that be a*
*   problem for him?*
Alan Douglas saw Harry as a house cat and not a

risk-taker, but Harry persuaded Sylvie Gilbert
to skydive with him.

Points in Harry's favor:
  Harry was charming, easygoing, never quarreled
    with anyone.
  Harry dismissed the idea anyone at the company
    killed Wilbur, including Susan.
  House cats are not lions.
  The brilliant decoy of Sylvie to create the
    appearance of a kidnapping seemed as unlikely
    as Harry suddenly playing a Stradivarius.

"Not so fast," I scolded myself. Harry might not be a whiz at algorithms, but he had an instinct for people, how to please them, charm them, motivate them to make the house cat purr.

Alan Douglas

Motive:
  The SIMPLE Car. Wilbur turned down the
    SIMPLE Car, but Alan claimed Wilbur agreed
    to waive the company's ownership. Now Alan
    counted on Ben making good on his father's
    promise. What if there was no promise?
  Alan's life appeared to be fairly monastic. Perhaps
    his only passion was the orange plywood model
    of his brainchild. He appeared diffident, even
    gentle, but how would he react if his concept was

not only dismissed but taken over as a work
product belonging to the company?

Points against Alan:
He was single-minded in his pursuit of a goal.
According to Todd, Wilbur decided against
creating the SIMPLE Car.
Alan cannot prove his claim that Wilbur gave him
permission to pursue the idea on his own.
He was quick to impute a motive to George Kelly.
Chess players are good at intricate planning.

Points in Alan's favor:
He appears to be gentle and diffident.
No one has said that Wilbur yelled at Alan.
Alan defended the innocence of Susan Gilbert as
well as Harry Hubbard and Todd Garrett

Alan Douglas was intelligent, quick, thoughtful, absorbed in the world of his mind. There was nothing threatening about him except for the intensity of his light blue eyes when I asked if he thought the proprietary claim against the car would be waived.

Todd Garrett

Motive:
Anger. Wilbur exploded at Todd and ordered him
to make the rounds at the civic club to say he'd
spoken without authority about the SIMPLE

Car. Todd took great pride in being the public
face of the company. Did the prospect of
humiliation in front of those he wanted to
impress push him to violence?
Stress. Todd tried hard to appear competent in a
demanding environment, but he knew he owed
his position to his long-ago kindness to a high
school outcast. His inheritance was enough that
he could remake his life, hunt and fish and never
have to be embarrassed again.

Todd Garrett opposed Alan Douglas's SIMPLE Car vehemently. Did he resent a younger man with only two years at the company receiving the respect and attention of Wilbur? Or was he opposed because he felt the plan lacked merit?

Points against Todd:
He was angry and humiliated by Wilbur's
order that he walk back his criticism of the
SIMPLE Car.
He hunted so he definitely knew how to handle
guns, very likely owned several guns.
His job was beyond his capability.
He was quick to claim he overheard a conversation
that provided a motive for Alan Douglas to kill
Wilbur.
The inheritance would afford him a life without
hassle or demands or insults.

Points in Todd's favor:

He was Wilbur's oldest friend and Wilbur had
treated him handsomely.
He defended Susan Gilbert.
Harry Hubbard insisted Todd was a good old boy,
a man who kept his word, protected the weak,
and valued the code of the Old West. Such a man
would not attack from behind.

Murder requires a hard spirit, a toughness that can be described as callousness. Murderers do not see other living creatures as special, irreplaceable, miraculous. Those who protect life and those who save lives have a reverence for the intelligence in every mind, the love in every heart, the utterly unique reality of each and every person whether a violin virtuoso in a Berlin orchestra or a seal hunter in Alaska or a new mother in the Amazon jungle. Imagining all the people in this world, each one with a beating heart and feelings of joy or anger or fear or hope, is as staggering as looking up at billions of blazing stars in the night sky. To escape the burden of that reality, many of us hunker in our shells like turtles, making the world small, manageable, narrow, focused.

A murderer doesn't see or feel the awesomeness of life. A murderer sees an obstacle to a goal.

Ben Fitch, George Kelly, Harry Hubbard, Alan Douglas, Todd Garrett.

Which one?

As Mama always told us kids, "If you knock your head against the wall and all you get is a sore head, you need a new start."

In the huge marble entrance foyer, the chandeliers were only dimly lit. A Tiffany lamp on one corner of the massive rosewood desk glowed softly. Rose Bower appeared closed for the night. I snatched up a *Gazette*. Perhaps if I read everything Joan Crandall had written I would find a new direction, a hint, a help.

I move from one place to another by thinking where I want to go. However, when transporting a material object, such as a newspaper, I must transport the physical item through space. I was midway up the marble stairway when I heard a clatter of steps that suddenly stopped.

I looked over the banister.

The pretty young attendant stood at the foot of the stairs. Perhaps her last task before leaving the desk unattended at night was a check of the second floor to make sure no room service tray rested on the floor outside a guest room. Rose Bower's kitchen was always staffed and ready to respond to requests. Even from here, I could see the utter incredulity on her face.

Earlier I'd let the sheets flutter to the floor, confident she would attribute the odd occurrence to the vagaries of the heating system. That solution didn't apply here. Even the most imaginative observer could not possibly believe the heating system buoyed a *Gazette* halfway up the stairs.

I had no choice. Firmly clutching the newspaper, I kept climbing though I increased my pace.

From her vantage point, the newspaper had been rising as if in someone's hand and now it rose as if the climber moved with alacrity. I reached the landing, started up the last section of steps, frankly as fast as I could manage, reached the second floor, made a smart left, and knew I was no longer observed.

With a quick glance up and down the hall, I hurried to Will's Room. I put the paper on the floor, moved through the door, opened the door, retrieved the newspaper. I settled in one of the expansive leather chairs—I could almost smell saddles and hay—and began to read. Six stories pertained to the investigation. I read every word. On one hand, I could take pride in the fact that I was aware of every reported fact. On the other hand, I didn't find anything to help me choose among the five men.

If I could at this moment contact Sam Cobb and tell him who committed the murders and how to capture him, I would have done so knowing, thanks to the *Gazette*, that Susan was not only saved, but her life was going to be wonderful. The stories in the *Gazette* pictured her as a stalwart aide to the authorities whose actions were praised by the Fitch family and her detainment a matter of her protection.

At noon tomorrow that picture would be as smashed as a delicate Dresden figurine flung from the Rose Bower stairway to the marble floor below. At noon tomorrow Neva Lumpkin's press conference would center on the arrest of Susan Mary Gilbert on two murder charges.

I pushed to my feet, began to pace. Gone was my exuberance when I first walked into Will's Room. The silence of Rose Bower was crushing, not soothing. I glanced at the wall clock framed in a wagon wheel. Eleven o'clock and all was not well. It was the time of night for reflection, perhaps a summing up of the day's successes, a preview of tomorrow's challenges. My gaze scanned the framed quotes in needlepoint, stopped: *Chaotic action is preferable to orderly inaction.*

⌀

I looked for Ben Fitch in his bedroom, went downstairs through the stately rooms and the dim family rooms. In the study, I noted for the first time a gun safe in one corner. That came as no surprise. I wondered if Ben knew how to open it. I wondered if there was one gun or two or perhaps a single gun and another that was missing. I was about to give up my search, thinking perhaps he might still be at the Gilbert house, when I saw light shining from an open door at the end of a back hallway. I found a stairway and smelled chlorine.

Bright lights illuminated the basement swimming pool. Ben was midway down the center lane of the Olympic-sized pool. I admired his freestyle stroke. He reached the end, did a flip turn, started back this way.

Another lap and another and another.

I hovered near the end of the pool. His face as he turned for air was blank, unreadable, cheeks flushed with exertion. Perhaps he sought forgetfulness or perhaps he hoped to oust grief with sheer exhaustion.

The huge damp chlorine-scented basement seemed filled with loneliness and sadness.

∽

George Kelly sprawled comfortably in an oversize recliner, booted feet elevated. Like most dark-haired men, his face had a heavy shadow of beard by late evening. His broad face looked confident and bold. His blue eyes were focused and intent. He scrawled a line with a blue felt pen. In his other hand, he held a half-full whisky glass. He took a sip. A muted football game, I assumed a replay, loomed on a wall TV screen. I nodded approval when I recognized the starred helmets of the Dallas Cowboys.

I hovered close enough to look at the legal pad. A listing of some properties in Latimer County, a notation to check whether the oil and gas leases were still current.

I took a last long look at George, who appeared relaxed and in charge in the big comfortable masculine room. I noted a gun safe in one corner.

∽

Harry Hubbard slept in a T-shirt and Black Watch plaid boxer shorts in a queen-sized bed, a red-striped comforter flung to one side. His handsome face was slack in sleep, but appealing as a napping puppy appeals. The room was surprisingly tidy and pleasant. In his living room I found no books except for a collection of crossword puzzles. I opened his desk drawer, lifted out a checkbook. His recent bank statement showed several charges for overdrawn checks and a current balance of seventy-five dollars. I checked the entire apartment. No gun safe.

⌒

The walls in Alan Douglas's living room were cream, the wood trim Chinese red. The room could have served as a furniture store display, everything matched, nothing out of place. A wall of books included several on quantum physics. A gun safe sat in the corner near a gray metal desk. A pen and pad lay on the desktop, perfectly aligned.

The only photograph was the night sky with faraway pinpoints of stars, cold and remote. Three paintings hung on one wall, large splashes of red and black, a tan maze, and a fiery eruption of molten lava brimming from a volcano.

Alan's short-sleeved polo shirt exposed bony arms. His jeans were well-worn, washed so often the cloth was more white than blue. He sat in a wicker chair, one long leg crossed over the other. He held a book very precisely, using both hands. He looked scholarly with his short-cut brown hair and ascetic face and brown horn rims.

The life of the mind can engage and delight, but the room lacked warmth and cheer.

⌒

Todd Garrett hunched at a workbench in one corner of the bedroom of his condo. His stubby fingers showed surprising skill as he delicately arranged a bass fishing skirt on a jig. To one side lay a half dozen crankbaits. He softly hummed "Delta Dawn." Instead of the defeated posture at his office, he was relaxed, looked like a somewhat heavy former football player with happy days on his horizon. Bass fishing can be all-consuming. There's no time for regrets or heartaches when you are trying to outwit a clever and elusive fish. The assorted crankbaits meant Todd was drawn to the brushy shallows of the lake.

I found his gun safe next to a desk in the living room.

Chapter 13

I stood at the end of the pier in White Deer Park. I'd chosen to appear in a soft blue cashmere cowl sweater and white wool slacks and blue heels. But the style and verve of my outfit gave me no comfort. I watched streaks of pink and vermilion and royal blue herald sunrise. This was Adelaide's oldest park. I'd stood here in 1942 when Bobby Mac was off in basic training at Fort Sill and I wrote him every day and none of us knew what would happen, what could happen. The big black headlines reported battles, the bombardment of Corregidor, the fall of the Philippines. There were Gold Stars in so many windows for the men who would not come home again. I'd stood here in anguish and fear and then hope.

I'd never stood here in defeat.

I'd done my best for Susan Gilbert. I began my quest cocky

and confident. I was the late Bailey Ruth Raeburn, forever twenty-seven, red hair bright and shining, green eyes eager and curious, and I was an emissary from the Department of Good Intentions, here to protect the innocent.

The whoo of the Rescue Express blew through me. The engine rumbled. Wheels clacked on the rails. Coal smoke as acrid as a long-ago Pittsburgh steel mill swirled around me. Cinders sparked from the funnel.

I felt forlorn. I could not climb aboard with a smile on my face or cheer in my heart.

"Bailey Ruth." Wiggins spoke in a kind and gentle tone.

Whoo, whoo.

I felt a rush of tears. "I fai—"

"Bailey Ruth, you have six hours yet." Wiggins was brisk.

I turned toward the sound of his voice.

Colors swirled and there he was, stiff blue cap atop reddish hair, high-collared stiffly starched white shirt with elastic armbands above the elbows, heavy gray flannel trousers supported by wide suspenders, highly polished sturdy black shoes.

"There's no way forward." My voice was bleak. Then my usual combativeness coursed through me. "It's maddening because I know one of them, one of five men, created this terrible trap for Susan and—"

He patted my shoulder. "You're almost there. I believe in you, Bailey Ruth." With that calm pronouncement, the Rescue Express whooed, coal smoke swirled, wheels clacked.

I stood alone in silence except for the chatter of a squirrel, a crow's raucous caw, the faraway hut-two at an early morning football practice. Bobby Mac was the quarterback of the Cougars. He was a good passer, and I remembered one game when he fell back and sent the football spiraling downfield. That's what I needed, a good play. The warmth of the memory faded. I needed more than a good play, I needed a miracle. I stood very still. A miracle . . . Roger Staubach at the playoff game between the Cowboys and the Vikings on a cold December day in 1975, a wind chill of seventeen degrees. Twenty-four seconds left in the fourth quarter, his team down 10–14, Staubach looked at the wide receivers running downfield, raised his arm, threw the ball, and said a Hail Mary. Drew Pearson locked the ball in his arms at the five and carried it into the end zone. Cowboys won 17–14.

Against all odds, Staubach took action.

Action . . .

I went straight to Susan Gilbert's desk in the alcove of Wilbur's study. I was glad she used an old-fashioned Rolodex. I took a sheet of copy paper from a bottom drawer, folded it in half. It took only a moment to write down five telephone numbers.

The living room of Carl Ross's garage apartment was as lifeless as Wilbur's study, two rooms not currently in use. In the kitchen I found a telephone mounted on the wall next to a counter. I put the sheet of paper on the counter.

I steadied my thoughts. I had one chance. I took a deep breath, tried out a few words. "Carl shouldn't'uv trusted you." I used a voice harder and flatter than my own, slightly nasal, with no resemblance to my husky deeper tone. Bobby Mac once compared my voice to Lauren Bacall's. Is he a smart man or what?

Which number first?

Only one number mattered.

I glanced at a kitchen clock. Seven minutes after seven. I closed my eyes, whirled my index finger in a circle, came down to the sheet, opened my eyes. I dialed. Caller ID would show the caller as Carl Ross. I didn't doubt the call would be answered.

"Hello." The voice was muzzy with sleep.

"You should'uv paid Carl. He would'uv kept quiet. You're gonna pay me—"

"What the hell are you talking about?"

"He saw you that night and he told me all about it and I wrote it down in my diary—"

The connection ended.

I drew a line though Harry Hubbard.

I closed my eyes, made a circle with my finger, tapped the sheet, looked.

I dialed.

"Hello." The faintest inflection of surprise.

"You shouldn't'uv shot Carl. He would'uv kept quiet. But you're gonna pay—"

"Lady, you got the wrong number. I don't know anybody named Carl and I never shot anyone." The call ended.

I drew a line through Alan Douglas.

I tried again.

"Hello." A cautious voice.

"You shouldn't'uv shot Carl. You should'uv paid him. You got the money and more where that comes from. But you're gonna pay me or I'll tell the police what happened."

"Who is this?" The voice was wary, careful.

"Carl's friend. Me and Carl been together off and on. We were back on. He told me all about you. What he saw. He told me he was going to meet you at the cabin and you was going to bring money. But you killed him. I want that money. You're gonna bring it to me. But I waited to call you 'til morning. I'm at his place now, but I'll be gone before you can get over here. Anyway, I waited 'til morning 'cause I'm not gonna meet you at night away from people. No way. You bring the money to the gazebo in the downtown park. There's always people there and the police right across the street. I can yell loud enough to get the cops over there pronto. You bring the money at eleven sharp or I'll tell the cops. In the gazebo."

This time I ended the connection.

⟡

After they married, Sam Cobb moved in with Claire in her huge old house. Now the gardens were neat, the trees clipped, the grass cut, the pond clear of algae. Claire was in the kitchen, humming to herself. I smiled as I recognized "The Church in the Wildwood." Bacon sizzled in an iron skillet, the old-fashioned kind of skillet my mama used. The kitchen smelled like bacon and cinnamon and happiness. As Mama always said, "Start the day happy and you march in seven-league boots."

I glanced around the breakfast room. Petunias were a spot of beauty in the middle of the white kitchen table. Two places were set. Sam wasn't downstairs yet. I found him shaving at the lavatory in the bathroom, attired in navy boxers.

"Sam."

His hand jerked. A spot of blood welled from a nick on his right cheek. He looked wildly around.

Heavens, I assumed he would recognize my voice, but, of course, he expected to hear Claire's voice here, and she spoke in a much higher register than I.

I darted to a rack, grabbed a washcloth, held it under the water. "Ouch." Of course the water was hot. I turned the hot water off, the cold water on, doused the cloth, held it up to his cheek.

He exhaled as he took the cloth, pressed it against the welt. "Couldn't it wait until I get to the office?"

For Sam that was grumpy.

"Sam, there's no time to waste. . . ."

༄

Sam Cobb rose through the ranks to become chief of police because he listened, evaluated, and dealt intelligently with whatever situation arose. This morning he skipped his shower, was dressed and on his way down the stairs in less than ten minutes. He poked his head into the kitchen. "Got a call. Have to go. I'll catch a bite."

Claire moved fast, popped warm cinnamon muffins into a brown paper sack, and filled a coffee thermos. She was at the front door as he pulled it open. She looked up and in her eyes was the fear police spouses know. "Be careful."

He took the bag with a smile, bent to kiss her cheek. "I'll come home. I promise."

He used the siren and cars swerved to the curb. In his office, he pulled a legal pad near, made several notations, began to issue orders.

I watched as a coverall-clothed workman climbed a ladder in the gazebo. Another worker held the ladder steady. A can of paint and a brush were set on the ladder's pail rest. There were several swipes with the brush, then a minute videocam was secreted in a rafter. The videocam was set to rotate to cover the entire interior once every two minutes. The recorder was scheduled to begin recording at ten forty-five.

I was in the park at nine a.m. when officers in street clothes began to arrive, one by one. A workman rolling a wheelbarrow. A young woman pushing a carriage containing a rifle instead of a baby beneath the closed top. Two joggers with guns in their backpacks. An artist who set up an easel with a good view of the gazebo. Four shovel-equipped workmen who turned over earth a few feet from a fountain. A sharpshooter in camouflage who climbed midway up a huge magnolia and wormed onto a broad limb that overlooked the gazebo. Magnolias, as all Southerners know, keep their glossy leaves year round, providing cover.

The park was perhaps three city blocks in size. The white-frame gazebo sat in the center. Elms, sycamores, redbuds, and magnolias filled the area north of the gazebo. To the south was a broad open grassy expanse, the grass now the dull brown of winter. The killer wouldn't come from the south. Wisteria, holly, yew, and red chokeberry shrubs dotted the winding walkways.

I had one more stop before I kept my appointment in the park.

Sylvie sat at the small kitchen table. A notebook lay open before her. Crumpled sheets littered the floor. I looked over her shoulder. Lists. Lists of what to do, who to call, what to ask Susan's lawyer.

I went to the front porch, pressed the bell.

I had only an instant. In the now-empty kitchen, I picked up the pen, wrote on a blank sheet in all caps: *NOON PRESS CONFERENCE. SUSAN'S RELEASE ANNOUNCED. CASE SOLVED. BE THERE.* I signed it quickly, Detective G. Latham. I'd no more than put down the pen when Sylvie returned.

She grabbed a half-filled mug from the table, emptied it in the sink, replenished the mug with fresh coffee, sat down again. She picked up the pen, went suddenly rigid as she read the note. She looked wildly, got up so quickly her chair crashed to the floor, and ran to the back door. She flung the door open, hurried down the steps, gazed around, then shook her head. She yanked her cell phone from her pocket, swiped. "Ben . . ."

I was pleased she already had his number on speed dial.

I made a last survey of City Park. All appeared perfectly normal. People walking. Workmen working. There was no indication the park was secured by undercover police.

At a quarter to eleven, I appeared in the ladies' room of Lulu's. I chose a black wig in a bouffant style, oversize aviator sunglasses, and a wide-leg pink pants suit beneath a shiny sequin-speckled leather jacket. I suppressed a shudder as I gazed at the image. No one would confuse this apparition with Detective Sergeant G. Latham or Private Investigator G. Latham.

It was five to eleven when I approached the park from the grassy southern expanse. I was too far from the wooded area to provide a good vantage point for a gunman. Shooting Carl Ross at a distance of perhaps ten feet didn't equate with a moving target at thirty yards. Moreover, I would be safe until I stood in the gazebo because my adversary had no idea of my appearance. He knew only that a woman knew too much, a woman was a threat, a woman had to be dealt with.

I didn't believe he would arrive to cajole or temporize or offer cash. He would be armed.

At two minutes to eleven I paused in the shadow of a red chokeberry shrub not far from a fountain where four city workers in baggy coveralls, with pockets capable of holding guns and ammo, stood in a semicircle gazing at the waterless spout. Were they awaiting an oracle? Was there an endangered grub worm in the vicinity? Oh, perhaps they were contemplating activity. One of them placed both hands on a shovel, wedged the steel into hard dry ground.

I was about fifteen feet from the gazebo. The white structure was elegant and old-fashioned with steps to the south and north. A wooden railing with columns supported a peaked roof.

I started up the steps. At the crack of a gun I would disappear. Eight steps in all. I took them slowly. I reached the elevated wooden floor, moved around the interior, gazed to the south and the fountain with one workman jamming a shovel near a bricked rim. A woman pushed a baby carriage on the central path. I walked around the perimeter again, looked to the north at winter-bare trees and the occasional shiny green magnolia and clumps of shrubbery.

He came from the shadow of a huge wisteria shrub, moving swiftly to the north steps. He was almost unrecognizable, head down, shoulders hunched, making it hard for an observer, if there were an observer, to estimate height and weight. A wool cap covered his head. A muffler wrapped around his neck obscured the lower portion of his face. A dark jacket. A black sweater. Dark trousers. Sneakers. His right hand thrust into the jacket pocket, a pocket that bulged. He came closer, stared at me. "You called me?"

"Carl told me. You killed Mr. Fitch. I know what happened and you're gonna pay me. You got the money?"

"You're as stupid as Carl. He thought he could blackmail me. At the cabin, he was sprawled in a chair like he owned the place. I let him talk, told him sure, I'd pay him five thousand a month. I said maybe we should have a drink to seal the deal. I got up and walked toward him and shot him and his shirt was bloody, a big splotch of blood, and I watched him slide to the floor and die. Now it's your turn." His hand jerked free from his pocket. The blue black of an automatic gleamed in a shaft of sunlight.

A shout blared from a megaphone. "Drop that gun. Police. Hands up. Police. We have you covered."

I flung myself to the side, disappearing as I moved.

A shot exploded, loud enough to startle grazing geese into lumbering flight.

Two more shots.

Sam's office bustled with activity. Detective Sergeant Hal Price swiped off his cell phone, spoke rapidly. "He's expected to survive. Harley's a good shot. Got the gun hand, knocked the .45 to the floor. It went off. A tech prized out a perfect slug plus we got two cartridges. They're in the lab now."

Sam reached for his phone, tapped an extension. "Any match between the cartridge at the Fitch cabin and the slug the ME dug out of Ross with the slug and cartridges from the gazebo?" His face was intent.

His office door burst open. Neva Lumpkin charged across the room. Today's pants suit was better cut, more flattering, but if I were asked for fashion advice I would murmur that black or gray are more flattering than cerise to a woman who weighs in at a good two hundred pounds. She jolted to a stop in front of Sam's desk. Her chest heaved. "I am preparing for the press conference—you do remember that a press conference is scheduled"—she looked at a gold watch in a sapphire-studded band—"to begin in four minutes to announce the arrest of that thief, Wilbur Fitch's secretary, and I am told that sirens shrilled right here by City Hall and there was a live-shooter incident across from my office and no one told me. And Howie says an important citizen was arrested and—"

Sam stood, all grizzled muscular six foot two inches of him, but his expression was genial. "You have arrived just at the right moment, Neva. I'll walk upstairs to the press conference with you." He came around his desk, politely took her arm. "We have just this moment received important ballistics information. I will explain to you as we go upstairs." He gave a quick glance at Hal. "Miss Gilbert, of course, is to be released promptly and thanked for her cooperation in the investigations into the murders of Wilbur Fitch and Carl Ross. And give Claire a call, tell her everything's fine, I'll be home for dinner on time." By now the word would be on radio and TV about shots fired in City Park across from the police station.

Neva frowned. "Susan Gilbert was at the scene of two crimes."

Sam knew his listener. "She was never a serious suspect. And, when you think about it, Neva, it would be pretty boring for the newshounds if we arrested a secretary. Now we have an arrest that will rock the town—" The door closed behind them.

⁓

The small room was jammed, seven cameras with handlers and on-air blondes, almost fourteen print reporters. I was sure I spotted a college student clutching a notebook and another with a microphone and recorder, so the college newspaper and radio station were here as well. Joan Crandall was in the center of the first row as became the *Gazette*'s star reporter. The AP bureau chief sat next to her. Deke Carson looked as scruffy as usual in a white T-shirt and dungarees with one ragged knee.

Neva and Sam stood just inside the door, Sam murmuring into her ear. She listened with widening eyes.

The downtown carillon chimed the noon hour.

Neva strode to the lectern. "I am Mayor Neva Lumpkin. Adelaide prides itself upon its safety and concern for citizens. Adelaide seeks justice without fear or favor, treating all citizens equally. Today the police arrested George Kelly, a leading citizen, and charged him with two counts of murder in the deaths of Wilbur Fitch and Carl Ross. The arrest was accomplished at shortly after eleven a.m. this morning at the gazebo in City Park. Acting on information received, police were in waiting when Mr. Kelly arrived and met with an unknown woman at the gazebo. Mr. Kelly drew a gun and attempted to shoot the woman. At this time the identity of the woman and her connection to Mr. Kelly have not been established. As police closed in on the gazebo and shots were fired, the woman apparently fled. Mr. Kelly was ordered by police officers to drop the gun. He refused and was shot in the right hand. His gun was recovered. Mr. Kelly has been transported to Adelaide General Hospital, where he is receiving care. He is expected to survive the wound. Mr. Kelly will be kept under guard at the hospital, and citizens can be assured there is no danger to the community. Outstanding police work"—she half turned and gave a gracious nod to Sam Cobb—"has already confirmed that the gun involved in the shooting at the gazebo is the weapon used to shoot Mr. Ross. I will take your questions now."

Sylvie Gilbert stood up, blonde curls wind tousled. She was young and cute in a pink sweater and rose slacks. "Where's my sister?" Ben Fitch rose, too. He looked eager.

Sam walked forward. "Ms. Susan Gilbert, who was instrumental in helping authorities with background information about Mr. Fitch, has been released from protective custody, as the arrest of Mr. Kelly concludes the investigation into the murders of Mr. Fitch and Mr. Ross."

Chapter 14

I was surprised to find both Susan's and Sylvie's cars parked in the driveway at their house and no one home. Oh, of course. I found them with Ben in the large living area behind the huge double staircase at the Fitch mansion. "I put champagne on to chill before I picked Sylvie up." He was buoyed by Susan's vindication, but his face also held anger. He filled three flutes, put down the bottle of Dom Pérignon.

He carried a glass to Susan. She stood next to a crystal sculpture of a dolphin. Sunlight streamed through a skylight, turning Susan's hair as glossy black as a raven's wing, giving the sculpture a sheen as if the dolphin had just emerged from the sea. Susan was slender and lovely in the richly red sweater and gray slacks. She looked up at Ben and her eyes held wonder. He handed her the glass and their fingers touched. She said with a catch in her voice, "You believed in me."

His blue eyes softened. "There was never a question. The first time I saw you, I knew you were good and fine. Dad thought the world of you. Dad was always right about people." Now there was a catch in his voice. "Except George. And in a way he was right about George. He never trusted George. He always told me you need a lawyer who's a junkyard dog. But the good thing is he was right about you and Todd and Alan and Harry."

"Hey, speaking of, I just got a text." Sylvie was excited, her voice light and bubbly. "Pour another glass. Harry's coming—"

A French door to the terrace opened. Harry Hubbard stepped inside, gave a fist pump. "I heard the news." He was preppy in an oatmeal cashmere sweater over a blue shirt and navy dress slacks. "I streamed the press conference. Glad they got the bastard. Glad they stopped being stupid about Susan. Anyway, Sylvie says there's champagne."

Sylvie looked at him with admiring eyes.

Susan, a tiny frown plucking at her striking dark brows, glanced from the champagne flute in her sister's hand to Harry, now standing quite close to Sylvie.

"On the way over here, I got to thinking." Harry grinned at Ben. "I know that will come as a surprise to you, esteemed step-bro. But Wilbur always wanted us to look ahead, make the company better. I've got an idea for a new look for Fitch Enterprises, like somebody splashed pink paint on a green billboard and flung a handful of glitter and turned on a huge spotlight. And here"—he pointed at Sylvie—"is the artist who can make everything bright."

∽

The Rescue Express streaked into a sky as richly blue as a Caribbean sea. Cinders sparked. Coal smoke swirled. The wheels rumbled like the Adelaide Cougar drummers at a championship football game. Going home. Susan and Sylvie safe. Going home. . . . The wind stirred Wiggins's russet hair. He spoke above the rumble. "I knew you would succeed, Bailey Ruth. You were as clever as C. Auguste Dupin." His tone was filled with awe.

But I knew the truth. Detective G. Latham was no Mike Shayne. "Wiggins"—this was a time for honesty—"I was at Roger Staubach's great game in 1975. Twenty-four seconds left. Fourth down. He launched the ball and said a Hail Mary. That's what I did, too."